Ishtar

Published by Gilgamesh Press
An Imprint of Morrigan Books
Östra Promenaden 43
602 29 Norrköping
Sweden
www.gilgameshpress.com

Editors: Amanda Pillar & K.V. Taylor

ISBN: 978-91-86865-01-6

Cover Design: Amanda Pillar © 2011
Internal Layout: Amanda Pillar © 2011

First Published November 2011

Ishtar

Kaaron Warren | Deborah Biancotti
Cat Sparks

Edited by
Amanda Pillar & K.V. Taylor

GILGAMESH PRESS
an imprint of Morrigan Books

Available From Morrigan Books:

How To Make Monsters
By Gary Mcmahon

Voices
Edited By Mark S. Deniz & Amanda Pillar

Grants Pass
Edited By Jennifer Brozek & Amanda Pillar

Dead Souls
Edited By Mark S. Deniz

The Phantom Queen Awakes
Edited By Mark S. Deniz & Amanda Pillar

Requiems for the Departed
Edited By Gerard Brennan & Mike Stone

Scenes from the Second Storey
Edited By Amanda Pillar & Pete Kempshall

Creeping in Reptile Flesh
By Robert Hood

The Whisper Jar
By Carole Lanham

Coming Soon From Morrigan Books:

Slice of Life
By Paul Haines

Dedications

DEBORAH, CAT & KAARON

The Red Hot Bad crew would like to thank our families and friends for inspiring and aiding us during this manuscript's birthing process.

Dedicated to powerful women everywhere, be they goddesses, grandmothers or girls.

KAARON WARREN

For Chris Gregory, my saviour in Suva, with thanks for his amazing library.

THE EDITORS

First — and most importantly — we would like to extend our thanks to the authors, the lovely Kaaron, Deborah and Cat. Thank you for writing such amazing stories! We'd also like to thank Mark S. Deniz and Lynne Green for proofreading this cracking collection.

Introduction

It makes sense to those who know me that I chose to start a publishing company that focused on questions about Assyrian literature, identity, culture and concerns. And they would find it of no surprise that I wanted to publish a book about Ishtar, the Assyrian goddess of love and war (especially considering the fact that Gilgamesh Press' mother company, Morrigan Books, has the Morrigan goddess as a figurehead — the Celtic deity of love and war).

So why didn't I simply name Gilgamesh Press 'Ishtar Press' instead? Well, it was the original name of the imprint, but then my brother-in-law was tragically murdered at the Swedish University of Örebro, in 2007. In honour of his memory, 'Ishtar Press' became Gilgamesh Press.

But Ishtar wouldn't leave me alone.

Ishtar was rather ubiquitous in the ancient Near East. Today, the descendents of ancient Mesopotamia are spread all over the globe, but they are a nation without a country to call their own. Ishtar is not worshipped by them any longer — she has been cast aside by the appeal of the various Abrahamic traditions that are followed by the Assyrians and the people who inhabit the lands where Mesopotamia once was.

Did Ishtar become bitter, angry at her dismissal? Did she fight tooth and nail to ensure her memory remained? Or had she accepted that her time had come, and gracefully faded into obscurity?

This idea — that of her ancient popularity, modern ignominy and future fight — gave me an idea. I wanted to publish a book that was comprised of three novellas, each one dedicated to Ishtar at different points in her timeline: her origins (ancient Mesopotamia), our present, and her future. Now, I just needed to find the authors who could create the Ishtars I could almost see.

Who better to write about Ishtar than three very talented women? I picked Kaaron Warren and Cat Sparks straight away; I'd read their work extensively and had tonnes of respect for their visions and writing. I knew I wanted their names on the cover of Gilgamesh Press' debut book.

Kaaron and Cat are both Australian, and I wanted to pick another Aussie to complete the triad. I knew of two other authors who could easily produce the story I wanted, so I emailed Cat and Kaaron and asked them their thoughts. The same day, I got their reply: Deborah Biancotti. Ishtar, or rather 'Red, Hot and Bad' (our working title) had begun.

Kaaron wanted to write the first tale. She was fascinated by the culture and mythology of ancient Mesopotamia, and had a mountain of research to complete before she could even put pen to paper (or fingers to keyboard, as the case may be). Cat was keen to write the futuristic story, and Deborah was more than happy to work on the contemporary novella. And so the timeline was set.

While I wanted to edit this collection, time and commitments forbade me from doing so. I asked Amanda Pillar and KV Taylor to take on the project: Amanda is an archaeologist with a speciality in Near Eastern religion and KV loves contemporary and futuristic works. With them on board, alongside Kaaron, Deborah and Cat, this collection was going to be outstanding. And it is.

You don't need to know about Assyrian mythology to love this book; you don't even need to know who Ishtar is. The stories in this collection are brilliant pieces of work that reflect their authors' visions as well as their talents.

I sincerely hope you enjoy this collection, and that perhaps, it will encourage you to delve a little deeper into the richness that is (and was) Assyrian culture.

Now come, meet the old, new and future Ishtar.

Mark S. Deniz
November 2011

Contents

The five Loves of Ishtar

Kaaron WARREN

My goddess Ishtar had five great loves in her thousand years of living. Many lovers; so many even I lost count, I, who can tell you the number of girdles in every household in the city.

But five men she loved, and five times she risked all for love.

Tammuz: 3000 BC
The Washerwoman Sharokin

I washed Ishtar's clothes in a stream, the waters high and cold after a winter of rain. She would complain if her robes weren't clean, but she did not have her fingers turned to frozen blocks. People who don't do the work don't understand the work. Not even a goddess.

The air was warm though, and filled with the scent of flowers; spring rains had begun and so we were assaulted with beauty. The pollen made me sneeze, but the colours, after the drab winter, made me sing.

I was looking my best, apart from my red, cracked

hands. My hair was sleek and clean. The warm breeze brought colour to my cheeks. *Kuttumu*, to veil a woman, may also mean to shut a door, but I didn't find wearing a veil so confining. I loved the freedom of being able to choose. I was lucky to have both; veiled and high class when I was with my mistress, low class and loose when I was not.

I splashed my face with the chill spring water, and my eyes felt sparkling and clear.

Downstream was a small flock of sheep. They were good looking creatures. Black of face, their wool the pale colour of sesame seeds. I watched them as I washed, happy for a distraction.

Their shepherd was hunched over, washing his feet in the stream. He stood up and stretched. Tall, strong and bare-chested, his skin tight against his muscles, the sight of him took my breath away. I covered my head, hoping he would glance over and see a respectable woman.

I thought of how sensitive his skin must be, how pleasure bumps would form if I ran my fingers over his chest.

He called to his sheep, a deep roar. They moved from the water and gathered at the greenish edge of the meadow. He walked amongst them, and for a moment, I could not tell his feet from theirs; his seemed cloven, too.

I worked, using rocks to remove the stains from the goddess' clothes. Perhaps I worked with more passion on this day, hoping he would look. If Ishtar were to walk in the pastures, this beautiful man would fall to his feet with desire for her.

My mistress was bronze in colour. Or copper. Or burnt gold. Her legs long and strong. Was I the only woman to have seen her naked, as she stood, hands on hips, demanding her jewelled robe?

All men fell to their feet. They didn't care that she was

cruel and murderous. They didn't care that she couldn't cook or clean.

She had people to do that for her.

I heard the shepherd laughing and looked up to find him watching me. "You are doing a very good job washing those clothes, though I'm wondering if your mistress will be able to wear them again."

I smiled. My tongue felt numb and my brain empty of words.

"Who is your mistress?" he asked me with such intensity it seemed like a lightning bolt.

I thought he already knew the answer. "I serve the goddess Ishtar."

He nodded. "And you will help me win her."

I had told him Ishtar likes clean clothes, but he did not listen.

"You are Tammuz? The Green One? I have heard nothing good about you," Ishtar said.

"They know me as Damuzi as well. They think I am two separate people, one hateful, one loving. One handsome, one ugly. One hard, one soft. I am all in one. But I am Tammuz; Tammuz is the name I am."

"You are a shepherd. You stink of sheep grease."

"Ah, but how soft are my hands?"

"Your hands are coarse like you. I couldn't tell them from a cat's tongue."

"Let me stroke you, goddess, and tell me if you still confuse me with a cat."

Ishtar had spent some time as a shepherd girl when I was young. I didn't wash for her alone then, but for the whole gang of sheep herders. Why were we there? Because her father the moon god wanted to teach her humility.

"I am the goddess of love and war; what need do I have for humility? The humble don't change the world. The humble would live in the dirt. The humble do not build homes. The humble don't live forever."

No need to gloat, I thought. Ishtar shed homes like a snake does its skin. Sometimes it galled me that she would live for long after I had died, and that perhaps my daughter would serve her, and my grand-daughter, and so on for a thousand years.

All we learned during our time with the shepherds was that they are like all men; kind and cruel in parts.

Tammuz said to Ishtar, "You have not seen beyond my sheep."

"*You* have failed then. Not me. Ishtar is never wrong." She touched her own chest gently.

Tammuz pressed her against his cedar tree, the mother of all others. Seeded at the beginning of time, it watched over us.

Ishtar placed a finger on his forehead and pushed him back.

"This is my mother!" He smiled. "Aren't you ready to meet her?"

"This is not the place to seduce me," she said.

Tammuz had an animal reek which filled your throat and your gut. He made my whole body pulse when he was close. I'm sure he did the same to Ishtar, but she kept him away. She knew she could reject him from afar, as a mere shepherd, but if she stood close she would fall back, wet and ready, and he would be the happiest man in all existence. He was blinded by her. He could have anybody, but he wanted her, who would take him and destroy him. The dust of his death; I could already see it around his feet.

Ishtar wasn't interested in death. Death was war, war was death, and she considered both to be consequences beyond her control.

Leaving him with his mother, the cedar tree, we walked towards the market.

"What of Tammuz?" I asked. "When will you reveal yourself to him? Are you worried about him seeing you in your underwear?"

A woman in her underwear reveals all. Ishtar was ashamed of her third breast and still worried it would turn men away. But what man would turn from Ishtar?

"I could ask my sister to make you some new underthings. Something clever, with flaps and hooks, which will leave your parts hidden if you want them to."

Ishtar stopped in her stride and turned to look at me. "You are more to me than a washerwoman. You know that, don't you?"

It was the greatest thing a god ever said to a mortal in all existence past and future.

Tammuz had his chance when Ishtar heard of a woman with a difficult pregnancy in the next village and we went to help.

Ishtar strode ahead, never looking down, so she did not see the scorpions, the *Zuqiqipum* or the snakes, the swarms of them in the desert. Her footsteps showed in the sand, but she walked without touching any creature; perhaps they crawled away at her approach. I walked as close to her as possible, yet still the *Zuqiqipum* scrabbled over my toes. At least they didn't bite; that is a terrible death to endure. You feel so ill you never want to eat again, and the sweat will soak the ground at your feet. Your heart beats like the fluttering of a bee's wings, and

5

your mouth is filled with spit. You vomit, and shit runs down your legs. Then you fall to the ground and shake uncontrollably until you die.

It's believed a drop of alcohol on the back will send a *Zuqiqipum* mad; they mistake the feel of the arrack for fire, of which they are mortal afraid. They will sting themselves to death rather than burn.

This woman had been pregnant for a year or more. This happened. It is said such women gave birth through their stomachs, though they always birthed alone, isolated, and would not talk about it.

This woman would not birth alone.

Ishtar called Tammuz, the Green One, to her. "This woman is ready to feel the quickening, and the sight of you, the smell of you, may bring movement to her womb."

It was arid and we trained ourselves to need less water or wine or beer, yet Tammuz took three huge draughts of ale, needing courage.

Dressed as a midwife, Ishtar entered in a golden glow, bringing calm to the birthing room. She stood at the mother's left side. "Your baby sits to the right," she said. A boy.

Tammuz entered the room, wary of so many women, so much sweat. Ishtar tugged his sleeve. "Come closer. Let her smell you."

He took small steps to the mat where the woman lay, tired, drained. He leaned over her, opened his lips and kissed her forehead wetly. She groaned. He stroked her hair, her left arm; he ran his fingers through the damp hair in her arm pit. Her breathing quickened and she pushed herself up.

Ishtar snaked her arms around Tammuz's waist and pulled him away. "You've finished here." She kept her arms around him.

He pulled her out of the room. She was red-cheeked; she had momentarily forgotten why she'd come.

I followed them to the doorway and said, "Goddess, this woman needs you."

Tammuz looked at me as if I were an ugly old woman. I wanted to take his hand, suck his fingers, take his loving so that he forgot Ishtar.

She returned to where the woman lay huge on the floor. Ishtar squatted beside her. The woman cried, "I'm so scared. My sister told me about a woman who was torn from cunt to breast, ripped open. My aunty told me about a woman whose baby got stuck and died drowning in the mother's own blood. I heard about a woman who was in such pain she threw herself from a window and killed herself, her baby and the three children she landed on. I heard..."

Ishtar placed a finger across the woman's lips. "These are stories women love to tell. Perhaps it is because they know you will feel great pain, the pain a man will never feel, and want to prepare you for it."

Then Ishtar quietened her by speaking of the ritual of birth. It was like a meditation, a calming list, a symbolic story. "You are steering a boat loaded with perfume, cedar, cedar fragrance, carnelian and lapis lazuli. The boat stops by the quay of death and the quay of hardship. My father, the moon god, waits for you there and will decide if it should carry on."

Lapis lazuli and carnelian as a combination were mostly seen at funerals. I think Ishtar evoked their combined image to warn of death, to let the mother know that she may not survive. Ishtar was a believer in being prepared.

"Ishtar, help me," the woman groaned.

"I beg my father for your safe passage and that he will see your future. He will see strong boys for generations, warriors. Soldiers. He sees our land safe because of your boys. He gives you safe passage."

The baby was part way through; its face was blue, her muscles tightened around his neck.

Ishtar pressed gently on the woman's stomach and the baby slipped out. The mother groaned; another came out when Ishtar pressed, then another, the last, a scrawny scrap of a thing no bigger than the spread of two small hands.

Ishtar threw back her robe and suckled all three, one each to a breast, while the midwives attended the mother.

"Why must we beg your father to keep our birthing mothers, our newborns safe?" one of the midwives asked. "Why does he make it so difficult?"

"My father doesn't like pregnant women because they have no moon blood. Moon blood is his; it fills him with fire."

Ishtar saved the three boys because they would be needed in war. They would all die in battle, but would add so much to the world. They would keep a hundred people alive by their existence and their courage; those people hundreds more. They would worship Ishtar for saving them and help her cult grow. I would not see this, but my descendants would. I wished I could.

Tammuz waited for Ishtar outside. He was shirt-less, shining.

"You take these birth clothes home to wash," she said, not looking at me. Her lips were swollen and she was covered with sweat.

I carried the huge bundle of filthy clothes on my back, bent forward with the weight.

"Grass stains, Ish?" I said when she returned. When she was tired I liked to talk to her. She didn't get angry when she was tired.

"I visited with my shepherd." Her voice was soft, as if she spoke through three layers of cloth.

"That must have made him very happy at last." I wanted details. My hands were rough as tree trunks, my skin like waxy dust; I did not have lovers lined up to worship me. "I thought you did not like the shepherd. You said he smelt of wool. That he was greased up and slippery."

Ishtar pinched my cheeks. Her fingers felt soft. "Oh, he is greasy and smelly and his cock is the size of a lamb's. But he told me that Anu blessed our union."

I laughed then, good and hearty with very little envy. "How many men have said the father of all gods blesses a union? Oh, Ishtar!"

I did not expect her reaction. She picked up her spear, which she mostly used for poking pigs, and pricked me with it. "Soap your mouth, washerwoman."

Mostly, I didn't mind what my goddess did. But I wished she had shared Tammuz. I loved him too, with a physical ache in my blood.

Without her, who knows? Would Tammuz have become the fifth king of the Land of the Rivers?

It was the kings who were written in history; Ishtar was only remembered for how she changed their lives and the lives of those around them. Every judgment Tammuz made, he made with her influence. He didn't like to judge alone.

"I have them all wailing in my throne room," he said one morning, shaking his head. They had loved together for a long time and could communicate without speaking sometimes.

Ishtar sighed. I myself hoped she would never pick

another man who lacked wisdom.

Waiting for them: a young girl curled up in a ball on the floor. An agitated young man. Two sets of parents, full of fury. And an older man, beaten bloody, near the door. He tried to crawl, leaving a dark trail on the floor.

It seemed that the older man raped the young girl, a virgin affianced to the young man. The couple had been engaged for many years, saving the dowry and the bride-price. The bride would have been twelve at the wedding, due to take place very soon. If her husband was a good man, the marriage would not have been consummated until she was sixteen. That was how a good man behaved.

"He has stolen their right to a pure love," the groom's father screamed.

Tammuz heard from each of them. The older man did not defend himself apart from to say, "She was so beautiful and the weather was right. I could not think properly." His teeth were so broken it was hard to make sense of it.

"Drown him," Tammuz said.

"And the girl?" Ishtar said.

Tammuz looked confused. "That is our problem, too?"

The families wanted judgment.

Ishtar stood. "I say the girl will live with me for one month. If her next bleeding comes, we know the line is pure. If not, I will ask my father to clean her, purify her, and whatever seed that man placed in her will be expelled like the poison it is."

There was silence. The families and Tammuz stared at Ishtar, in awe of her great wisdom.

"And also," Tammuz said to the father of the bride, "You may take that man's wife and rape her." This was standard in the law.

The rapist, who had accepted his own death sentence

with fortitude called, "No!"

The girl's father shook his head. "I do not wish to take up that right."

When the family left, Tammuz called for beer. He was Tammuz of the beer, of the *ababu*. Then he and Ishtar drank and made love for all to hear. Usually, after making love with Ishtar, the Green One walked in the desert and in his footprints sprang pennyroyal, mint; beautifully aromatic herbs.

For her part, after making love, Ishtar loved to have doves flying around her. Their cooing calmed her.

This time though, they stayed together and drank beer. Ishtar poked at her lover. "Do you think of your sister when you are with me, Tammuz? Do you think you are entering her as you did when you were young?"

His sister was the wine goddess Geshtinanna. Sometimes, I knew, Tammuz got his women confused. It was as if they were twins to him. Or the same person. Sometimes, the women would use it to their advantage. There was much between them, though. Jealousy and mistrust.

Tammuz wouldn't answer Ishtar when she asked these questions.

Some would say Geshtinanna did not cause trouble between Ishtar and her brother, but she made suggestions, placed hints, which led to trouble. Led to the Underworld, and to dust and to death and to starving children. Crop failure. Many would not blame Geshtinanna, but I asked: Why not blame the one who is to blame?

Tammuz did not expect to die. He expected to live forever. But you should not anger a goddess. He sat, drinking wine and laughing with his sister's friends. Geshtinanna, annoyed that those women, who had come to visit with her, sat laughing with Tammuz instead. She ran to Ishtar, a *beru* or more away.

"They adore him," she told Ishtar. "You can almost hear the laughter from here!" Geshtinanna knew that Ishtar did not like women to make him laugh; he should laugh only with her. It was pure trouble-making to tell Ishtar.

Ishtar picked up a hoe, rusty but still sharp, and spun in a circle, twisting and twisting until she was a blur. Then she let it go, and it shot like a star through the air, vanishing from sight.

She closed her eyes, put her hands on her hips. "There. That will strike that viper down."

I wanted to run to him, gather my skirts and run through mud and stones until my feet were shredded. But I knew she wouldn't allow me that. "Should we follow it?" I asked. "Perhaps he will have some last words for you."

"Washerwoman, you are right. He will whisper something; of course I should be there to hear it."

But all he whispered was, "It hurts."

Ishtar was not given to guilt, but she was a terrible victim of loneliness. She did not change her clothing for two weeks after the death of Tammuz, and I began to wonder if I should look for other work. Finally, I managed to strip her, give her new clothes and convince her to bathe.

"I wonder if he is suffering down there?" she asked.

"We are suffering up here," I said. At least in the Underworld you were free from the sun. In summer, this world was dry and unliveable, although of course we lived. The plants died and no one could work. We did not converse because we were too hot and thirsty.

It was the sun god's great power which did this to us.

With Tammuz in the Underworld, dead babies slipped through their mother's cunts, skin, bone and blood. Root vegetables rotted in the ground, fruit fermented on the trees, stored wheat had the taint of mould. The people starved as they had never starved before. In summer, there was usually an end in sight. When the winter comes, or when next year comes, or when the crop grows or the cow calves. There was nothing for us, though. With Tammuz the Green One dead, all lay fallow. His mother the Cedar Tree began to coarsen, the smooth planes of her bark now rough to the fingers.

As to who really did descend into the Underworld, that is for history to tell.

Geshtinanna came to Ishtar and said, "I know that the earth is dying because you sent my brother to the Underworld. I will go there to ask for him back."

"I will go," said Ishtar. "But not this week. This week I have things I need to do. My father will not let me go."

"I will go," Geshtinanna said. "I will go now. This day."

"I will go," Ishtar said. But her mother, wise and loving, whispered to her from the clouds, "Let the other one go. She is no goddess. Let her go."

Ishtar dressed Geshtinanna in layer upon layer of beautiful clothing. But she only got as far as the first gate; *this place is not for you*, she was told. *There is nothing for you here. It is Ishtar, Ishtar who must enter.*

Geshtinanna pulled out her pins and tore her dress with them in fury and frustration.

All was not fair in the Underworld. You carried with you all that you had done in your life. In life, if you were good, you had family and friends. If you were bad, you ended up alone. In the afterlife, a good man was attended by his loving parents and by his wife, once she travelled there.

The bad lived on the dusty cold streets of the Underworld. I saw such people in Aššur, tragic in their loneliness.

Ishtar always had me. I followed her no matter where she went. Except into the Underworld, where I would be stopped. Not worthy.

But Ereshkigal, goddess of Irkalla, the Underworld, hated Ishtar. Ereshkigal liked things to be straightforward, with no need to assess. Things were what they were. She thought that Ishtar blurred reality with sex-lust and blood-lust. She thought Ishtar filled the Underworld with people not ready to be there.

Ishtar hated her in return, though without such passion. Their last meeting ended with Ishtar saying the words: "I am the one who will be remembered. You will only be known for your habitat, for having a home thick with dust."

It would not be a happy reunion, but Ereshkigal wanted Ishtar in her own domain.

Ishtar returned from the Underworld, triumphant against Ereshkigal, Tammuz tired and happy to be breathing fresh air. Ishtar could barely move for the dust thick in the folds of her hair, her clothing. She told me she had been forced to strip naked, but she had enjoyed it, that the freedom of bare skin bolstered her rather than weakened her. Her nostrils were clogged with sand, her ears filled, so she breathed though her mouth and could not hear me.

Once home, she stripped and bathed, a long, long bath lasting almost a day. Her servants fetched jug after jug of water and we took it in turns to scrub at her.

The dust seemed immovable. Ishtar told me that in the Underworld, surrounded by it, she felt like she couldn't move or escape. Nothing could grow in it, so those dead folk ate it, yet took no benefit from it.

When Ishtar saw Tammuz, thick with the dust of death a day later, she felt such relief that she wept tears enough to fill a bowl of lapis lazuli. Tammuz caught her tears and wiped her eyes with a piece of red wool. These colours calmed her. The two stripped naked, their clothes merged in a pile.

I beat their clothes at first, but the dust didn't move. Water turned it into a thick and sticky mud, which dried back to dust. This stuff sat in your lungs.

No matter how hard I had scrubbed, I couldn't get the bloodstains out of his shirt. I didn't want to know how the mess got there, but I knew all the same.

A washerwoman knows everything.

Ishtar told me to give the clothing to the impoverished, so I took it home to my sister. The poor often wore the clothes of the dead. This was how it should be. Washed out, dried in the sun, washed again; there was nothing diseased about a dead man's clothes, although a deep, rich stench of the Underworld came off them still. Somewhere, there was a beggar with a long shirt carrying a dark, faded stain of the blood of Tammuz.

When I gave them to my sister she said, "What have you slaughtered? A great black cow?" In return, she gave me a beautiful piece of cloth she had woven, the colour of the sand at dawn.

I took the cloth to Ishtar and she fingered it

distractedly.

"The colours," I said. "Aren't they bright?"

She tossed the piece to the floor. "Where I have been, there is no colour."

Ishtar told me how Ereshkigal realised her mistake in bringing Ishtar to the Underworld and stripping her naked.

Ereshkigal called Nergal her consort, though I heard he didn't agree. He was a god of fertility, fever and death, and he had almost murdered her. She offered him a shared place in the Underworld and he allowed her to live.

Nergal loved singers, though this love was what sent him to the Underworld in the first place. On special occasions, when he was alive, he would have criminals set free to sing for him, if their voices were heavenly. To him, the voices meant innocence. One of these men sliced Nergal's throat for the rings he wore.

In the Underworld, singers fought to be his entertainer.

Ishtar said, "I did not find Nergal attractive. So pale. Bloodless. But Ereshkigal was still jealous. She regretted her decision to strip me of my clothing. She thought it would make me vulnerable to disease, to shame. That without clothing I would be barbaric. I stood there, dressed only in the dust of her terrain, and her man smiled at me so foolishly I thought his brains had been sucked out through his nose.

"That's why she gave me Tammuz back again; she didn't want me stealing her man."

Ishtar was so thirsty when she came out, nothing could quench it.

We did not know it at the time, but this would happen

time and time again and into the future. Tammuz died and lived again, as did the fruit and the grain, and Ishtar would have to bring him back. Eventually, though, Tammuz and Ereshkigal became lovers, and that made life easier for all of us. Ereshkigal was a fickle lover and a few weeks of him was enough. She would send him back, only to miss him and want him again.

Fickle.

It was never the same for my goddess and Tammuz after their trip to the Underworld. He would weep as she took other lovers, his tears making the ground too salty to grow vegetables.

Ishtar became so popular that women would queue for days to say one sentence to her. Many of them said: "Stay with us for all eternity, because your strength means we are powerful too, and we will be able to make all our own ambitions reality."

Ishtar did not know or care of my life when I was not near her. She imagined we all stopped moving, that we shut down, when we were not serving her. She was not alone in this; there was not a god alive, nor a wealthy person in all of the Land of Rivers, who worried for the welfare of the people. My belief was that this would cause their downfall. To live without caring was a dangerous way to exist.

I believed the only way that humankind would ever have a future was if the starving masses were given a voice. We were so close to savagery. Three days without food, maybe four, and neighbours would be slashing each other's throats over a sheaf of wheat.

Ishtar took many lovers. They could not say no. Even knowing the outcome, they could not say no. When she tired of them, she destroyed them in ways I didn't want to remember. She turned them into sea creatures, she blocked their veins so the blood didn't flow, she jellied their bones and softened their brains. She did not feel that love making was complete unless there was suffering.

Despite her disinterest in death, Ishtar dealt in it on many days. I remember that one evening, she arrived on the doorstep with the impression of a hand on her back and her garments stiff with gore. Her face was drawn; some nights, being unable to control the consequences of war seemed too hard for her to bear. Her fingernails were dirtied with it, and the creases of her skin. She wanted her clothes washed, even though I was ready to go home to my family. She liked to wake each day with everything washed away.

I hung the small items from the thorn bushes. Ishtar watched me work. I didn't like that.

"You are getting older. You should have a child."

"I have sons."

Ishtar shook her head. "You need a strong daughter. I will send someone to you. Your husband is no good for it."

I did not know then what she had in mind, but oh, wonderful goddess. Oh, kind and generous goddess, so loving.

She sent Tammuz, who made love to me in a way my poor husband would never match. That is how the gods did it! Still, I would have to take my husband that night, because there was no doubt, no doubt at all, that I was impregnated.

It was late when I walked home. The town changed in the evening. Goodly working folk were at home, settling their children, and out and about were the other sorts, the ones who would drink beer, *ababu*, for their evening meal. None knew what I had done. Who I had lain with.

I knew my husband would like some *ababu* with his stew that night, and I wanted to be sure he would make love to me, so I walked one street wide, to the inn where my sister worked. She told our mother she was a cleaner there, but she worked on her back more often than not, and I couldn't judge her. Ishtar gave it up for free any time of day; why should not my sister be paid so she could feed her family? I wished my hands were not so rough, my face so lined, or perhaps I would make some money myself.

She was at the bar. "Sister!" she called. We were always happy to see each other, regardless of the secrets we carried. Secrets made us strong. Secrets gave us eternal life. We kept the secrets from our men, because they were innocent souls who didn't need to know everything.

I spent some time with my sister at the bar and left, numbed with beer. I hoped Ishtar would not call for me; my tongue was filled with truth and I would not be able to hold it.

I went home to my children. Four boys I had, and they were all hungry, though this hunger was only a day old. Other children went hungry for weeks, until they lost the desire for food. The mother would scrabble along the street in piles of refuse; the father would catch rats to boil. With enough yoghurt and salt, you couldn't tell what you were eating.

Some days when Ishtar had her friends for a meal,

they were so busy laughing, drinking wine, preparing for sex, that they would not eat much more than a few mouthfuls.

The cook and the table-clearer took the food home with them; that was fair. Sometimes they would sell a piece of bread with tooth marks. People will pay good money for the discards of the gods.

My husband was sleepy, but I gave him beer and I made sure we spent the night together.

Ishtar was happier after my girl was born. She did not incite war, and she took fewer lovers and was less cruel to them afterwards. She wanted to make the world a better place for my daughter, she said. This was during a time of terrible flood; we lost mothers, fathers and children to the raging waters. Ishtar's father told her it was because of peace. That some must die and it may be in war and it may be for lack of food. Regardless, people must die.

Ishtar took it upon herself to plant wheat and other crops to help feed the people. Dressed in drab robes, she walked from home to home with new seeds. She was not sure if the floods were her fault, but it broke her heart to see hungry children crying.

"What sort of place do we live in? We are dry for most of the year, and our crops struggle. Then we get all our water in a downpour of three or four days and our crops are washed away. Those seedlings left behind cannot grow in the depleted soil and the sun beats down to cook them."

Her father would not discuss the weather with her. He was a harsh man, like my own father. They knew how much struggle was required to survive and that only the strong can bear it; they wanted their families to survive.

Regardless of the lovers she took, and the boredom she sometimes felt, Ishtar returned to Tammuz. I'm sure she still loved him, and she certainly loved the position, the mortal power of being consort to the king.

Then one of Ishtar's former lovers came begging.

He came, *napištu*, to present himself to the king. Tammuz knew about this man. Ishtar laughed at him. But he had been caught with a young girl, and the girl was not happy. Now he came to beg for his life.

"*Napištu*. I give you all I have, Lord Tammuz."

"You should have been here last week. The time for *napištu* was then."

"I got sick and couldn't ride my wagon until yesterday."

Ishtar and Tammuz laughed until they wept.

"This is a man you lay down with?" Tammuz asked Ishtar. "Why? Look at him! You made poor choices before you found me."

She shrugged. "He was better looking when he was young. And it's possible I damaged him."

Like the camel spider, Ishtar sometimes devoured her mate, or at least bit off his limbs, when she had finished.

"I doubt there is anything you can tell us to save your life, but you are welcome to try," Tammuz said.

Ishtar rose and spoke into the accused man's ear. I knew of what she spoke, since her lips swelled as they did when she thought of sex. The man's erection was taken as proof of guilt.

She crouched beside him, and rather than defend himself, he told far more than they had known. Far more than he had ever admitted to any living soul, more than just about the girl.

"I had to kill those children," he said. "They bewitched me into thinking they were grown, that I was worshipping the Goddess. When I discovered they were actually children who had seduced me into taking their innocence, I had to kill them to save other victims."

She bent over this man, put her lips over his eye socket and sucked. She spat out his eyeball and a cat batted it around the room. Then Ishtar sucked out the other eyeball. He was insensible. Some men lose all feeling when in contact with Ishtar's skin. Ishtar said later, "A man like that, feeling nothing? He barely suffered." She felt she had failed.

I am dying now. Glad to have my sons and daughter to carry my blood into the future. Glad to have served the goddess as I did, to have witnessed all I did. This last thing I saw: a great secret. Ishtar would curse me through all possible futures should I tell anyone.

This secret began when Ishtar took a mortal lover, one of those who desired to be immortal. Ishtar liked those men because they believed she would help them, and she liked to see men make fools of themselves.

This man, Etana, had a chance to grab the plant of life and failed. Not only that, his wife gave birth to only stillborn babies. One after another after another. A dozen, maybe more. Ishtar felt sad for the wife; all those dead babies. So she went to her uncle, Ninurta, who, as the god of fertility and vegetation, could heal the sick.

"I cannot bring back the dead, Ishtar. Only Gula can do that, and she has no reason to do so in this case."

Ishtar's aunt, Gula, had always been a great friend to her. She had the ability to restore life, but to also kill on a whim. Ishtar understood too well the conflict between these impulses, and the passion both inspired. She knew the conflict of death and war, sacrifice and love.

Ishtar said, "What if we brought those stillborn babies back to life? For that poor woman with no children."

"Those babies would not be like ordinary children. And what of the other babies born dead? Who is to say they do not deserve life as well?"

Ishtar considered what Gula had said. "Let's bring them all back to life."

Ishtar decided that these children, these stillborn children, would be her army. One day she might need them. But she didn't understand the consequences and believed she would have power over them.

This is my secret: Ishtar's army of stillborn children, who grow stronger every day, yet never know more than the knowledge they are born with.

I die leaving my daughter in charge. She will help Ishtar make the transition between life and death. Help her to rest with her army until it is time to rise again and be at the forefront of affairs.

Ishtar does not age. Her skin glows and she makes young men cry.

She likes to rest, though, even if just for a short while.

At the same time, she is restless, seeking her place.

Seeking her next lover.

GILGAMESH: 2510 BC
The Washerwoman Atur

One of my ancestresses was known for saying that humankind will only have a future if the starving masses are given a voice. We have no voice today, yet still we exist. With all the terrible wars, the killing of men young and old, still we exist.

If only Gilgamesh, the great flood king, had loved her when and how he should, many thousands of families would have been saved. If only Enkidu, his dear friend, had not caused such jealousy in Ishtar. My brothers, my uncles, they all would not have died in war; the only male left in my family a cousin, who was crippled and weak and vicious in the brain.

When Ishtar first heard of Gilgamesh, she had been living quietly for almost 400 years. The lovers she destroyed were unimportant men; unremembered, unremarkable. I had been with her for twenty years, taking the role as washerwoman when my mother died. She was a lazy washerwoman, my mother, with no pride in her work. Nor in her cooking, nor in us, her children. For me, this job was one of freedom. I could be myself: washerwoman to a goddess.

It was known amongst us, the washerwomen, that she would have five great loves. This one, this Gilgamesh, was to be the second. When she heard of him, she had me wash her most desirable clothes in a mixture of rose water and the glands of a cat. She bathed in honey so her skin was soft and sweet. The Ishtar I know was never clean, no matter how hard I washed. I cleaned her clothes and yet she came home soaked in blood again. Blood and gore, with things in the seams, crusts on the hems. She didn't care for her appearance when war was in the air.

But Gilgamesh resisted her. He was a smart man; he knew what happened to her lovers. He looked out onto the street. There were bats in the massive date grove which filled the square. "One of your lovers, Ishtar?" he asked.

She peered out. "I wouldn't recognise him."

Gilgamesh laughed, but Ishtar didn't joke. He said, "You think I want to become an animal? A wolf like that poor fellow, hunted last week?"

"That will only happen when I tire of you. Perhaps I never will tire of you."

"I do not want to be a sad man. You enjoy eternal life as if it is a glass of beer. You sip and swallow and barely notice the taste at all. You simply enjoy being drunk. Why do you and your kind have this and not me?"

"You will taste the beer if you lie with me. Come out now, to the desert. Come with me."

She led him out, away. I followed, carrying a bedroll.

Ishtar stood in the cold, desert night air. Her great inner heat kept her warm, and around her feet small fires formed.

Standing there that way, with fire at her fingertips and her toes, who could refuse her? Gilgamesh watched her and she thought she had him. But he said, "If you can withstand my father's demonic *sangarliness*, I will make love to you."

He wanted to test her, he said. I think he wanted to weaken her. His friend, Enkidu, tried to pull him away from Ishtar and he was the one who devised the test. I think that man knew how much power she would have over Gilgamesh and he didn't like it. Some men do not like to share their friends.

Gilgamesh lived in fear of his father and thought perhaps this would appease him. His father was a priest of terrific reputation. Unforgiving, he took the slightest blink in temple to be against his gods, and his punishments were legendary. Gilgamesh himself was scarred across the back and the tops of his thighs. He said sometimes that if a week went by without his father damaging him, he felt as if the world was asleep and that he was dreaming along with them.

It was to this priest — Gilgamesh's cruel father — that Ishtar presented herself. I had washed out her drabbest robes, ones that my mother had washed many times and perhaps even my grandmother. They were threadbare in places and here we draped more drab cloth, until she was swathed like a baby. She went this way to the temple of Gilgamesh's father. She kept her eyes downcast so he could not see their fiery light, and kept her hands under her robes so he could not see their sensual length.

Ishtar hoped her disguise was so good that he would not know her, and that she could pray for a day and leave without being noticed. But Gilgamesh had warned the men to watch out for her, and so they did; one tendril of her hair, the sway of her bottom, and it was enough for her to be known.

Gilgamesh's father, whose robes were reeking and unwashed for many years, stood behind her and pressed his groin into her back. She did not know how to react to this, nor to the blows he felled on her, using a stick he always carried. "Whore!" he called her, and she knew then she could withstand his cruelty. Whore was no insult to her; whoring was a profession she supported and loved. And so Ishtar allowed this man to beat her and abuse her. She was in control because she allowed it, and although she believed nothing was proven by the pain she suffered, she knew that Gilgamesh would relent, and that his guilt would work in her favour for the entirety of their time together.

Here, history will say that Gilgamesh withstood her to the last, but this was not true. He was weak, like any man, and they took to bed like two mating lizards, hot from the sun and lazy and slow with it.

Gilgamesh said to Ishtar, "You can't tell anyone. Not a soul. If you speak of this, I will do all I can to destroy you."

"Are you ashamed?"

"Yes, I am."

"You are too busy to waste time destroying me."

And he laughed in her face like an insane child. But it was too late for him. He was caught.

He was a different man than others she had been with. He was fickle and bored easily, and he was distracted by the next idea, the next thing.

I could not wait to tell Ishtar news of Gilgamesh and his conquests. Was it bad of me to enjoy her crest-fallen face? I took such sweet-smelling clean clothes to her, and as she enjoyed them I told her the news. She paid, in this way, for all the times she hit me, for all her harsh words. She should know that even a goddess can suffer, and that even a washerwoman knows more than a goddess does. Even my eight year old daughter knew more.

The Washerwoman Ninlil

A man who dies suddenly spends his afterlife lying on a couch, drinking water. A man who falls in battle will be comforted by his parents while his wife cries. A man with no family or friends will eat only scraps and crumbs and rubbish from the gutter.
~ Proverb

I was eight years old when my mother disappeared. Ishtar said I was to wash the blood from her tunic sleeves. My mother told me one day I would do this, but I thought I would be grown. A woman. Ishtar laughed when I told her I was eight.

"Your mother should have thought of that, shouldn't she?"

Ishtar said my mother ran away to find a god for a lover, because she was desperate for fame and excitement. I wished Mother had said goodbye. It made father very angry. Father came to me and touched me in that way, which I didn't like. Gilgamesh had Father banished when this was discovered. I, too, would have been banished, but Ishtar, my goddess, saved me. She told Gilgamesh, "Who else will wash my clothes?"

I was happy to serve Ishtar, though. Perhaps I would not have to marry in her service. I was not keen on marriage.

"I do not like children," Ishtar said, and while I did not become an adult the moment she spoke, it seems to me, looking back, as if I had no childhood.

Drought struck us, and by the time I was eighteen, the ground was so dry and for such a depth, that even the thorn bush was dying. The seed pods, which kept many animals alive during drought, did not renew themselves, and the bushes were all thorns.

Yet still men fought, dying for a strip of land so easy to cross, so vulnerable to invasion. Gilgamesh was not a man to give an inch and Ishtar was bored. They went to war with no thought for the consequences.

Gilgamesh, king of Uruk, summoned his troops. Morale was low; they saw the city crumbling, no gains made. He told them that conscription would be rewarded with state land; that they would assure their children's future by pledging loyalty. Most men were loyal. They understood the importance of protecting their city. Even the mercenaries, men who killed only for the money, felt devotion to the city, to Gilgamesh.

They rode with chariots and mounted troops. They marched with axes, adzes and piercing spears. Bows and maces were so worshipped they were given names.

The men would consider themselves divinely blessed if they won. They did not contemplate losing.

Our side fought alongside Ishtar's private army. She would not say where they came from, but no man could go near them without illness, without thinking of or longing for death. Her army was dead behind the eyes, like no man you have seen before. I say man, but they could be woman. They had no sexual features, as if none had ever grown. They were all the same, they marched as one, single minded. They ate rubbish. Stones. They ate whatever lay in their path and did not need water. They rode on horses, their flesh hanging in shreds off their yellow-boned legs.

This was how Ishtar's army marched. She told me they were the stillborn babies of a thousand women, brought to life by Gula and reared by barren nursemaids. Ishtar kept them in the desert, in tents, and she did not visit them.

The recruitment of the other soldiers, the living ones, was torture to watch. They had to be purified before they become soldiers. They were beaten with a switch, starved for five days, and made stand for three. After that, they could march with pride alongside the stillborn army. Who would tell them, after all that, that they still looked weak beside Ishtar's troop?

Such a great deal of dust was raised by the warriors. Gilgamesh asked Ishtar, "Is this how it is in the Underworld?"

I would never speak to Ishtar at such a time. At war, especially one she instigated, she is at her cruellest and most determined. But Gilgamesh was filled with pride and strength; he could say anything.

I tried to work in the shade, but the sun moved quickly. My washing dried as soon as I draped it over the wall, but it dried stiffly, as if frozen into position. Using rocks helped, but still I had to knead the clothes to soften them or Ishtar would be angry. She said I could be the best washerwoman she ever had. She told me that already I was far better than my mother had been, and certainly better than my grandmother.

We marched too, we washerwomen, carrying our buckets and our soap, while it lasted. The men didn't bother us unless they wanted release, and then they would notice we were women. There was no love in these encounters. They barely looked us in the eye. But we considered ourselves to be in Ishtar's service, so it was worthy work.

We were paid to mourn as well as to wash. We were happy to do it, bringing on tears by rubbing our eyes hard with our calloused hands.

"There is no place for feeling in battle," Ishtar told me as I washed blood from her leggings. "You cannot balk. The one who balks loses."

The flies were thick like a blanket, and the bushes had no fruit, so that the soldiers took the few remaining leaves and sucked them for flavour.

We came across a well which had been cursed. All who drank from it died of black throat. Around the well there were skeletons, men so thirsty they ignored the warning. The stillborn army drank, though they needed no water. Why did they do it? Ishtar said they liked to drink poison. I thought they saw what the men had done and they copied. Gula once again saved stillborn babies every day and they were trained from rebirth to fight. Their numbers grew.

The peasants fought too, with farm tools as weapons. Ruthless. Terrible. And so very loyal to the king. There are always spies, though. One was caught while Ishtar and I were in camp, and we watched as he was tortured, stripped of skin and flesh, until all that remained were his spy senses; his eyes, his ears and his tongue.

"It doesn't matter if he warns the enemy of the stillborn army. They will never be able to withstand my babies," Ishtar said.

The stillborn troops reached the broadest part of the Euphrates River. They stopped, bumping and falling because they feared a body of water this size; crossing such a body of water could transform you. And these soldiers did not want to transform. Or perhaps they feared the water itself; the rush of it, the wetness. I have crossed water many times. Perhaps I am subtly transformed. Perhaps with each crossing, I changed my future and that of my descendants for many generations.

Behind them, Gilgamesh's men pushed and agitated. "Weakness at last," they muttered to each other, "Let's leave them behind. Better that and risk losing the war."

Gilgamesh ordered his men forward, saying to Ishtar, "Move your ghouls."

She tried. Ishtar saw the sense in his order, and she really tried to move the stillborn army. Instead, they turned on Gilgamesh's men, tearing out living throats with yellow teeth, breaking necks with a single twist, running swords through three men at a time.

Gilgamesh called a retreat.

"Control these creatures, Ishtar, or I will have you killed and killed again for all eternity."

I knew that Ishtar was not frightened of the threat of a mortal man. But she liked that he made it.

"Feed your men. Rest them. I will look after mine."

Ishtar sought advice from her father, the moongod, on how to manage the stillborn army. "They are beyond your powers now. All you are is the creator. They will march until their feet are worn to nubs. They will fight until they have nothing but a head and torso. Then they will bite into the enemy's thigh and sink their teeth in; to remove them, you will have to cut them out."

"Why did I create them?" Ishtar berated herself. She could show weakness with her father. I had seen her weak before. I stood beside her, hoping to give her strength, but she flicked her arm at me as if I were a fly she barely noticed.

"You thought you could control them. You thought you could control war. But blood-lust is all engulfing."

"This is about land, not blood."

"All war is blood-lust, daughter. Each death becomes part of the next."

"They were supposed to fight on my side. Defend Sumer."

"They are on no one's side. They fight simply because they want to."

"I was not the one to create them. It was Gula who revived them."

"And now you have learnt never to trust another god."

Ishtar said, "I am the heart of the battle. The arm of the warriors." After her conversation with her father, she ordered bodies and logs lain across the river, telling her army, "You won't get your feet wet."

On the other side, the enemy waited, lulled into a false sense of security by the army's long pause on the opposite bank.

Gilgamesh and Ishtar spoke quietly to their armies, asking for stealth. They spoke of the evil enemy, the cruelties, how a loss would spell the end of the world as they knew it. Ishtar's army didn't care. They had decided *en masse* that they would cross the water, and for them the time for talking had passed.

Taken by surprise, man by man the enemy were run through, throats bitten, hearts ripped out. Just the touch of one of those stillborn soldiers was enough to turn the blood grey. When it spilled, it sat sluggish and dusty, attracting the flies.

The stillborns suffered some wounds but they shrugged off the loss of a limb as if it were an interesting itch. They knew that before long, new limbs would grow.

Our army, our living army, followed afterwards, finishing off the enemy. There was little joy in it for them and they knew they were not covered in glory.

They raped at will to place their seed. Was there ever a conquering army who did not do this? But at least those women were spared rape by the stillborns. Imagine that seed; it would destroy the womb for future children. I shuddered to watch them. They didn't defecate or urinate and they showed no interest in the women or the children, even those naked, tied spreadeagled, even those wet with blood and open for penetration.

This was not the first and would not be the last time a river ran with blood. This time though, the colour of it was enough to send nightmares to your grandchildren; grey.

We washerwomen walked the battlefield, collecting discarded, filthy clothing. Nothing went to waste. Ishtar and the armies marched ahead, leaving us to the smell of death, the awful debris left behind.

I saw limbs and other pieces of flesh, but these we left behind. I did not want to think about some of those pieces, the ones chopped off the stillborns, wriggling, pasty and slick.

The stillborn army moved amongst us, collecting their body parts. I didn't like to think what they would do with them. The stillborn washerwomen moved slowly, but the strength in them was enormous. They washed without water, simply squeezing the garment until the dirt dripped out, as dry as the Underworld.

That army marched almost without rest, pausing only when they reached a town or village to devour like a plague of locusts. Only the rats were left behind. The people were used to going hungry, but this took them to death.

There was sustenance in a rat, but much sickness as well.

In the path of war, as always, lay suffering women and children. Starving villages. In these places they had to make hard decisions. Some harvested the cereal when still green, and this grain, this *abaḫšinnu*, was used for bread that made the stomach ache. Harvesting early damaged the crops for the next year. Were we so hungry that we would eat the roots, thus ensuring starvation for generations to come?

Since humans rose from Gula's mud-stained hands, people have starved meal after meal in order to ensure food for the future. The army was starving. They made porridge from the pods of the thorn bush. But many plants were already lost to drought and what was left was soon depleted.

It was only when the watermelons ripened on the vine that the hunger abated. Then there was fruit to eat, the juice cooling and quenching, the sweetness bringing smiles.

Even the stillborn can smile. When they did, that was the beginning of the end of the war. But Ishtar felt great tenderness for the war dead, great pity. After one battle she touched a thousand foreheads. She had been to the Underworld, so she knew what awfulness awaited them.

Afterwards, she took her army to some caves she favoured and knew they would wait until she called them again.

Gilgamesh buried a document in the foundations of Ishtar's greatest temple. He said, "Words will last forever. No one will have to guess at your name."

Ishtar was bored by records and rolled her eyes. "I want bodies in there. That's how I'll be remembered."

Gilgamesh insisted, though. "There have been enough sacrifices in war, don't you think?"

For Ishtar, there was never enough sacrifice. As grateful as she may feel for the dead, as filled with pity for the loss, there was never enough.

Gilgamesh was very keen on inscriptions and documents. He would have them carved on stone or metal, on marble, on gems and on bronze plates, but mostly on clay.

Preparing the clay to write on was an art in itself. First it had to be ground to powder, then mixed with water and moulded into tablet shape. Slightly curved. Once it was dried in the sun, it could be inscribed upon. Ishtar thought it a waste of time.

What a mess that clay created! It clogged the water and made our washing difficult.

Gilgamesh ordered a five-year count of our busy city, because he liked to know what he owned. Forty thousand people, or a number close to that. But people distrusted being counted. It did his reputation little good.

Gilgamesh lived in a mud-brick tower, so he saw the great sprawl when he looked out of the skin-covered windows. People didn't like his tower. The hunters and gatherers in particular hated it; they had paid for it in trade taxes. It stood tall, reaching for the gods, and with its many rooms, its lavish decorations, it was built with great skill and cunning.

The moment Ishtar's new temple was built, people came to feed the gods dishes of honey, rolled sweets, balls of savoury, and dishes of hommos. They wanted blessings.

Ishtar was annoyed. "Does no one feed me out of pure love? Do they all want my blessing? Or a boon?"

The *sangaresses* bowed their heads. "We are here because we love you, Ishtar. We want nothing but to be allowed to love you."

Ishtar chose to believe her priestesses, but she would test them along the way.

Gilgamesh came more often than he openly admitted. In disguise. He watched Ishtar, the great goddess of war who had helped him to a great but costly victory. He was grateful to her, entranced, so smitten he forgot how she treated her lovers when she tired of them.

"You are so regal," Gilgamesh said, and Ishtar and I knew that meant he finally adored her, as all men should. "You make all the demons vanish with your smile."

"My sister lost her virginity to a demon," Ishtar said, though I knew of no sister-loving demon. I sensed a trick, and it made me smile. She was clever, my goddess. She could have anything.

Ishtar closed her eyes as if it was a difficult memory.

But her lips had swollen, reddened, and her cheeks were heated. Gilgamesh could not help but move closer to her.

"My sister and I caused our father some heartache when we were young. Even a god is not immune from difficult children. She was the leader; I was very accommodating then.

"Our father had selected a husband for her: kind, old, wealthy. None of that mattered, of course, because love can come regardless. But we heard from his own washerwoman that he was endowed with a weapon the size of a little finger, and that it did not get hard, ever, ever, ever. We also heard that he did not believe in touching women tenderly with tongue or digits, and so my sister was faced with a lifetime of frustration."

Washing Ishtar's underthings in soft water under the window, I listened proudly. Thank the washerwoman for that information! We know everything!

Ishtar said, "She did not know how to express this to our father, because you do not talk about such things. Our mother did not talk of it. She gave us to believe it was her duty, that lovemaking was something to be endured. But we had heard her in their chamber, and her cries were not those of disgust.

"My sister and I discussed this; that our mother was a sexual being, and perhaps she could understand. She was known for her gentleness throughout Sumer. She listened as my sister spoke, fumbling, then took her into her arms and tried to comfort her. 'All men can be taught certain techniques,' she said. 'Once they realise how much pleasure they will receive from your pleasure.'

"Our mother surprised us in this way, and my sister went into the marriage with some hope.

"A demon will always know, though. A demon can sniff out uncertainty and considers it his duty to take the virginity of a woman like this. Perhaps to spoil her for the sad, dull lovemaking which will follow; who knows?

"On my sister's wedding night, we did not have a guard. Her new husband did not have young friends; his were too old to sit on the floor. So my sister laid waiting for him on a nest of a thousand pillows, her hair spread like silk around her, her body oiled, eyes closed. She thought of the goatherd she saw every morning, with his torn pants revealing muscular legs, his broad, bare chest, his sweat, and his dark, lustful eyes.

"The demon sniffed her out. He appeared at the end of her bed, slim, muscular, his weapon hard like a club, reaching up stiffly to his stomach. He smiled at her; no demon wants to take an unwilling woman, as part of their pleasure is in the acquiescence. He touched her toe, stroked it with his forefinger, then drew his finger up her leg, so softly she thought it was a gust of wind. She did not want to open her eyes and ruin the picture she had, but the smell of him was so different, so unexpected, she had to look.

"Using his thumbs, he stroked her thigh, her breasts, her shoulders, as if he were moving the flesh into a position he liked. She gasped, but already her breathing was too quick for her to speak. She knew what he must be. But the smell; of perfume dripped onto hot sand, of sweat — the sweetest, freshest sweat, was too much. He glowed. He kissed her and it was like eating a date dipped in honey. She was not sure if she breathed, but she must have."

Gilgamesh was torn, I could tell. He wanted Ishtar so powerfully, but my goddess could always spin a tale.

"He clutched his fingers into the hair between her legs, combing it, tugging it, then he sank his thumbs inside her, spread her apart and bent his head to drink her juices. This is what she had imagined, exactly what she had dreamed, and she could not help the shudder which shook her whole body.

"Meanwhile, her husband? The demon had sorted him out, sent him terrible stomach pains which had him crouched over the waste hole in agony. He would need to bathe well before coming to my sister, he knew that much at least.

"My sister reached for the demon, wanting to feel his weapon. It was smooth, hard, silken. He held her chin and raised his eyebrows. Demons need an invitation; that is something we don't usually tell you men. They will not enter without an invitation.

"'Please,' she said. 'It's time.'

"There was no pain. He was a gentle demon and he moved to fit her perfectly, so wondrously. 'Remember this,' he said, the only words he spoke. 'Remember this.'

"She would, too. Every night when her husband came to her, she would remember the demon and then she could manage to be a good wife."

Gilgamesh and Ishtar enjoyed each other greatly that night.

Gilgamesh was weak for Ishtar and weak for death, too. He couldn't understand why he wasn't a god, why he wouldn't live forever.

Ishtar said, "Only Adapa refused immorality. When offered the bread of life, he didn't take it."

"He thought it was the bread of death, didn't he? And he was obeying the command of his patron, Ea. He made a mistake. I would not refuse."

Yet Gilgamesh failed when he had his chance. He found the bread of life, but set it down for a moment. A snake took it; slithered away with immortality, just like that. This is why, like Tammuz, the snake will shed its skin every year.

Gilgamesh came back, not only having failed at grasping his chance at immortality, but with both ears bright red and deaf with infection. We ground the thorn bush to powder and applied this to his ears (our nurse did, at least. But I washed the bandages), and he was cured of the deafness if not of mortality. Ishtar comforted him, held him in his fury and sorrow, but later, to me, she confessed relief.

"To spend eternity with him is too much to ask. He should know that and know my choices."

"Your choices?" I asked quietly.

"I made the choice to house my army in the caves. That was a good choice."

"What else could you have chosen?"

"Immortality for Gilgamesh or for you," she said. I knew she joked but she took my rough, damaged hand. "I would choose you, Ninlil."

This was the first time she had used my name. She could only be telling the truth.

"I could have chosen to house them in the Underworld, but I don't want to be beholden. Especially not to her."

I will go down to the cedar forest...the jungle...I will open it.
~ Epic of Gilgamesh

That is why Gilgamesh began his great adventures. Out of punishment, atonement. Anger at his own failure. He went into the Giant Hugeness, the King's Forest, *Ababu*, with his friend, Enkidu, for wood to build Ishtar a house. Did he think to domesticate her? Did Enkidu suggest this to keep her trapped? Ha! A house the size of a city, with all the magic and attractions, all the food and drink, all the lovers and things to watch and running water, and all those things he imagined would not keep her there.

For this he needed wood. This is the real reason he entered the forest. The *Ababu*.

The forest was off limits to ordinary people. By mimicking actions of gods, Gilgamesh hoped to become one. Enkidu, too. Those two men, seeking what they could not have. Even the death of the Bull of Heaven could not grant them this desire.

It was all to no avail, anyway. Enkidu died, and on his own deathbed, Gilgamesh shook with fear. "I don't want to go to the Underworld."

"I'll be there, my love," Ishtar said. "I will come to visit you."

Of course, this was what he was scared of. Her very great power, that she could come and go in the Underworld as she pleased. He was scared that she could come to him whenever she chose, but that he did not have the freedom to get away.

Those who said that Gilgamesh never succumbed to Ishtar's charms were wrong. He had known she would tire of him. And so Gilgamesh sat in the Underworld, proof that there was a union. Ishtar knew he would be waiting for her.

Time passed, and the world changed before another king was born whom Ishtar could love again. Whom she could make great.

Kaaron Warren

SARGON: 2270 BCE
The Washerwoman Shamiran

It is the men who are remembered in history. Women are found as consorts and in cults.
~ The Washerwoman Shamiran

I am not emotional like my ancestresses. I use my knowledge to record history, not my place in it. To tell the real story. Before me they remembered invention, adventure.

I remember truth.

Ishtar met Sargon when he was very young. A child. The cities all around were ever-watchful. She kept close by as he grew, waited until he was old enough.

It was said Sargon was found drifting in a reed boat when he was a newborn. That a gardener adopted him, and that he was born in the land where herbs grow. Not all believed this; some thought he was the son of a simple farmer, with no king-like inheritances. Ishtar knew she would want him as a lover from the moment her eyes clasped on him, and that without her, he would not wage war as he should. She kept close by as he grew, waiting.

He was not difficult to seduce. She dressed simply so as not to frighten him, drab robes clinging to her. She was covered with a light sheen of sweat. She had always sweated a lot. If I hadn't rinsed her clothes out well they would have rotted. Her skin beneath glistened as if covered with fine sand.

He didn't have a hope of resistance.

For the wedding of Sargon and Ishtar, the boats lined up for weeks in the docks. Most sailors like to use the Euphrates, with its lower banks and less violent floods.

Life must be different along the Tigris, rough and fast as an arrow.

They brought apples and cucumbers. They brought red carnelian to stop blood, should Ishtar fall pregnant or Sargon be injured at war. They brought lapis lazuli, the stone with which men dot their beards, twisted into dozens of tendrils, in order to seduce. I liked a man with a twisted beard. A beardless chin meant a lack of potency. Male slaves had shaved chins or beards too short to be twisted. Shaving an enemy's beard shamed him.

Men were funny about their beards. Grow another one! It didn't matter how new the beard was, as long as there was one.

There were female slaves on the ships as well, and I thought perhaps they were the strongest people aboard.

Captains were always male.

The poor lined the docks, waiting for the scraps. They cleaned ships for a handful of wheat. They were whipped away often, but still they came back. One of my ancestresses believed that the only way that humankind will ever have a future is if the starving masses are given a voice. Yet still they stood, unheard.

With Ishtar's help, Sargon was made king. She easily convinced the city's rulers, saying, "We need one man to lead us through the emergencies of existence."

Sargon had no dream of immortality. He was king of the earth; his descendants were his immortality.

Sargon was a very handsome man. He made whores stutter, so lovely was he. His eyes were always half-closed as if the lids were heavy with perfumed oil. If they widened you would need to beware; it meant some great fury rose in him, and whoever stood by would bear the brunt.

Ishtar told me his eyes opened this way as he was about to release himself.

"Wide open in surprise, as if such a wonder has never occurred to him before." She sat on a smooth, flat rock by the Euphrates, watching me work. The stone was warm enough to dry her thin shawls in moments. The heat turned her bare buttocks a pleasant reddish colour, though sometimes her internal heat changed the colour of her skin, too.

"And his lips, too, will part in surprise." Sargon's lips were thick and pouty. They often looked amused, but this was a terrible trick.

I remember one young man who brought a message about a late sheep delivery. Pale-skinned, this was a sheltered boy unaware of the ways to read a face. He was angry at his father for sending him as messenger, so when Sargon said, "And is your father sorry for this?" and lifted the corners of his mouth, the boy was tricked.

"Him? He is never sorry. We are not a sorry family, all in all." The boy thought this was clever. He smiled.

Ishtar entered the room then. She had been listening; she heard all, when she concentrated.

The rainless sky made us all irritable. Sargon smiled back, and the boy said, "And you know he thinks he could be king? If only he had the chance?"

Sargon drew back one arm and with a blow knocked the boy across the room, where his head crushed against a solid urn. Something shook loose; the boy would only smile from then on. Was only happy. Not such a bad punishment, really.

But I had more clothes to wash.

Ishtar talked to me a lot. She had no female friends and

she did not trust her servants. She said, "Sargon is the most attractive man I have been with because of his lack of — his disdain for — humility."

"We Akkadians are proud. Never humble," I said. "This is why we will live forever. There will be Akkadians on this ground till the end of time."

"This is true." She was not like other women, the ones who were happy to share, to live in a harem and wait for the man to desire them. She needed to be with a man when she needed it.

I think she played in her own harem once, but she found the deception too exhausting.

"I only love the powerful men who come close to matching me," she told me.

I was with her always. Did she rely on my mother in that way? My grandmother? It was perhaps so, but Ishtar and I, we were friends, despite our age differences. I was not the youngest washerwoman; during the reign of Gilgamesh, one of my ancestresses was only eight when she began. She never married. Ishtar does not talk about it, but I know that she was raped by one of Gilgamesh's guards and that she gave birth to a daughter. Perhaps Ishtar ordered this; certainly her desire was that each washerwoman was the daughter of the last.

Ishtar and Sargon liked to tour the city and environs, incognito, dressed in drab. They come back covered with food, other stains.

As they walked, Sargon talked of how difficult Akkad was to defend, without natural boundaries apart from the rivers and the mountains.

"You should turn the river red and they will be too frightened to cross," Ishtar told him. She had learned a lot in her many years. "Turn the water the colour of blood."

So thousands of animals and prisoners were slaughtered to keep the enemy away.

In this way, they prepared themselves. I had been told about the travails of war; how dirty the men get and how much they liked to pull on clean trews. I would do my job well; boil those clothes so hard the black fat bugs roiled to the top.

When Sargon built Akkad, he also built two walls around the city. Little did he know that between these two walls, resting, was the army of stillborns. Ishtar had moved them there, thinking she wanted them close. There they waited for their next war. Akkad was Ishtar's city. As long as it was strong, so was she. She would do all she could to protect it.

I don't know what will be written in the future. We write of our enemies in the past in the worst possible light. We talk about invaders as being so cruel. And we are spoken of in the worst possible terms. Some believe Sargon demonic in his cruelties.

There are many different versions of the truth, but these things I saw myself. I saw children, women and men impaled alive on tall, sharp sticks in the ground. Impaled at the top, they slowly sank to the ground. One woman survived for three days, writhing on the ground, the tall stick through her belly. She was a strong woman. She begged to be released, but no one would risk the wrath of Sargon. Her family were all dead; not as strong as her.

Ishtar watched, fascinated. "What makes one woman so strong? What gives her the desire to live when she is in agony?"

Many others were skinned alive. Why did Sargon order such torture? To be powerful. To incite fear and obedience. To ensure loyalty, and to cause a smaller ruler to pause before considering an invasion of Akkad.

Are we different from any other powerful race?

Ishtar had her own secret weapon. They waited between the two walls of the city; unbreathing, unthinking, waiting. The stillborn army, depleted, but still living. She told me that when they needed further numbers, they sliced a limb off and grew it, but that these soldiers were...ugly. Small. Malformed. Ishtar learned to keep the numbers of her army down so that she could control them, and used them for night attacks. She sent them to enemy collaborators or to those who talked of treason, and they used small knives and their sharp teeth. Ishtar told them to leave the traitors alive because she wanted them to talk, to spread the word about the law.

It was these creatures who first performed the cruelties, deaf to pleas for mercy and cries of pain. But Sargon did nothing to stop them, did he? And when he saw the fear, the instant capitulation amongst survivors, he took to the ways of the stillborn army without regret.

And so war was done and won.

In peacetime, people complained. Not one a day, but many. Ishtar became irritated to the point of fury.

Sargon loved her angry. It inspired him.

"It is so dry," whined a woman.

I couldn't help myself. I whispered in Ishtar's ear, "And yet I find the water to clean your clothes."

It was enough for Ishtar. She roared, "I will stir the waters of the Abyss for you," and she lifted her arms. Tilted her head until the back of her skull touched her spine. Opened her mouth so wide I thought she could swallow the whole court. We watched as the woman choked on sand, and when one of the soldiers slit her throat to help her breathe, fine golden dust poured out. No one touched it; no one dared clean it. We watched over the days as small gusts of wind spread the grains through the city.

Even Sargon was frightened by this. "She's bored," one of his childhood friends said. No one else would dare. "You need to find something for her to do or she will destroy you." To keep her occupied, he asked her to visit the neighbourhoods in disguise, to see if there was any talk of war.

"Who would dare war with you now, Sargon?" she said. "Unless I ask him to?"

But she did go out. And in a tavern three towns away, she did hear conspirators in their talk. She laughed at them because they were weak, arrogant men. The worst sort.

She took her time getting back to Sargon and by then the men had run away. The wine seller was put to death in their place.

"It is the law. The wine seller heard this and did nothing." Did Ishtar feel guilt? I don't think so. At most she regretted her lazy journey home because it allowed the men to run.

Regret was the beginning of the loss of power.

When people came to beg favours, Sargon said, "I am the King of Earth. I do not represent the gods."

Ishtar smiled at that. She knew what happened to arrogant men in the afterlife.

One of the men who came begging slipped through, hoping for work in the kitchen. With all my listening, and with all Ishtar's knowledge and Sargon's power, still the poisoner got past us. Almost got past us. If it wasn't for the food tasters, Sargon would have died.

There was no doubt who the poisoner was. There were witnesses (and these, too, were punished. Certainly it was not obvious until all the pieces were put together; but still, they should have stopped the man). The poisoner was caught resting in the shade of a thorn tree and terrible illness struck him. He no longer had spit on his tongue. It was like all the water was sucked out of his body. His insides dried up and curled in on themselves like a dead worm. His weapon released white dust, not the cream of babies. His life's blood dried to a thick paste inside his body. He died in a most uncomfortable state.

Strange that he should be so dry at neap-tide.

"You should answer the questions, King Sargon," the poisoner croaked as he died. "Was it a reed boat you were found in? Were you really rescued by a carpenter, a *nagar*, and brought up that way? What was your name before you overcame the King of Uruk and built Akkad? 'King is Steadfast' is not the name you were born with."

Sargon didn't like to be questioned about his past. All life began when Ishtar blessed him, he said.

After that, Sargon never trusted his cup-bearer. He changed them every couple of days, never telling them beforehand. When he had been cup-bearer to the King of Kish, not a day had passed without plotting, so Sargon knew how little these people could be trusted. His counterpart, King Lugalands of Lagash had been poisoned, and survived, but with his skin turned blue and each breath a pain. Lugalands' washerwoman told me it was his wife, Queen Baranamtarra, who poisoned him. She said he was a dull husband who did not appreciate a good woman. Even Sargon, who did not criticise other kings in case he needed them as allies in the future, had no time for the man.

I told Ishtar all, and before long the two Queens were friends.

Were they lovers? Some would say so. Some said that Ishtar placed her favoured women in ruling positions, and some said that she transformed them into men and placed them in many positions of power.

The Queen had three daughters and five sons, and Ishtar, watching the children around their mother, came to wish she could inspire such unequivocal love herself.

Ishtar said, "In all my years I have had no desire for a child. But now, this Sargon, this powerful man. If I had a child with him, imagine where the line would go."

I didn't speak of the dangers of a goddess and man having children together. That the child may be born a monster, because he should not have been born at all. If we washerwomen have learned anything, it's that our mistress only wants to hear what she wants to hear. But I knew what this would mean for Ishtar, allowing herself the role of mother: once she cared for another human being, her power would be diminished.

She did not discuss the idea with Sargon, but merely told him it was time to make an heir. He was so nervous he could not speak for three days. What if he couldn't perform under such pressure?

"This is how it must be," Ishtar said. She devised rituals to calm him, keep his focus.

Ishtar hid away for her pregnancy. She didn't like the way she looked, she didn't like the way she felt. She stayed in her home and shouted orders. She was restless, angry and I know that more than once she regretted her decision. She made Sargon suffer for it, though he showered her with gifts and love. He told her she was beautiful more times than any man should. We were all greatly relieved when the time for confinement came. She had me wait outside.

I spoke with midwives as I readied the sheets. "I would not need to do this if so many newborns didn't die." The sheet she birthed on would be stitched into a baby pillow, a mattress, to keep the baby safe through its first three months, the most dangerous time after childbirth.

"It is not our fault," one midwife said. I think she was more witch than midwife.

"You think it is the fault of the gods?"

Nervous laughter. "Of course not. Maybe it's the rituals. Our rituals are wrong." They spoke in husky voices.

I told them they needed to drink, to ensure they were strong for the ordeal ahead.

As her pains begin, Ishtar, impetuous as ever, moved from room to room, dwelling to dwelling. "I don't want the baby now," she said quietly to one of the midwives. "I really don't want it. Take it away as soon as it is born."

The midwives looked at her attendant, who was frozen with horror and indecision.

"Many women feel this way as the baby begins its journey. It will be different when you see your child," one midwife said.

Ishtar roared at her, wide open face, skull showing. The midwife's eyes teared up in terror. They would never stop tearing as long as she lived.

The midwife calmed her by telling her stories of the calf or pregnant cow and the powerful, king-like bull. The circle of life shown with the calf suckling from the mother, the mother licking her calf clean.

"I can imagine another circle," Ishtar roared at us. She wanted to be lover, not birth-giver, to use her opening for pleasure, not pain. She wept, then.

"Many women do this. Like them, you will never be the same," the midwife told Ishtar with some glee. Ishtar struck out, twisted the woman's nose until it broke.

"Evil gossip," she said.

Her body was changed. But what did that matter? A woman is as sexual after as she was before.

"I just want a healthy child," Ishtar said through her tears.

"Woman have said that forever. We are all terrified at this time, Goddess. You are not alone. You are a sister to all of us."

As Ishtar wailed, the midwife said, "This is good pain." These words have annoyed birthing women since the beginning of human life, and it will continue to do so forever.

"Come on, heavenly cow," another said to her.

This made Ishtar laugh.

Ishtar had never suffered like she did in childbirth. "Is this what death feels like? I should not be feeling this. Sargon wants to destroy me." One side of her mouth went slack and she stopped speaking.

"Don't let yourself be distracted," the midwives said.

Her fingers went cold and she felt as if she couldn't move them, as if her heart stopped beating.

Sargon's attendants called at the door for entry. "He wants to know what is happening."

"Get out!" shouted the midwives. Men in the birthing room could lead to disaster. They could attract Lamastrum, the she-demon who killed babies. Sometimes a male exorcist could be used, if the Lamastrum would not leave.

Ishtar later told me all she saw and felt. She was in a fever, and there is truth in fever. "I thought my baby would die and that I would be left deformed for all my eternal life."

There was a smell in the room. It was a quiet smell, the smell of burning dust.

"You heard me scream at the cleaning woman, didn't you? How could she leave this room dusty?"

But then the smell grew stronger and there stood Nergal of the Underworld. The forgotten god, Ishtar called him.

The god of fertility, fever and death. Though Ishtar still found him unattractive, Ereshkigal remained jealous. So Nergal disliked Ishtar both for rejecting him and causing him trouble.

Still, she hoped he would not let this make his decision. She had said to me on more than one occasion, "Why would they let a man like him be in charge of those three things? No wonder women die in childbirth."

Beside him stood the female demon Lamastrum. The demoness had a hairy body, the head of a lioness, donkey's teeth and ears, long fingernails and fingers, bird's feet and sharp talons.

"You are consorting with this one now?" Ishtar hissed.

The midwives pressed oil to her forehead. They took the waters of labour and sprinkled them over her torso.

Ishtar threatened the demon, "I will cover you in death's dust. Fill your mouth, cover your face." Her great internal heat filled the room, so we all sweated.

They called for Lamassus: the protective spirits, the doorkeepers. Lamassu have an intelligent man's head, a strong lion's body and a brave eagle's wings.

They exist as the opposite to Lamastrum. At that moment, as I gathered bloody rags from her bed, Ishtar seemed as vulnerable as any woman. Not the goddess of war, feared by all.

The law books carried admonitions to those who hit a mother and caused the child to die. People who committed this crime were led on by the cruelty of Lamastrum. That was how she worked. She liked others to do terrible things in her name. As Ishtar shouted and thrashed and cursed us all, the Lamassus and Lamastrum did battle in the skies. Nergal, a weak man, allowed these others to do the fighting, while he watched Ishtar with a mixture of love, hatred and desire.

Finally, Ishtar's father called halt.

"This is my grandchild!" he roared, and the whole earth was silent for a moment or more.

Finally, the baby emerged, with the cord across her mouth. They cleaned the face before all else; a face covered with the muck of birth brings trauma to a new life.

"She will be good with words. That will ease her life," the midwife said, lifting the cord gently away from the baby's mouth.

"She already will have a good life," Ishtar said. Sensitive goddess.

"What will you call her?

Ishtar closed her eyes. "I have not decided."

"You must name her soon. She has no identity without a name."

The first day, Sargon was kept out of Ishtar's bedroom. He was furious, wanting to see his daughter. Ishtar knew she should feed from her own breasts and she struggled to do so, though in a way which made the midwives roll their eyes. They didn't say anything, but I knew they were thinking *a mortal woman manages this but a goddess chooses not to.*

She gave perhaps five mouthfuls of milk to the baby then gave up. "Hire a wet nurse. I have no milk. My breasts are there for beauty, not to be used as vessels."

Alone with me, she wept. "Once I fed three boys from these breasts and they did not struggle! Then my milk flowed." She rubbed at her breasts as if to wipe them away. "Is that right?" she asked me, as if I had been there. She always did get us confused. "Did I feed those babies? Or did they just chew at my nipples?"

The next day Sargon was allowed in, and the first

thing he did was to carefully examine the child's genitalia. Many babies are born girl-boy and these people, while not unhappy, are separate. They were considered fortunate to have the best of the two sexes, but they were also seen with suspicion.

The girl was beautiful, and had her own way from the moment she could burble. With her position in life, she could become whatever she liked, though she always said she had no choice.

They named her Enheduanna, meaning Chief Priestess of the Ornament of the On High. Ishtar left Enheduanna increasingly to the wet nurse. This woman secretly took another child to feed as well. She sat there with one at each breast as if there was nothing wrong with sharing the tit meant for a goddess' child.

I had to tell Ishtar. The wet nurse was tortured before a crowd; her breasts cut off, her head shaved. Her fingers broken.

A new wet nurse was found.

For all of that, Ishtar knew her daughter would need a friend, and that having shared the milk, the two babies would share a life. This was true, although the other child grew to be dull, humourless and tongue-tied. Her mother was a businesswoman with her own silver sewn into the hem of her coat. She dealt in buying and selling property, and Ishtar was quite happy to talk to her, because she was strong and vital.

As the girls grew, Ishtar's daughter Enheduanna became a poetess and the other girl became a weaver.

Sargon was a great and powerful king in his city surrounded by mountains. Yet he turned to feathers at the sight of Ishtar and his daughter, Enheduanna. Both he and Ishtar were weakened by parenthood, as was natural. We pass our strength to our children.

Sargon had near six thousand men keeping the peace around the city. They were a strange bunch. Idle soldiers were always difficult; they found things to do which were not always pleasant. These soldiers knew about the army in the walls and some would stare in through a crack and poke sticks through to try and rouse them to action.

But the stillborns would not rouse until Ishtar asked them to.

Ishtar placed my sister in charge of the army of washerwomen needed to keep Sargon's soldiers clean.

"I protect you from such a chore," my goddess told me, though I would have loved to wash more than her bloodstained face cloths. My sister marched to war with the army. She told us terrible stories about Sargon's cruelty in battle. He liked to destroy completely, to take away any chance of rebellion, of people rising up to take revenge. She told us of the stillborns, how at times their skin would drop off from burns or dryness, and new skin would grow back in an instant. We saw this as we followed behind; Ishtar, her daughter and me.

Akkad had soon filled with desperate, displaced people. Ishtar tutted at this. "He is not very nice. Why destroy their homes so completely there is no point rebuilding? They don't respect him more because of it. They are just tired. You, where are you from?"

"The Land of Rivers, lady." The young man was close to starvation; all of them in the long line were.

"Where, fool? Where is your place?"

"Kazilla. But there is not even a bush left for a bird. Your Sargon has razed us."

"He is not mine," Ishtar said.

56

The young man spoke of an army so terrifying, so ugly, that he would have nightmares all his life. She helped feed these people and spread word they were not to be harmed. Later that night, she let Sargon know what she thought. "Why do you take their homes? You may as well kill them."

He kissed her, eyes wide open, dark and mesmerizing.

Ishtar's temples were very busy and there was money being made. The girls liked the soldiers because they were strong and determined. They sometimes sewed a small sprig of hair into a man's shirt, casting a love spell.

Ishtar would dry their cunts up if she found out.

Daughters of kings and rulers were sent to Akkad seeking husbands. Sent to spend time in Ishtar's temple. They were easily seen, with their raised-rim caps, their folded garments, their jewels. Some carried a staff with the insignia of their fathers.

I was happy there. There were gutters for taking away the dirty water. Even when it had not rained for some time, we were not thirsty.

Our houses were built from oven-baked mudbricks. Some had stairs inside, one room above another. Our streets were wide and well planned, and we had secure places to store grain. Cats killed all the pests.

But always, of course, there was war. I don't know if there was a week without it, in the reign of Sargon.

Sargon's advisors told him that Ishtar needed to produce a male heir if she wanted to remain 'first wife'. Ishtar did not care. She laughed at Sargon, made him angry. Scoffed at his law-making, which she said made him a boring man. At the same time, she told me he was the most virile lover she had known. This contrast interested her, despite herself. Great lover, dull lawmaker, cruel leader.

Ishtar felt unattractive; I know because she wore loose, ugly clothes and kept her hair unwashed. She would sit in her own temple and wait for one of the men to notice her, but they didn't.

Until the beardless traveller came.

No other girl would touch him. "A man without a beard won't pay. He will steal your sandals and be cruel."

Ishtar slept with him. Found him sleepy and lazy. He was funny, though. She liked him. When Sargon found out, he was disgusted that she had lain with a beardless man.

She said, "You bore me so much. You are so worried about your filing. Your administration."

This is what I mean about Ishtar. She didn't understand the importance of records.

He brought sense to us. In the market, there were standards of weight which were not there before. He did this. Ishtar thought this was dull, but I knew his work would be remembered.

Sargon wanted a boy. Ishtar said she risked death if she had another child. Sargon did not believe her. He thought there was a problem and they needed to have a sheep's liver read to find out what it was. He wanted to travel to the Oracles of his childhood, those he trusted more than anyone else.

"It is so far and war is so close. We should stay here," Ishtar said. "We do not need another child. We need to protect our city. We have our daughter who you will adopt as a son. Enheduanna will transform into a man, and she will manage all our kingdoms."

An advisor suggested they send a clay model of the sheep's liver instead.

"That is the lazy way. We will accompany the sheep,"

Sargon said.

Ishtar disagreed. "We have fortune tellers here. This one can read the patterns of oil poured on water."

But when a calf with two heads was born, Sargon knew he had to go to his Oracle.

We travelled twenty double hours, taking forty sheep, because they died so easily and Sargon wanted plenty to choose from. He would boon some of those not needed, and order a great barbeque pit to cook the rest.

I loved meat cooked like this. You could tear strips off and chew them as you walked or worked. If I chewed sheep meat while washing in a field, I was never bothered by animals; the smell of the flesh frightened them.

The desert was searing and swarming with snakes. A great dust storm lifted as we travelled. Though Sargon's men were well-practiced, four of them died while putting up shelters of thin wood for protection.

The smell of hot sand filled me. At night, when we stopped at last, we built beds of the hot rocks, and they kept us warm throughout the chilling dawn.

We led animals and prisoners with us. This was called *abaku*. They did the work and were sacrificed if need be.

The sheep turned from white to black, a terrible omen. If it was not for the love of Ishtar and Sargon, the caravan would have dispersed.

As the dust storm eased, the sheep nibbled at camel thorn bushes. Their memories were so short it was as if the storm had never happened. Some men we lost to quicksand, that sucking brown death you couldn't always see. Mostly, I was aware of the filth. The beer they drank on the way, and the washing this caused, with the vomit and the shit and piss as they fell down drunk.

We came across a flock of flamingos and watched in wonder. Our omen reader was confused by the good and bad. "We shall eat three of these birds," he decided. "Or thirty. Those we catch deserve to be eaten."

Sargon arranged trade with the communities we passed through. Metal ore and goods, textiles. His brilliance at negotiations was close to his brilliance at war, and even Ishtar could not help but be impressed. He controlled the trade from silver mines in Anatolia, lapis lazuli mines in Badakusha, and the cedar forests of Byblos. These forests gave him the biggest headaches, because of the difficulty in transporting unwieldy, heavy cedar. At least there was less risk of theft. Although I have known a caravan, sleeping over night, to find itself awash with fortune tellers seeking to read the future in the texture of the bark.

Finally we reached the Oracles, and they greeted Sargon as if he were a young boy; they had known him that long.

They cut open one of our sheep and read the liver.

If the liver was loose, they said, a prince would be slain in the palace.

But one part was distended, and this meant that the son of a king would take the throne.

"I have no son." Sargon roared so mightily that his exhausted men collapsed to the ground. "That is why we have come to you. Where is my son and why does my goddess not wish to bear him?"

They slaughtered another dozen sheep, consulted for three days, and finally told Sargon that the goddess of love and war would have two children, a girl for love and a boy for war. There was no doubt about this.

Ishtar said, "I will fill my cunt with thorns before I have another child."

Foolish Sargon to think a fortune teller could convince Ishtar otherwise. "Women have five or six children, Ishtar. Not just one."

"They are women. I am Ishtar."

"But if our daughter dies?"

"Our daughter will not die."

And so it was said, and we all returned to our ordinary lives. Of course, the ordinary life of a worker was very different from the ordinary life of the elite.

Ishtar's domestic staff might include, apart from myself: one hundred and fifty slave women, spinners, woolworkers, brewers, millers, kitchen workers, a singer, a musician, six women to grind grain for pigs, forty men, six women in brewery, the wet nurse and nursemaid when her daughter was young, personal servants and a hairdresser. The ruling class had no real idea of our daily existence. They thought we disappeared when they closed their eyes. They should be horrified if they saw the homes we live in, how mean they are. Except they would not care.

Ishtar liked to take Enheduanna to her temple, to let her feel the worship. Let her daughter see how women should be treated. Women went to be worshipped by serving the goddess.

Enheduanna liked to walk alone through the city, but was angry when taken for a prostitute. "You think I would be here and not in my mother's temple?" In the temple, women were worshipped for their sex, but in a brothel, there were naked women all over the walls, many in degrading situations.

In the brothels, men were worshipped as Tammuz once was, receiving the passion — the love — that the god deserved. Enheduanna did not care for this. She watched as farmers brought their wheat and got a shekel coin. Wheat on one side, Ishtar on the other. They would come back at festival time and spend the shekel on sex with a *sangaress*, to ensure fertility of fields. Fertile fields meant wheat for the temple, and so it continued.

Enheduanna wrote a poem to Ishtar, describing her mother as powerful and passionate. This poem, it left no doubt her words would be remembered forever.

She loved jewellery and wore it with great majesty. Large, golden earrings. Silver arm and leg rings. She paid the price of solitude to the god of writing, Marduk's son, Nebo, because she would never marry. She would marry her words.

Then the river changed its course. The land became drier, and the people blamed Sargon, who was not used to their anger. He had no other time of unrest in his entire rule. "Am I in control of *An*, heaven? No, I am not. I have power over *Ki*, the earth, in that I can move it, and I can build on it, and I can spill blood on it. But I cannot control the water. This is not in my power."

They listened to his voice of reason, and he helped to move the earth so that the river flowed through Akkad again.

Sargon reigned for fifty-five years. Or perhaps sixty-one. Nothing in history is certain. He aged, while Ishtar remained so beautiful it hurt your eyes to look at her.

He took another wife, and another. They had son after son. Ishtar, tired by life itself, did nothing more than send Sargon a perpetual rash to make his beard itch. That was suffering enough, she thought, for all those wives. She left him to his young women and his sycophants.

"I am tired of the smell of old man," she told him.

He sacrificed his great love, Ishtar, to have a son.

When Sargon was a hundred or more, the cities around Akkad finally banded together to fight him. He still won. Afterwards, he walked down to the river, alone, carrying only his great sword.

I was already there, my back aching, as I rinsed out my goddess' robes. We stood side by side, the King of the World and I, washing in the river. He did not want ceremony. He simply cleaned his weapons, as if to say, "I am done. I have conquered all."

He gave me a smile. "Enough," he said, and he went to his bed and did not rise. As he died, he threatened, "Whoever lays hands on the cursed stones of Akkad — should she fall — will find pain for many generations."

Touching a stone of Akkad is called *Qatu*. Perhaps my descendants will know of what happens to the stones.

When he died, there was such grief that the men drank more beer in a day than they would drink in a week. Men lay stultified in the streets, women huddled inside, all of them weeping at the loss.

At his funeral, perfume and fragrances were part of the ritual, and desiccated fruit was laid out to be chewed for sweetness. At the back, quiet, grey-faced, stood line after line of inhuman soldiers. They stood stooped but not tired, smelling of ash and vinegar. They watched — the stillborn army of Ishtar — with no emotion on their faces. They merely ensured that no upstarts tried to take the throne from Sargon's son to another woman.

After the funeral, Enheduanna and I helped shift the army to large, dry caves. Ishtar faded visibly; she needed rest. We made her a bed in the caves amongst her soldiers, and we left her there to sleep.

And that son, once king, was killed by his own servants. Did they use him as a scapegoat for all his father did? I don't know. Ishtar and I no longer lived in his tower, then. Once Sargon died, we had no reason to stay.

His daughter, Enheduanna, was removed as High Priestess when Sargon died. As if she had never held that position in the first place. "The words chose me. I am a poetess and that is all there is."

She wrote this poem:

Me who once sat triumphant, he has driven out of the sanctuary.
Like a swallow he made me fly from the window. My life is consumed.
He stripped me of the crown appropriate for the high sangarhood.
He gave me dagger and sword — "It becomes you," he said to me.

It was in your service that I first entered the holy temple,
I, Enheduanna, the highest sangaress. I carried the ritual basket,
I chanted your praise.
Now I have been cast out to the place of the lepers.
Day comes and the brightness is hidden around me.
Shadows cover the light, drape it in sandstorms.
My beautiful mouth knows only confusion.
Even my sex is dust.

SHULGI: 1990 BC
The Washerwoman Ninevah

On that day, the storm howled, the tempest swirled,
The North Wind and the South Wind roared violently,
Lightning devoured in heaven alongside the seven winds,
The deafening storm made the earth tremble,
Ishkur thundered throughout the heavenly expanse
The rains above embraced the waters below
Its little stones, its big stones lashed at my back
But I the king was unafraid, uncowed.
~ Shulgi[i]

Four generations passed. My mother, my grandmother, my grandmother's mother.

Ishtar's temples multiplied and grew in importance. There was also an increase in the violence against the

Sangaresses and the temples; a greater fear. Was it because the *Sangaresses* learnt to read, write and count? Did the men think this would destroy society as we know it?

Ishtar complained to me: "I hear a whining noise. Most irritating. I think it is the pleas of men who have never visited my temple. Hard to imagine why they think I will help them. Perhaps I will consider them my enemy instead. Perhaps I will send them great mismatches, like the scorpion, the *Zuqiqipum* and the crab. I will send the bite of the crab to their genitals, and it will not release its grip until they rot in the ground. The crab is very stubborn."

At Ishtar's main temple, there was a brick altar in front of her statue. Sometimes she sat there observing, unmoving. Leading to this room there was a long hall, lined with rooms for the *Sangaresses*. The temple was made of mud brick, dusty inside, but cool when it needed to be. Mosaics covered the walls and roof. Women made this art, painstakingly cracking the tiles, sticking them together. I watched them as my work dried and it was remarkable to see; none of us washerwomen believed it could form a picture. But it did: Ishtar, naked at the gates of the Underworld.

Music and singing filled the temple, so there always seemed to be happiness, regardless of the reality. There were eunuchs, serving Ishtar as well as any priestesses could. And there were virgin worshippers, ready to serve. There was some opposition to this from those who didn't worship Ishtar. Those who disliked Ishtar's temples said, "You damage your city because you damage the family. You are neither stable nor predictable."

There is an Akkadian proverb which says, "The one who does not support a wife, who does not support a son, is a dishonest person who does not support himself."

The family was holy and we in Ishtar's service were considered by some to be against that. Families looked after their own. A settled family caused less trouble. So the preservation of the family was vital to a society and took precedence over individual needs. Wise King Shulgi knew this.

But all roads led to the temple area. Ishtar, or at least, the cult around her, was at its most powerful. In homes, housewives built their own shrines, and I believe their husbands did not complain. Any wife who loved Ishtar loved to lie with her husband as well.

An adulterous wife once lingered in Ishtar's temple much longer than she needed to. Yes, she came to take a man, as all married women must do for their marriage to hold, but this woman did not want to leave. By law, her husband could choose her punishment, up to and including death.

Her husband loved her so much that the punishment he chose was for her to spend a year in Ishtar's temple before returning to him. He knew that this would be pleasant for her, that it was no punishment at all. He took pleasure from it himself, and I told him details, things which made him sweat and brought the breath fast in his lungs. I told him that his wife said to every man, "Come, cross my bed post. Climb into my bed."

He loved to hear such details.

Ishtar's advisors told her to banish these women, who loved the physical nature of Ishtar's temple too much. Before she did so, Ishtar took the time to understand the women. She sat with them as they laughed at their husbands' lack of virility. "No beard below," they said.

"What of the men who visit them?" I asked about the banished women. "These women did not make love to ghosts."

"They can't help themselves. They are men."

I knew she had not loved since the passing of Sargon and the death, long ago, of her poetess daughter. King Shulgi, so bright in the eyes, so clear in his head, drew her to him, although he didn't plan this. He didn't know of her past; he was not religious, nor superstitious.

Ishtar couldn't be understood in simple human terms. We knew her a thousand years, my mother, my grandmothers and I, and still I could not predict what she would do. She was always conflicted; did she protect or destroy? She was better than some about allowing the poor people a voice, but still, as washerwomen have believed for many centuries, mankind will fail unless we are given the chance to speak.

She was so changeable, capricious, in love. What made her love a man also made her hate him. All lovers felt such emotion, but with Ishtar, all things were exaggerated

Shulgi was not difficult to seduce. Gilgamesh — with his fear, his knowledge of her — took much to bed. But Shulgi spent a lot of time with the *sangars* because he loved books. In their library they had seventy-two volumes called *The Illumination of Bel.* They had geographical lists and maps of the known world, they had catalogues of animals, plants and minerals; they had calendars and grammatical works and books of words and training books for the scribes.

But Ishtar distracted him. For all his wisdom, he was as shallow as any man in the things which attracted him; he began building a tower at the age of ten, thinking this would earn him a place eternally in the minds of men.

Ishtar darkened below her eyes with guhlu, made from burnt camphor, and wore a pendant of carnelian which hung between her breasts. She reddened her nipples simply by touching them. Her pubic hair was lush, her genitals swollen. These things a man could not resist.

He was wise enough still to see that in marriage she would give him strength and power. He said he had a divine right to rule, given to him by Sin, god of justice and truth. He did not know this was Ishtar's father. But he knew that the goddess of war and love would help him to become great.

He made a simple promise in the ceremony. "To cover her with cloth and hat." We laughed, the other servants and I, because Shulgi made the vow surrounded by his vast wealth.

We did not laugh too hard, though, because Shulgi was a good man. He laid roads between his cities and he always protected the interests of the downtrodden. He straightened the highways, enlarged the footpaths. Travel was vital to trade and communications, he said. The easier the travelling, the better the trade.

It opened up the land for expansion, made it easier for people to return home for visits. He built rest-houses for travellers, pleasant places where experienced minds could meet and solve problems.

He dreamt of the Silk Road and other great lands. He dreamt of a land far beyond Kemet, the land of the backwards river. He didn't like to sit still, he liked to travel. It was not the journey; it was the destination.

He put the destitute to good use. Doing jobs others didn't want, like handling the dead. He'd been building a tower since he was ten, one he hoped could keep the whole population safe in case of danger. Solid and high, it was. For many years they built, and for many years people thought this was Shulgi's folly. Who would live in such a tower, reaching for the sun?

Ishtar found him fair and his interpretation of the law open and intelligent. He was not war-like, and when he smiled at her it was because he was amused or happy.

He began the process of writing down the law. Ishtar could not see this, but I knew it: writing down the law was another reason why she weakened. More laws meant fewer wars. Fewer people praying to her for help. He said his laws were approved by Sin. I thought that Ishtar was jealous of her father, of the respect he gave him. But Shulgi adored Ishtar and would listen to her, every word she said, foolish or otherwise.

"He is so wise," she sighed to me. She slept more often these days, and sometimes only got out of bed because I wanted to wash her sheets. "You didn't know Tammuz, but your ancestress loved him, washerwoman. I thought he was a wise man but how we learn! Now I know Shulgi and I see that nobody before him had his wisdom." She closed her eyes and sighed. "I remember when I was the wise one. I made the good choices."

He was not always kind, though, when his dignity was offended. The men who broke treaty with Shulgi were cursed. "As the mongoose hates the snake, so shall your wife hate you." The curse brought infertility, locusts, man-eating lions.

Treaties were respected after that. This held us all well when the storm came.

It was so dry in the year before the rain that people arrived to beg with their eyelids open, too dry to close them. First we had to give them water, let their bodies absorb it, before any words could be spoken.

"If only there would be rain," people said.

"The storm is coming," the seers said. "Then you will beg for the rain to stop."

We had known since the last storm, a thousand years ago, that another was coming. There were people who watched the sky every day for signs. Some children were paid in sugar to watch the reed marsh for turtles. It was said that if a turtle left the marsh for the river, the reed marsh will dry up. If the river dried, that was a sign of a great storm to come.

Shulgi had his builders work to make the city walls unshakeable. He talked of the weather which weakened Akkad, drought and dry storms. He talked of the coming flood, had talked of it since he was a child. He had them pile rocks and sand around his tower, strengthening it. There was no time for rest.

I asked Ishtar, "Can you call on your army? Or are they only for times of war?" She had shown me her stillborn army, safe now in the caves of a mountain three *berus* journey away.

"Only for war. And for me," she said.

He knew what work lay ahead of him and his people, not just preparation for the flood, but for the time we knew would come after, the long years of *ubbulu*, the drying of the field. Mud and debris would keep the grains from growing and make life uncomfortable for us all.

All cooperation was needed to build the city higher: "A place for those who contribute and their wives and children."

Though the wives and children helped too, gathering the materials, cooking the food. The washerwomen had less to do because people did not change their clothing very often. They fell instantly into exhausted sleep, woke, two, three hours later and rose in their clothes to go back to work.

Ishtar stood with her face tilted to the sky, her eyes closed. She sniffed, her nostrils flaring as they usually did when she was angry. "Can you smell it? The sky should not smell like that. Smells like the storm a thousand years ago. Zu stole the tablets of destiny then; perhaps I can steal them back if I can find them."

When we saw bright, shining light flying through the

sky, we knew it was almost time.

When the Black Wind came, I felt as if my nightmare walked with me. The storm raised black dust and it blocked the sun, the clouds, the sky. All was dark. The animals, confused, slept. They ceased production in their daze. How were they to know the time of day? To know when to eat or sleep?

Ahead of the storm, a pack of wolves ran in a great dust-raising mob. Their howls could be heard from half a *beru* away, and as they ran they snatched up food in their jaws: snakes, small dogs (*kalbum*), and in the villages, an abandoned baby here and there.

When people accepted there was a flood coming, there was a great exodus. Many left to set up elsewhere, as if elsewhere would not flood.

"Abhu. Abhu," the wagon driver called. He would transport people to high ground for half their earnings. Many were frightened of him. Abhu meant not just travel on earth, but travel to the Underworld. It meant death. The wagon driver liked his passengers frightened. They complained less, he said.

As the water continued to rise and it became obvious that this flood was different, panic set in. People began calling on Shulgi to make the rain stop. He was no Adad, god of the thundercloud, who could bring rain to a friend, and destructive storms to an enemy. What could Shulgi do?

Flood water smelt different than other water. It was full of the things it had washed in its path; the houses fallen, the horses drowned, the children. These things flavoured the torrent like soup.

Initially, children played in it as it rose, laughing at the idea of water where it shouldn't be, in the school rooms, the tents. But as it rose higher and higher, more were lost. They were lost laughing.

King Shulgi, wise and fair, let all of us and our families into his high tower. All of us who worked for Ishtar. Some high-born shouted, red-faced at the idea of a washerwoman, a carpenter, and a refuse-taker filling space while the high-born drowned.

"Who do you imagine will rebuild the city and keep it clean?" Shulgi asked.

Was there ever a king as wise or fair? If I could sneak into his room dressed as Ishtar, keep her clothes unwashed so I took the smell of her with me, I would. Imagine the child we would grow, Shulgi and I.

If we survived this storm. It rose above the lower floors of his tower. We could hear it lapping below, a gentle, destructive sound.

It was the hungry who died first. Those who only had enough for the next meal, perhaps, and once that was gone they scrabbled for the next. The hungry and the poor had no stores. Stores gave you time to rest from thinking about food.

Shulgi had thought there would be room for all inside his tower, would prefer the tower he began building at ten. None were to be left behind, but the population had grown faster than he could build. He could never keep up. He could not save them all; in fact, he saved very few.

Ishtar was angry with Enlil, blaming him for the flood. "Is this him again? Last time he did this on a whim, tired of the roar of Man. Has he ever come close and heard the words spoken? It seems a noise from afar, but each voice has merit."

My mistress preferred mortals to gods. She said they had more of interest to say.

When Enlil failed to respond, she called for Zu, the god of storms, but he did not come either. "He is too frightened to face me. He knows that I will take him to the floor and he will shake with desire, and I will take back the tablets of destiny. At least he is not a fool, but he has no courage."

Oh, the water. Such endless pounding. It made my head ache. The moistness in the air rotted our clothing and turned the places between our toes green. We were lucky in our tower; we could watch as people drowned, as cattle and sheep drifted past.

The flood waters around Ishtar boiled. She could boil the Tigris, make beer and wine bubble over, and so she thought she could boil the flood to steam. Instead, she was filled with such a deep inner chill she could do nothing but shiver.

When the rain finally stopped, they sent out a bird from the top of the tower to find dry land. A wise move by Shulgi. It came back with a twig from one of our ancient trees.

Shulgi said, "My grandfather sat at this tree and learned our family's history from his grandfather. It is a very old tree."

We knew then that we only had to wait until the water subsided, and we could rebuild our city.

After the storm, Shulgi spent many days and weeks surveying his land, riding on his chariot. He was enlivened by the flood, and the people loved him.

On his way out he looked to the left; on the way back he looked to the other side. He was not superstitious but sensible; he liked to make sure he observed both sides well.

The people liked to see him out this way, amongst them, for him to see the suffering and to perhaps give them aid.

He saw the land owned by soldiers from past wars. This land he did not worry about. The land he was interested in was that owned by aristocrats, who had used their connections to *sangarhood* — to the priests — to gain land. These he thought were undeserving.

Ishtar was not likewise impressed by land ownership. She knew how easily it could be taken away. She could render these wealthy, lying men homeless by sending Shulgi to war with the *sangars*, stealing their power.

But Shulgi did not like those who hadn't earned their land.

At fallow fields women wept for Tammuz. Ishtar said, "I am no longer responsible for him. Ten thousand lovers he has had since me. Each one of them can die for him and travel to the Underworld to replace him."

After the great storm, people cursed Ishtar for not saving them. They said that Ishtar drowned alone and that her body was found, battered and marked, once the water subsided. I knew better. I was Ishtar's washerwoman; I knew all.

Ishtar said to me, "What do they want from me? I am not all. I am only Ishtar."

She no longer gave me clothes to wash. She said she did not need me, that she was done for, and all she had to do was sink into the dirt and dissolve. It was the fact that she was almost forgotten, I thought. I adored her and always would, but others no longer cared.

"You have your army," I said, knowing that my love alone was worthless. "They need you and will respond to your every move."

She nodded at that, but there was a slight twist to her mouth. "Men not even born," she said. "That is what I am left with for lovers."

I washed her clothes nonetheless, made sure she had fresh garments, should she choose to wear them.

And one morning Ishtar was gone. I was glad to see she took the clothes; it meant my life was worthwhile, that I had not wasted it. She left behind a jewel for me. She didn't tell me where she was going.

Without her, Shulgi sickened. He read too much. He read of a disease and thought he had it, then the next. He lost blood, and his urine contained crystals, and his stools were liquid. The priests did what they could. I did what I could, keeping his clothing clean, making sure disease didn't pass that way, but to the great grief of the people, Shulgi died.

Ungoverned, people soon turned to anarchy.

The land where Akkad sat was taboo for centuries.

ASHURNASIRPAL: 883 BC
The Washerwoman Ashurina

The first Sumerian king ruled for twenty-eight thousand years, his son for thirty-six thousand years, but that makes no sense in books. Or in the scrolls or tablets. Time was different until they wrote it down.

People lived shorter and shorter lives. Once we would have easily seen three hundred. Now we were lucky to live to one hundred. As the number of people grew, we lost our ability to stay alive. Perhaps there were only a certain amount of years to go around and now they had to be shared by many people.

Is history propaganda or truth? Only Ishtar knows, and she is prone to lying. I know too, but who would ask me? I am nothing more than a washerwoman. Though that is something to be proud of, now more than it once was.

"What is it like to live forever?" I asked Ishtar.

"Don't you know?" She touched my cheek. She would not have touched the washerwomen of long ago, but she was less of a goddess now. Less of everything since she woke from her long sleep in the mountains. Now we were more equal than once we were. "Haven't you lived with me all these centuries?"

I wasn't sure if she really believed this, that she didn't know me from all those who have gone before me, or if she was playing with me.

She said, "You get tired. But each life is its own. Each new place is a life, each new friend. As long as you change, you do not get bored."

I was not even convinced this woman was all of Ishtar. Perhaps her spirit was in pieces, and the strong one lived elsewhere, leaving just this weak and helpless part behind in the mountain with her secret army.

My great grandmother told the story differently, my mother said.

I'm not sure why, of all the men she could have chosen, it was Ashurnasirpal who took her attention. He was not a good man. Of all her lovers, he was the one without quality. Gilgamesh believed in himself so powerfully that all around him benefited, and Tammuz had had his innocence, his Greenness. Sargon, for all his cruelty, had Akkad at his heart; Shulgi was a master builder and planner. Ashur had only himself and, once Ishtar won him, he had her at heart as well. I think Ishtar loved him because he worshipped her as a goddess, not a woman.

Their wedding banquet was talked about by king after king into the forever. Ishtar took three days to prepare, fussed over and poked at by a dozen attendants. Oh, the gossips they were.

"I heard she was hung by hooks in the Underworld. For two hundred years!" I heard one say.

"That's where the scars came from," another told her.

"Ishtar would never stay still for so long, you fools," I told them. "Those scars are from where her wings used to be." And there; information passed which may or may not be true.

Ashur adorned his palace with wood because he loved the feel of it, the smell. Box, mulberry, cedar, tamarisk, poplar. The utensils. The musical instruments. Napkins of wood shaved finely, used to wipe the grease from chins.

Around the wall were bronze-fittings, bolts holding things in place. "Our craftsmen are very talented." He was proud of this; those men and their families would not die of hunger, regardless of circumstances. Ashur did reward talent.

There were beams of Byblian cedar for roofing, high tamarisk doors furnished with bronze fittings, gleaming bronze friezes in doors. Statues of red gold and precious stone. The room had a bluish glow from the blue enamel baked brick.

There were inlays showing his conquests. The serving girls, slaves one and all, didn't like to look too closely because the pictures made them sick. Images of their own people in pain and defeat.

In the garden, these things grew: cedar, cypress, box, fir, medicinal plants, juniper, lamer-oak, date palm, ushu-willow, mulberry, bitter almonds. Grown from torn bodies in the ground, sprouting between the bones of his enemies.

In the storage room were man-high jars for food and drink, made of baked clay and etched so that the servants would know what they held. All this food and drink was to celebrate his goddess.

Food offerings came from everywhere, carefully

sourced; no point in giving food if the goddess didn't know from where it came. Ishtar brought enormous wealth to the marriage, but Ashur did not want this. As his bride price he chose just one thing: the long pin Ishtar wore to symbolise her freedom.

As part of his speech, he spoke of the three fears of a man:

That his lady would perform black magic against him.

That she would pass on words that should be kept secret within the palace.

And that she would open her thighs for another man.

Ishtar promised him many times that none of these things would occur. I could not understand, though, how he didn't bore her. She would be better with a stone cutter, or a soldier, than this dull, jealous man.

The wedding lasted for seven days, and then the people starved again.

Ashur did not care. "Are you hungry, my love?" he asked Ishtar.

She shook her head. She spoke less than ever she did, as if each day she forgot another word.

"Then that should be enough for the people. Anyone who says he is hungry is committing blasphemy against the goddess."

When Ishtar worried about hungry people, he said, "You are *satadaru*. Worried. You should not be." Ashur did not like to be around worried people.

If Sargon was cruel, then Ashur, half his size, was cruelty reduced to a potent paste. He took pleasure in pain, saying that inflicting it made him feel god-like. "I would be a good god," he said.

He had his enemies flayed over days; he loved to cut men and watch them bleed. He relished destroying families. I saw it more than once; men so distraught at the violent deaths of their loved ones that they wept themselves to the Underworld. We were so dry, so waterless, that the loss of any moisture could kill you, let alone the rivers of tears from those men.

At least there was no blood to wash from their clothing.

He had children dashed to mush. Babies. He had them crushed and pounded until there was nothing left of them but a mess in the dust.

This was the man Ishtar chose to marry.

Was it his wealth? She had wealth enough of her own, all she could ever want. Was it because he could protect her? Keep her worshipped?

His palace was so well-made that when a dust storm came, the inside was untouched. After it was over, we went out to find all covered with black.

He burnt many libraries. He was a fool of a man. Didn't he realise that by burning a clay tablet you preserve it? He was too lazy to step inside and smash them himself. Yet, because of Ishtar, he preserved the texts about Gilgamesh. My daughter will see them written into one volume, perhaps, or my granddaughter.

He recorded the stories of the land. He recorded the great flood, and the reign of Sargon. He recorded the decisions of Shulgi. All things Ishtar had witnessed and played a hand in, yet she was not recorded as such. She said, "And Tammuz? You must keep his story as well."

She spoke of Tammuz as if he were still here. Her grasp on time was slipping. I asked her, "Was Tammuz your lover or your son?" and she was both surprised and horrified. Oh, history, how it blurs.

Ashur took Ishtar's continued presence for a mandate, that her divine love gave him the right to do anything: cut off the hands of those who offended him, destroy entire villages on a whim, allow his people to starve, burn buildings and begin wars. Ishtar did not care. She was tired.

Ashur had many girlfriends, a harem. They were terrified of Ishtar and kept their pins sharpened to keep her away. Pins were used for personal protection — I think they gave the illusion of an armed society, ready for war. Pins were also worn in the grave, but those were far longer. Our loved ones were buried with all their jewellery, and the pin pointed up towards their chins.

A virgin wore a garment pin which would be loosened after marriage.

Ishtar called Ashur her garment pin. The effect that had on him! It could make him go weak at the knees, just to hear her say that. Pins were Ishtar's weapons. She liked them.

I always said they left holes in the fabric.

Sometimes, if she was feeling maudlin and remembering her past loves or her daughter, she would scratch herself deeply with them. She spoke so sadly of her daughter, how she had too much secret knowledge. That was never understood in a woman.

Some days, when Ashur was away and would not ask questions, she would go to be amongst her army. They were pale, now, paler than ever before, and their muscles were slack, their flesh soft. They waited for her command, but she did not know against whom to set them.

This, perhaps, was the worst of it.

Oh, it was dry as a stick. Ashur worshipped his goddess even in this drought, anointing her feet with cedar oil. "I am your main worshipper. You need no other."

Did she think this would make her stronger? But he

treated prostitutes, her priestesses, terribly — with such disrespect and violence that her temples became dusty with misuse, the women too frightened to work there.

Had men changed so much? Were they now so frightened by the power of a woman in pleasure that they would give that pleasure up themselves?

In the time of Gilgamesh, Ishtar said, the husband would take great delight in pleasing his woman. This was long before the time when female pleasure was considered a sin. Oh, Ishtar, how powerful you were. Once you left, women lost the power of lust, didn't they? They lost the truth of desire, although that desire remains.

Now, womanhood was used as a curse. Ishtar heard this once; a man cursing another to become a woman. She was so furious she struck the curser down and turned him into a maggot wriggling in a sour, stinking dead camel's stomach.

Can you see what this meant to women? That to be a female was to lose prestige and power.

Time came when Ishtar knelt beside me washing the clothes. She was so faded, so empty. I had no children; we two old women stood beside each other and we rinsed out the blood of the people. I think she believed this way she would escape destruction, the end. But she did not realise, she has never understood, my ancestresses' prophecy: that mankind will fall if no one worries for the welfare of the people. With her becoming one of us, what will happen? Who will care?

So those were the five loves of Ishtar. Five mortals, five gods, who can say? She liked them better if she knew they could die. She didn't like the idea of forever.

She went to sleep with her stillborn army in caves and tunnels. She slept, bitter and angry. Dry and unloved. There they lived, guarding her, waiting for a time when they would be called to service again.

Biography

Kaaron Warren's short story collection *The Grinding House* (CSFG Publishing) won the ACT Writers' and Publishers' Fiction Award and two Ditmar Awards. Her second collection, *Dead Sea Fruit*, published by Ticonderoga Books, was shortlisted for a Ditmar Award and an Aurealis Award. Her critically acclaimed novel *Slights* (Angry Robot Books) was nominated for an Aurealis Award, shortlisted for the Ned Kelly First Novel Award and won the Australian Shadows Award fiction, the Ditmar Award and the Canberra Critics' Award for Fiction. Angry Robot Books also published her novels *Walking the Tree* (shortlisted for a Ditmar Award) and *Mistification*, which launched in June 2011.

Her stories have appeared in Ellen Datlow's *Year's Best Horror and Fantasy* as well as in Australian Year's Best Horror, Science Fiction and Fantasy anthologies.

She has recently been named Special Guest for the Australian National Science Fiction Convention in 2013.

Kaaron has stories upcoming in *Visions Fading Fast*, from Pendragon Press, and a series of four stories from Twelfth Planet Press.

And the Dead Shall Outnumber the Living

Deborah BIANCOTTI

Chapter One

"Sorry, we're not hiring." The Madame is slim and wears
a suit. Her hair is coiled faultlessly on the top of her head.
Her makeup is perfect, too: evening-smoky-eyes-going-
to-the-Oscars makeup. It's two o'clock in the afternoon
and the brothel has the faded, dusty look of a place that
shouldn't open before dark.

Adrienne flips out her badge. "Business not good?"

The Madame's perfect face doesn't move, but it's clear
the badge has adjusted her thinking. "Business is fine,
Detective. We're busy. We're legal. In these lean
economic times, people limit their spending. The jobs are
getting smaller, more...modest."

Adrienne finds it a funny choice of words.

"Lower expectations?" she asks.

"More easily satisfied," the Madame confirms. "Is
your interest business? Or pleasure? We have some
delightful ladies—"

"I'm looking for Nina," Adrienne says.

The Madam doesn't even blink. "Nina is occupied, but you're free to wait—"

"It's a social call," says Adrienne.

At last an emotion shows on the mask of the woman's face. It's surprise.

"You a friend?" the Madame asks. "Nina doesn't have many women friends."

Adrienne notes that they're ladies when she's a customer, but women when she's a friend.

"I'm one of a kind," Adrienne says.

"Well, then. Leave a number, I'll pass it on."

Adrienne drops a card on the desk and takes her leave. Down the plush burgundy carpet hallway, through the heavy curtains at the front, and out the glass doors onto the street. A customer would go out the back door, discretely — or is it shamefully? — exiting into an alleyway behind the local shopping centre. She's not a customer, so she goes out the front. She puts on her sunglasses. An old man gives her a wink like they're friends.

She stares him down.

The glass windows of the brothel feature the painted image of the king and queen of hearts — the queen with cleavage up the wazoo (as Nina would describe it), the king looking particularly cheerful. Oddly, both king and queen are ducks. Adrienne wonders if it's rhyming slang.

She walks the thirty minutes back to the city in the crisp, cold July weather. Her fists are plunged into jacket pockets, shoulders hunched. She shivers until the energy of her walk begins to warm everything but her toes.

Nina calls late that afternoon.

"You should get a phone," says Adrienne.

"Then people would call me more. Where are you?"

Adrienne mentions a coffee shop near the office and Nina hangs up.

She's on her second cup of decaf by the time Nina arrives. Nina moves like what she is: an ex-dancer with a few too many years on her frame. She's tall and curvy, with a prominent bust. But it's her cheekbones that really stand out, lending her face a wide, predatory coldness.

Nina says, "Haven't seen you in a while. What's it been?"

Not even a hello.

"Ten years?" Adrienne suggests.

Nina reflects, tipping her hard face to the side. She hasn't softened with age. "Maybe twelve."

"Guess I'm older than I realised."

"Aren't we all? Can I smoke in here?" Nina shakes open a box of cigarettes.

Adrienne inhales the tobacco promise and tries not to salivate. Nina raises an eyebrow in invitation. It's then Adrienne notices how pale her brow is, plucked into almost-obscurity. Her face is clean and her skin is pink like she's been scrubbing at it.

"It's no smoking," Adrienne says. "Listen, I've got a problem."

"What, pregnant?" Nina gives the first smile Adrienne's seen from her in something more like twenty years. "Too old to be worried about pregnant, surely? I mean, not too old to *be* pregnant. Just too old to give a goddamn."

Adrienne places a plain manila folder on the table and pulls out four photos, close-ups of faces made of grey clay.

"What's this?" Nina asks.

"Facial reconstructions. We found these guys dead, bones shattered. All their bones."

"All?" Nina looks confused. A dancer, a whore, a med-school drop-out. Somewhere along the line, she appears to have picked up a passing familiarity with bones. "Impressive."

Adrienne nods. "And no, we didn't find them at the base of cliffs or the bottom of the ocean. We found them in the street."

In the street, left to rot in alleyways or behind buildings. One in an empty construction site, the developer having gone bust years back. No weapons, no tools, no marks on their skin. Just four jellied dead men with calcium paste for bones.

"Well," Nina says, "it's nice you thought to look me up, and all, but why are you showing me dead people?"

She squints and a spider web of lines fans out from the corners of her eyes.

"At least one of them is a prostitute. Unconfirmed on a second."

Nina looks at the photos. "These guys?"

"You used to run the sex workers' union. Do you recognise any of them?"

"That was a while ago." But Nina peers into their plastic eyes. "Wait, I know this one. And this guy, yeah. Both rent boys." She points to two men Adrienne hasn't been able to identify. That makes three out of four dead men prostitutes. The fourth guy looks too old for the game, and Nina says so.

"Someone's killing prostitutes?" she asks. "Male prostitutes?"

Adrienne nods. She gives Nina time for the idea to sink in.

"That's weird."

"Isn't it?"

She feels herself slipping back into the familiar ease they had when they were young. Before life got to them.

Adrienne takes a deep breath to quell the fear in her belly, the fear of getting old, the fear of death. It was fear that drove her into the police force, but nowadays it's fear that's driving her away. She keeps thinking of settling down in a nice house with a garden, hiring a cleaner and a gardener, and spending her days on the verandah sipping cocktails, feet up on the balcony. In her head, this daydream always gives way to another one, where she's swapping witticisms with Dorothy Parker, wearing 1950s-style trousers and planning a trip to Spain. She's not even sure where the images come from.

Nina says, "I'm guessing you've got no leads. I mean, if you're here talking to me."

"I've got two leads," Adrienne says. "Both crazy."

Nina part-way succumbs to the nicotine pull and picks a cigarette from the box, letting it dangle between her lips. She gives the waitress a reassuring wink as she thumbs the lighter, and indicates the spot on the table where she'd like a cup of coffee. "I like crazy."

Adrienne takes a long breath. "One is a liberation group."

"Sure."

"Liberation of the oppressed who trade sex for cash."

"Hear hear," says Nina. "I'm all for anyone who promises me a raise. And the other lead?"

"The Cult of the Goddess. They like to sit around and wait for their goddess to arrive. And be naked. They say she's coming back at the end of the Mayan calendar."

"Sounds like a long time to be naked." Nina indicates the cold, grey sky outside, the people hunched in their coats. "Not good weather for it, either."

"The Mayan calendar ends the twenty-first of December, 2012. This year," Adrienne says.

"And then?"

"Who knows? The end of the world. The ascension to

the next plane. The evolution of the soul."

Nina is thoughtful. "That ascension stuff rings a bell. This naked group, they worship Ishtar, right? Goddess of love and war."

"Love *and* war?" Adrienne raises her eyebrows. She hasn't paid the cult much attention. Had them pegged as being all show and no go.

Nina keeps thumbing her lighter, clearly fighting the urge to light up. "What, you don't think love and war are related?" She grins. "Prostitutes get into this cult sometimes. They like the themes, I guess."

Adrienne makes a note while Nina continues. "Way back when, Ishtar had these sexual sacred rituals. Prostitution, of a kind. So, some of the girls—"

"That's working backwards, isn't it?" Adrienne interrupts. "Fair enough, people do crazy things for sacred reasons. Goats and human sacrifices and whatever. Sex, sure, I guess." She tries to get her thinking straight. "But if you're a prostitute already, why pretend you're doing something sacred? Isn't that like retrofitting?"

Nina snorts. "We can't all be upstanding detectives of the police force. You're missing an earring, by the way. Makes you look lopsided."

Adrienne reaches up to pull on her earlobes. "Shit!"

The earrings aren't valuable; they're just the only ones she has.

The waitress brings over a coffee and Nina spins the cup slowly, eyeing the beads of froth on top of the black liquid. Then she looks at Adrienne, her face composed. "Goddess Cult, hey? You know, my money's on them. Waiting for their goddess, or whatever."

"Why's that?"

Nina picks a piece of tobacco off her tongue with thumb and third finger. "I got a hunch the bitch is early."

Chapter Two

"Did Nina say why she thought we should go for the cult?" Steve asks.

Steve is the only other member of the newly-instituted Gender Crimes section. Amazing; you kill a dozen or so female prostitutes, no one sets up a special police division. Not since Scotland Yard. You kill a handful of male prostitutes, suddenly there's a new division, and she's the lead. Adrienne figures she's being set up for a fall.

"She said it's a hunch," she replies.

Steve looks out the car window at the site of the last discovered body. St. Peter Julian's is one of the ugliest Catholic churches in existence. The design must have been based on a war bunker, but then they'd gone and put the whole damn thing above ground. Thick, uneven cement and pale white struts are set evenly into the walls. It looks like a concrete piano. The front features a crucified Jesus with crown of thorns that hangs three storeys above ground, old-copper-green with exposure. He's frightening. A god with a serious 'don't fuck with me' attitude.

"Pretty big hunch," Steve mutters.

"She's going to put me onto a guy. A prostitute friend of hers; might know more about the victims."

"Tight-knit community, is it?" Steve asks.

Steve's a young man, but hefty. Loves his junk food, been on a diet since she met him eight months ago. He's not what you'd call jolly. His humour is a callous, bitter expression part way between funny and despairing. Adrienne likes him.

They're parked on George Street, the city's main thoroughfare. Buses intermittently obscure their view and pedestrian traffic presses close to Adrienne's window. The smell of sweat and city pervades the car.

"Cults are weird," Steve says.

Adrienne shrugs. "My sister joined a cult."

She's forgotten temporarily that Steve went to school with her younger sister, so when he says, "Who, Grace?" she's taken aback.

"Yeah, Grace." She shifts in her seat.

"What kind?"

"The kind that takes your money and your mind and gives you a shinto-load of crazy in return."

Steve is quiet.

Adrienne wracks her brain for the name. "Allatu, it was called."

"Allatu? What's that mean?" Steve asks.

"Some religious thing, I guess. The guy leading it suicided after a string of sexual abuse claims. Then...I think it fell apart."

"Where's Grace now?"

"No idea," Adrienne admits.

Steve is about to respond when a car pulls up beside them. It waits for the traffic to ease, then it turns right into the church carpark and rounds the building, hypothetically coming to a stop in back.

"That's gotta be him," Adrienne says.

Inside the church is nicer than outside. It's a large, square shape with white polished floors and a scattering of wooden pews. The altar is set at floor-level, not raised, with a red tablecloth and two vases of flowers.

Father Thomas is mid-forties, neither fat nor thin, and just tall enough not to be considered short. Given his surroundings, he's surprisingly — almost disappointingly — normal-looking.

"We're looking for Candice Angers," says Steve.

"Yes?" Thomas's voice is mellifluous, well-trained, incongruent to his plain looks. "And you're looking for her here?"

"She hasn't been seen in three days. Not since her police interview the day they found the body," Adrienne says. "Seems she never made it home. Can you tell me about her?"

The priest takes a breath. He isn't wearing priestly garb. His clothes are faded from wear and washing, and his arms are crossed over the beginnings of a convincing pot belly. "She's one of mine."

"One of your what?" Steve asks.

Thomas gives him a bemused smile. "Flock."

He turns his gaze back to Adrienne. They've been playing tag-team, she and Steve, but when it's clear Thomas considers her the boss, Adrienne takes over the questioning. "She attended mass here?"

"Every week, usually twice."

"She was quite religious?"

"That's the funny thing about people who are regular church-goers," says Thomas, "they're often quite religious."

Adrienne ignores the comment. "So you knew her pretty well?"

"We talked."

"About?"

"Her, largely," Thomas uncrosses his arms, spreads his hands. "And god. And her relationship with god —"

"Is her prostitution a problem for that relationship?"

"Well, it isn't an enhancement," he admits. "She told me she wanted to quit. But, much in the same way anyone unhappy talks about quitting. It was a 'one day' kind of thing. One day I'll quit, but not today. You know the type?"

"Like St. Augustine?" Adrienne asks.

Thomas laughs. "Give me chastity and moderation, but don't give it to me yet? I see you have a little religion yourself, Detective."

Adrienne neither confirms nor denies. "What's Candice's mood like lately? Any changes?"

Thomas shakes his head. "She's spooked. She was the one to find the body."

"And what about relationships? Partners, friends, anyone we can contact?"

"She doesn't talk about relationships much."

"Because she's a lesbian?"

Thomas presses his lips together. His eyes flick to a particularly imposing statue of Jesus, like he thinks it might be listening. "As a representative of my Church, I cannot condone relationships that are not deemed holy..."

He lets the silence lengthen long enough that Adrienne realises there's another answer he's itching to give.

"And as a man of principle?"

"I find," says Thomas, "I cannot *not* condone a relationship between two loving, consenting adults. Of any persuasion."

Adrienne nods. "If you see her, get her to call me." She hands him a card.

Thomas takes it and turns it over a couple times in his hand.

"One last question, Father," says Adrienne, "and you may find it impertinent."

"The answer is no," he says.

Adrienne starts.

"You were going to ask if I'd had a sexual relationship with Candice." Thomas eyes her levelly. "Weren't you?"

"Good guess," she admits.

"Sex is always considered an impertinence when discussed with a priest. Though whether you meant impertinent to me or to Candice, I'm not sure." Father Thomas stands, the wooden pew creaking at the shift in weight. "Because she was a prostitute, you also assume she's promiscuous. Isn't that right?"

Adrienne hesitates. She's thinking that surely anyone who has sex for money is promiscuous, but maybe that oversimplifies it. Maybe promiscuity for the financial gain is different from promiscuity for sexual gain. But she's not sure. She feels she's blundering into a world she doesn't understand. She hasn't had a sexual relationship in years. She resists counting how many.

"You must know," says Thomas, "that Catholic priests are still celibate, even in this age."

"You follow the Church's ruling on that, too, Father? Your conscience doesn't smart at following out-of-date rules intended to suppress natural humanity? Still," says Adrienne, "it's probably not your conscience that's the problem with a deal like that."

Thomas stares blankly at her for a second. Then he smiles. "You have a lot of anger." But he doesn't offer to address it, and Adrienne respects him for that.

They walk towards the square of daylight that marks the outside world. Steve is ahead of them, heading for the door like a man with purpose. Adrienne figures he doesn't like churches. She can't blame him.

"Could be worse," she says to Thomas. "You could be a nun. Celibacy *and* poverty, I understand."

"They make great sacrifices to serve God, yes." But Thomas won't be drawn into any more discussions on morals.

As they leave, they pass a corkboard full of photos, some faded with age, many curled around the pins that hold them. "More of your flock?" Adrienne asks.

Thomas nods. The photos show a mishmash of faces, from a group of grinning hikers to the room of a nursing home, residents ensconced in wide chairs. They're clapping and smiling toothlessly.

"What did Candice tell you," Thomas asks, "about the man she found?"

Adrienne shrugs. "Just that she thought she knew him."

"How did he die?"

"We don't know that yet," Adrienne says.

"You don't know?" He gives her an incredulous expression. He clearly thinks she's holding out on him.

Truth is they know how he died. Massive internal trauma. They just don't have a clue how so much trauma could be inflicted without breaking the skin or leaving an external mark.

It's like he exploded inside.

Back in the car they're idling at lights. Steve is asking, "Where to now?" and Adrienne is thinking that's a Hell of a question, she'd like to know the answer herself. Her phone rings and she's grateful for the distraction.

"How'd you go with the priest?" Nina asks.

"We got nothing," says Adrienne.

It's the answer she has to give — Nina is a civilian, after all — but it's also true. She's relieved to find a friend in this landscape. Not the familiar hard-edged landscape of the city, but the landscape of weird deaths that's been overlaid on it. The inexplicable crimes, the unnerving environment of belief and religion. Not for the first time she thinks about quitting.

One day.

"Well," says Nina in that purring drawl of hers, "I got an address for you, for the Ishtar cult."

She gives Adrienne an address in the upmarket end of Balmain. Adrienne notes it down with a distracted,

"Thanks".

"I've got something else for you, too. But you won't like it," Nina says.

Adrienne likes very little about this so far, but Nina declines to explain over the phone. "Come to my place. I know someone who can explain it better than me."

Nina opens the apartment door wearing a long shirt and soft trousers, her feet bare on the floorboards. Her hair's a mess and she wears no make-up. The skin on her neck is soft. She looks old and vulnerable.

"Transference," she says without introduction.

"What?" Adrienne asks.

The apartment is a one-room event, kitchen and bedroom and dining space combined. Shelves line almost every wall, books and boxes and souvenirs from a life already half-lived. A large frame dominates the space above the stovetop. It's littered with photographs and postcards, ticket stubs and receipts. Figurines from Europe and Africa are lined up on a window frame. Scarves hang thickly from a hook by the door. It's a visual assault. Adrienne gets lost in her own vertigo and has to ask Nina to repeat herself.

"I said, this is Chapel. He's a friend. He knows — knew — one of the victims."

Adrienne starts, finally noticing the man at the dining table. He's tiny, almost a stick figure, with narrow wrists resting on crossed leg. His skin is pale brown, maybe Indonesian.

"Hey, Chapel." Adrienne remembers to introduce Steve, but Nina gives her a strange look.

"Yeah, we covered that bit," Steve says. He stands like a stone in the middle of the chaotic apartment. They haven't been invited to sit down, but then, there are only two chairs. Steve and Adrienne lean over the room's other occupants.

"Sorry," says Adrienne. "I think I'm caught up now. So, transference?"

"It's a theory," says Chapel, "that a personality can be transferred from one body to another. Or a soul, if you like."

"Uh huh. And what's that got to do with anything?" She doesn't mean to sound harsh, but she sees Chapel exchange a look with Nina.

Nina winks in reassurance and he continues, "Transference usually ends with the host dead. When the personality or spirit leaves, the host body can break down."

Adrienne is trying to hold onto her patience. She looks at Nina and reminds herself to be civil. She asked Nina for help, after all. She shouldn't reject what's offered. Even if it's making the whole thing stranger.

"How does it break down?" she asks.

Steve gives her a pointed look, but she ignores him. She'll cop an earful later for letting the crazies take up their time. Steve checks his watch and stares blandly out the window.

Chapel shrugs. "Different ways, depending on the power of the transference. Some have aneurysms, where the brain basically explodes."

Adrienne is listening now. "Explodes?"

"Yeah," Chapel nods. "Sometimes there's broken veins, broken bones."

"How many?"

Chapel looks at her. "What?"

"How many broken bones?" Adrienne asks.

"How many you got?" Chapel asks.

Good answer. She asks, "What's your job, Chapel?"

He purses his lips, gauging her. "I'm an entertainer."

"Prostitute?"

Nina cuts in. "Let's just say we've worked together."

"Vice isn't my department," Adrienne says. "So let's assume it's all perfectly legal."

Chapel chuckles. "Not in some countries."

When he smiles, his narrow face becomes unrecognisable. His teeth are wide-spaced and lopsided, and a vein in his forehead pops. He goes from distinguished to clownish in a second. But then his hilarity dissolves and the subdued expression returns.

Adrienne gestures for the folder Steve's holding and pulls out the photos. "Do you recognise any of these guys?"

Chapel pushes the photos around on the table with thin fingers. He looks at each one, apparently hunting for something familiar, something that can be translated from the cold light of the lab overheads to the flattering half-light of the street after dark.

"Yeah, these guys I know." He indicates three of the photos. "My God. Are they all dead?"

"Afraid so," Adrienne confirms.

He's chosen the dead guy from the church and two other unnamed men. Mick Spencer, he tells Adrienne, pointing at the first photo. But the other he refers to only as Teddy.

"Never needed to know his name," Chapel shrugs.

"You work with them?" Adrienne asks.

"Mick, yeah, I worked with him. Teddy wasn't a working girl. He was a john."

"A customer? Any of them have enemies, that you know of?"

Chapel is shaking his head slowly. "I can't believe they're dead. These guys, they had broken bones?"

"Right."

"How many?"

Adrienne shrugs. "All of them."

Chapel gives her a look. "And you're wondering if it's *not* an aggressive spirit?"

Adrienne doesn't answer.

"Detective," Chapel pushes the photos back towards her, "forget looking for their enemies. Face it; you're in over your head."

"You seem pretty sure of that." Adrienne tries not to sound defensive.

"You didn't even know their names until now. I'd say you're desperate," Chapel returns. "The point is, if you've come this far, you may as well go all the way. Start accepting the stuff you think is crazy. And then leave it the hell alone."

Adrienne feels her face heat up. She doesn't spend her days pursuing justice for nameless corpses, just to have her efforts denigrated by some pissant skinny little lollypop with bad teeth who makes his living screwing strangers.

"Thanks for your time." She marches to the door, Steve following.

Halfway down the first flight of stairs Nina catches up with them. "Hey. You asked me for help, right? This is what I got."

"You found a witch doctor with a doomsday obsession and you thought you'd give me a call?"

"I knew you wouldn't get it," Nina says.

"Oh, I get it," Adrienne says. "I sure as shit don't believe it, though."

"Well," Nina moves back up the staircase, talking over her shoulder, "if it turns out to have a simpler explanation, it's still something you should think twice about messing with. Unless you like flour for bones."

Adrienne waves a mock 'thank-you' and keeps walking.

They get to the car and Adrienne's phone rings. It's Nina.

"What?" Adrienne fights to keep her tone neutral.

"One more thing," Nina says. "Chapel says at least two of those dead guys had something else in common. Apart from prostitution."

"What's that?"

"They exclusively worked women."

Adrienne stops. Steve is unlocking the car door and giving her a quizzical look. He mimes a 'What is it?'.

"Are you sure?" she asks.

"He's sure. He says they didn't do gay."

Adrienne pauses. "Good to know."

When she repeats the conversation to Steve, he raises his eyebrows. "How'd they make a living?"

"You think there's not enough women to keep those guys employed?"

"No," Steve doesn't hesitate, "I don't. I mean, sex aside, even with straight escorting, I don't get how they could survive."

"Maybe they had other jobs. Maybe they got into the drug trade," Adrienne theorises. "Maybe one wealthy woman is all you need."

"Yeah." Steve starts the car. "Ain't that the truth."

When every bone in a face gets broken, the face itself becomes unrecognisable. It's like a plastic bag full of water — flat and swollen, all defining shape gone. The contents of the head spread out like toothpaste, mixing with marrow and the blood released from broken bones. Clots form, cells spend seconds repairing damage before the whole thing stalls, a result of the unresponsive central nervous system. The body begins to settle and deteriorate, committing itself to the next stage.

Reconstruction in clay comes from guesswork and whatever evidence of wear can be found on the skin, where perhaps a cheekbone or jaw sat, where the brow might've protruded, where the redness on the sides of the nose were found. But the real face, the real body, has to be scooped and rolled up into a bag and carried carefully, sloshing like soup, to a freezer before forensic work can begin.

"There it is," Adrienne points.

From a distance it looks like a circus, blue and white police cars, blue uniforms, yellow tape flapping in the wind. A sunny carnival atmosphere prevails, TV cameras and journalists parked a reasonable distance away. Everyone waits for the big top to go up, the next act to begin.

They approach. The officer recognises Adrienne and waves them through. Behind blue plastic sheets they find the body below street level. It's floating in a stormwater drain and visible through a one-metre square grate.

"What've we got?" Adrienne asks.

"A man. *Was* a man, anyhow. Looks like jelly now."

Detective Tarling is senior to Adrienne by about fifteen years. He's an old dog with an impassive face. They go back a way. Tarling was at her first precinct. She'd recognised him as a man of quality and started shadowing him, looking for a mentor. Looking for an example. Rumours began about the two of them. Claims they were an item.

Tarling told everyone it was absurd but he didn't tell them why. Fifteen years back you didn't ask and you didn't tell. Most people who made the assumption probably figured it was Adrienne who was the gay one.

In the end, Adrienne asked for a transfer. She never did find another mentor.

"Same M.O.," Steve observes.

"Thought it might be," Tarling says. "Hard to miss. Any leads?"

"Apparently," says Steve, "it's evil spirits."

Tarling is unperturbed. "Usually is."

"So, I guess no one's moved the body recently?" Adrienne asks.

"You see any buckets?" Tarling asks.

She crouches and grips the edge of a drain outlet, peering in. The stench is unbearable. Every shitting, vomiting junkie in the city crammed into one room couldn't smell this bad. The body looks like a sack pushed up against the grate, spread out, blocking nearly the whole outlet. Water rushes around it, making the skin ripple. It's naked, and the dark hairs on its chest and arms and legs, the dark V of hair around its genitals, are pressed flat by the weight of water. The insides must've floated away by now, out to sea.

"Kids thought it was a balloon or a clown suit or something," Tarling says. "Until the face rolled round and looked at them."

"Counselling?" Steve asks.

"Oh, years of it, I'd imagine," Tarling says.

"I guess there were no flash floods lately, no spelunking deaths or losses?" Adrienne asks. It's a stretch, even she admits it. No spelunking death ever looked like this.

The others reply there's been nothing they've heard of.

"How'd it get in here?" Adrienne examines the grate between her and the body.

"Reckon it was dumped in a stormwater drain and floated here," Tarling says.

"How in hell do we get it out?" Adrienne murmurs,

more to herself.

"Same way it was killed," Steve suggests. "Supernaturally."

Adrienne gets back to her feet and wipes her palms against each other. "You two are a big help."

She goes to talk to the officers who first took the report. They're both still at the scene, faces pale as ash, chins rigidly upright. Clearly can't wait until they're dismissed so they can crawl into a couple of pint glasses. They don't have a lot more to add to what she already knows. Found by a couple local kids who freaked out, thought it was the bogey man. She thinks how glad their parents will be, to have acquired two kids with new, improved attitudes.

"Have you requested the underground maps from the city?" she asks.

"On it," one officer confirms.

He looks pleased to have something to do. She leaves him to it.

The body doesn't look like it's been in the water for longer than a day or two — the skin is intact, pale but not discoloured — but there's no telling exactly where it was dumped.

Adrienne watches the police divers arrive. They're in full wetsuits, hesitating on the side of the drain.

"Reminds me of a story," Steve says.

Adrienne's heard it before, but Tarling listens with grim enthusiasm. The story goes: The body of an obese man was put in a morgue locker too soon, while it was still inflating from post-mortem gases. When they went to pull it out hours later, it was stuck. Wedged in tight, its bloated arms and belly filling the locker, blocking any hope of removing it. They pulled and pulled on the gurney to no avail.

Finally they had to saw off the arms, leaning into that

stinking metal cavity with a bonesaw. First cut they made, the insides exploded all over the young intern tasked with the job. Rumour has it he's in obstetrics now. "But if you buy him a beer," says Steve, "or three, he'll tell you the story. Right down to the colours of the muck he had to wash out of his hair."

Tarling chuckles. "Nice."

Off to one side are the gawkers; onlookers who've been attracted by the police presence, the tents and trucks. But behind them is a different group. A smaller group, three men and a woman. The woman stands in the middle with the men surrounding her like a security detail. She's small, with black, curled hair piled high on her head and heavy make-up that makes her lips glow red and her eyes look like spilled ink. What's most unusual isn't the woman's exotic presence, though. It's the fact that in the middle of the sharp winter day she's wearing a sleeveless evening gown, gold with a gold star under her breast that gathers the cloth from shoulder and waist and bunches it into a cascade spilling towards the ground.

"Who're they?" Adrienne asks.

Tarling turns. "Looks like a pop princess."

Steve shrugs. "Concerned member of the public?"

"Hey!" Adrienne starts towards them.

The men ignore her but the woman looks, dark eyes glowing almost red. She sizes Adrienne up and then she turns on her heel. The men part to let her through and then they follow her to a black limousine parked behind them.

"Hey!"

Adrienne breaks into a jog. She dives under the police tape and pushes through the line of gawkers. She runs up the hill and reaches the car just as it's pulling away. She thumps a fist against the window and pulls out her badge with the other hand.

"Open the door!" she shouts. "Stop the car, open the door."

The car continues to move forward, the men staring mutely away from her.

"I'll smash in the damn window!"

It's only the woman who meets her eye through the glass, only the woman that gives a deep nod, as if of recognition. Adrienne feels a powerful wave of nausea pass through her, her insides turning to bile. As the car careens away, she doubles over and retches powerfully into the gutter, arms and legs shaking. Juddering groans push from her body and tears pour from her eyes. Her left hand burns. Between thumb and forefinger, the skin is red and inflamed and there's an image there, like a tattoo. Or a brand. An eight-pointed star with a circle in the middle, like the one on the woman's gown. She doesn't know what it means, but she knows she got off lightly.

Her bones are intact, for one thing.

The woman in the car must've taken a liking to her. Or to something she said.

Chapter Three

"You okay?" Tarling is crouched beside her.

Steve runs to her side, out of breath and gasping, sounding almost worse than she does. "What the hell just happened?"

The nausea has passed, but Adrienne feels hollow and torn apart, like her bones are about to slide loose of her skin. She keeps flexing her left hand, exercising the burnt webbing on the side of her thumb.

"Recognise this symbol?" she asks.

The others shake their heads.

Tarling says, "If it's a tatt, I'd say it's infected."

Adrienne tries to breathe deeply. "Did you get the license plate?"

Tarling taps his breast pocket where his notebook sits. "I got it, but are you sure you want it?"

She does. She radios in the plates. Her belly feels pummelled, like someone's done the Houdini-death-punch on her. Her muscles ache. Not to mention the burn-tattoo throbbing on her hand. That *thing* in the car, it hadn't even touched her. What would happen if she came skin-to-skin with that monstrous being, that all-powerful bitch?

She's pretty sure she doesn't want to find out.

She shows Steve the text from Nina, the one with the address for the Cult. While he drives, she Googles 'eight-pointed star symbol' and gets a long list of possibilities. There's an eight-pointed star on the Iraqi flag, and an eight-pointed Christian Star of Redemption. She pinches the skin of her hand to ease the ache. Further down the page, one reference leaps out.

"Inanna, or Venus, later Ishtar," she reads, before her voice trails off.

"What?" Steve asks.

"Keep driving."

"Nearly there, boss."

They've reached Balmain. The car skirts the main street. There's a heavy traffic of baby-strollers and trendy cafe-goers. They twist up and down hills and past winding streets with their mix of old and re-furbished pubs. It's a difficult suburb, the streets are narrow, confused and crowded, crammed into a space that's too small for all the life oozing out of it.

They go the wrong way up a one-way street to reach

the house, an unimposing two-storey cottage with a token veranda at the front. Jasmine spirals around the balustrades and up the ornate faux-iron structure to the second storey. The balconies are white and the front door is a deep red.

It looks perfectly normal from the street.

After the fourth knock the door opens, just barely. A young woman peers through the gap. She's mostly hidden behind the door and it's only then Adrienne remembers the whole nudity thing. She can't tell if this woman is naked, but she feels it's an uncomfortable possibility.

"Detective Garner." Adrienne holds out her badge and then gestures to Steve. "Detective Mack. We'd like to talk to the residents, please."

The woman's eyes widen. She shuts the door without a word.

"Do we wait?" Steve asks.

"I guess we wait." She fingers her ribs experimentally, checks the star-shaped burn on her hand. It doesn't look any worse. It doesn't look any better.

After a minute, a woman in a satin dressing gown pulls the door open. She's older than the first woman, fresh-faced with grey-and-black-streaked hair loose to her shoulders. It's clear she's not wearing anything under her gown. The cloth slides over her hips and shoulders smoothly, leaving little to the imagination. Even her cellulite shows.

"I'm so sorry, the gentleman will have to wait outside," says the woman.

Adrienne turns to Steve. He's pale with surprise, brows high.

"Sure," he says.

He turns his back on the woman as if he intends to guard the house, shoulders rounded, hands clasped in front of his groin.

Adrienne steps inside. It's hot, and when the woman directs her to a coat rack, she gratefully takes off her jacket. The woman waits expectantly, but Adrienne isn't planning to remove anything else.

Despite it being the middle of the day, the house lights are on. Maybe to counter the fact all the blinds are drawn. The woman slowly, and with great gravity, leads her to a room painted in deep red. There's an assortment of unmatched chairs lining every wall. Five other women are already in occupation. There's no sign of the young woman who first opened the door. These women are older, tipping into a collective age of about three hundred. And they're naked.

Not nude, nude implies cunning, surprise, manipulation. They're naked just because they're naked, and they sit on the floor or the few chairs or the arms of the chairs and they smile or don't smile, offer tea or wait with patience for Adrienne to speak.

"Would you like a chair, Detective?" asks one woman, offering to vacate her own.

"I'll stand," Adrienne says.

A ripple of restrained laughter echoes across the room.

"What can we do for you?"

"I'm investigating a series of murders."

No reaction from the women. It's as if whatever happens outside their walls is irrelevant. After a pause, one of the women speaks, the one to offer her chair. "I'm so sorry to hear that, Detective." She crosses her legs unselfconsciously and leans back, hands on her thigh.

"What's your name?" Adrienne asks her.

"Ishtar," she replies.

Adrienne freezes.

"We all go by that name here," says the woman calling herself Ishtar. "The original goddess, the every-goddess.

We are all—"

"Okay," Adrienne cuts her off. "But if you worship her as a god, isn't that blasphemous?"

"Goddess," Ishtar the woman corrects. "And no. She is honoured."

"Really?" Adrienne says. "Have you asked her?"

The woman laughs. "I'll ask at the very next opportunity."

"When do you think that might be?" Adrienne keeps her face stone-still.

The woman pauses, her own smile fading. "Are you making fun of me?"

"Afraid not," Adrienne replies.

Something happens in the room then, some shared emotion that isn't surprise.

Another woman asks, "You think she's...here?"

"Could be. What would you say to that?"

It's hard to gauge what the women are feeling. They stare at her, mute and tense. Adrienne thinks it's probably a mix of her no-nonsense cop demeanour with the longed-for-but-not-quite-believed implication of what she's saying. Ishtar herself might be available to them. Ishtar might be here on earth.

"Have you seen her?" asks the woman, the talkative one.

Adrienne lets them stew before answering, "Say I have. Why would she be here?"

The woman gives her a thoughtful look. "It's 2012. The Age of Aquarius is returning, the time of the god Anu. Gods and goddesses are set to roam the earth, to jostle for power in the new millennium."

"That explains the timeline," Adrienne says. "But not the location. Why *here*?"

"Maybe," the woman speculates, "this is far enough away from her homeland that she feels she's safe to start her bid for power. Hidden from the other gods."

"And what's her bid for power gonna entail, exactly?"

She dreads the answer. She's already seen what the goddess can do. The aches and burns, the gut-wrenching nausea from her own encounter won't easily be forgotten.

Ishtar's followers look between themselves uncertainly.

"You don't know, do you?" Adrienne asks.

"The transition from one age to another is unpredictable. Disruptive—"

"How disruptive?" Adrienne asks.

"As disruptive," she says, "as you can imagine. Floods, earthquakes..."

"The gods can cause that?"

"If she's here, now," says the first woman, "there's a chance she's the first. That makes her powerful. And vulnerable."

"I don't get the impression she's particularly vulnerable."

The woman doesn't smile. "She's vulnerable to jealousies. Attack by gods or humans who are, perhaps, pushing their own gods."

By now it's clear the women don't know enough to lead her to Ishtar, but maybe they can point her in another direction. Some way to stop that mad goddess. "Which humans would that be?"

"Anyone with faith these days might be an assassin for their god," says one of the women.

Adrienne thinks of the Catholic priest. She doesn't buy it. "How many gods should we be expecting?"

They look at her, their faces blank. "How many do you need?"

Adrienne returns their stares sourly. "Shit."

Back in the car, she gives Steve an earful. No reason for it, she's just mad as Hell and if she keeps up the anger and the verbal ranting, she can escape the other knowledge pressing on the back of her skull. She's afraid. She hasn't been this afraid since she was twelve and thought she was drowning in a neighbour's pool. The sensation of water closing over her head, sealing her in, that's exactly what she's feeling right now.

Steve listens calmly. When Adrienne pauses for a breath, he says, "What you need is a nice walk by the seaside."

Adrienne's blood is freezing solid under her skin.

"There's been another one, hasn't there?" she asks.

Steve nods. "Bondi Beach."

"Shit!"

Shitshitshit.

"Fuck!" She glares balefully at the closed door behind which the naked Cult of Ishtar sits swapping stories and offering each other tea. "I left my jacket in there."

"Go back for it?" Steve asks.

"Nah, fuck it, never liked that jacket."

She rocks back and forth in the passenger seat while Steve guns the engine.

Chapter Four

The body reveals nothing more than the others, though his clothes are found inexpertly buried on the beach.

"Klaus Bartoch," Steve reads, fingering the discovered wallet. "Colourful name. Drivers license, Hunters Hill. Not likely to be a prostitute, then."

"Maybe he was visiting a prostitute. Maybe the killer has moved on from prostitutes."

"Yeah. Maybe she's looking for a more sensitive

lover," Steve says. "Could be my chance."

"You don't want anything to do with this bitch," Adrienne says.

Steve gives her a quizzical look. "It was a joke."

Klaus Bartoch lies in a shallow indent in the sand. He looks like a human puddle, his mouth long and stretched revealing a bloated tongue and powdered teeth. His eyes swim like uncooked yolks. Judging by his driving license, he was always ugly. This, however, is a cut above. In the winter sun he stinks like rotting hamburger.

"That's how they found him," one of the local cops tells Adrienne. "By the smell. A couple, cleaning up after their dog..."

He doesn't go on; he doesn't have to. Adrienne wonders herself whether there's any reason to go on, whether the goddess has just got them beat hands down. Maybe they should leave her to it and get out of the way.

There's another group gathered around the body.

"Who's that?" Adrienne asks the cop.

"Anti-terrorist team."

"Terrorist?"

"Yeah," says the cop. "They think it might be chemical weapons."

"On non-events like Klaus, here?" Steve asks. "He's nobody."

"I know he's not much to look at," says the cop eyeing the mess of Bartoch in the sand. "But he could be target practice."

The anti-terrorists are plain, wouldn't-stand-out-in-a-crowd types, but they're the focus of attention as they don gloves and begin to poke and pinch at the body on the beach.

Adrienne gets a phone call from an unknown number.

"It's Chapel. Nina gave me your number." On the phone, his voice is clipped and snide. There's noise in the background, and at first Adrienne thinks it's the TV. But she soon realises it's sobbing.

"What's going on?" she asks.

"I got something for you."

She's caught between frustration and politeness. She wants to tell Chapel to take his know-it-all tone and stick it where it's likely to do the most damage. It's an immature response and she knows it, so instead she asks him to explain on the phone. He refuses. There's someone she needs to meet, he tells her. "Someone who might've met your killer."

That clinches it.

"Clean this up, would you?" she says to the local constabulary.

"Any idea how?" the cop asks.

He dips the toe of his boot into the puddle of Klaus Bartoch and the body wobbles like badly set jelly.

"I'll leave it to your imagination," Adrienne replies.

Then they're back in the car and on their way south. Steve sticks to the coast, even though it probably takes longer. Not because of the distance, because of the traffic. There are plenty of tourists taking the scenic routes around the city. While he drives, Adrienne watches the ocean. It's late on a bright winter day, but even now the beaches are busy with sun-worshippers. The sand glows dully and the water is a deep blue-green, waves breaking on the white sand. It's so picturesque the cynic in her is momentarily silenced.

"So, you haven't heard from Grace?" Steve asks.

Adrienne starts. "No, I told you." She pauses, then adds, "What makes you ask?"

Steve gestures at the ocean. "Just that she used to say

she was going to be a journalist overseas. You know, she really emphasised the *overseas* thing."

"Yeah, she did. She did become a journo, though. At some point."

Her name appears in the national papers sometimes, so Adrienne figures she's still alive, still out there someplace. She doesn't think much about her sister. More, she thinks about what it's meant to her own life, the decision to stay local.

"Why's his name Chapel, anyhow?" says Steve, changing the subject. He pronounces it '*sha*-pel', not 'cha-*pel*', the way Chapel did. "I mean, it's a place of worship, right? But he's got all these bullshit stories about transference and spirits...doesn't sound like something you'd believe if you attended a chapel."

"I suspect," Adrienne says, making it up as she goes along, "it's meant to be ironic."

"I think it's a variation on a stage name," Steve says after a while. "Like, Chapel by day, Schapelle by night, maybe?"

Adrienne chuckles at the idea of the tiny Indonesian man naming himself after a famous Australian drug mule doing time in a Balinese prison.

"I like it," she says.

When they get to where they're going, it's a redbrick apartment block in Coogee. Same as every other redbrick in Coogee. Plain on the outside, plain on the inside, but with a sea breeze Adrienne would kill for.

The door is open and Adrienne can hear sobbing, the same as on the phone. She enters in a crouch.

Inside, Chapel is sitting on a lounge beside the crier. It's a man, round as a beach ball, his jeans hooked high on his convulsing belly. He rests his head in his hand, elbow on the arm of the lounge, face averted.

Chapel is sitting with his legs crossed, looking blandly at his own nails. He catches sight of Adrienne and Steve as they enter. "Detectives."

He looks glad to see them, but probably because he's bored with the crying.

"What's the problem?" Adrienne asks.

The sobbing man finally looks up. His fat face is contorted, almost a caricature of grief. He looks at the detectives without comprehension.

"This is Timothy," says Chapel. "He nearly died today."

Timothy looks to be late forties, hair short and shot with grey.

Adrienne lowers herself to a chair. She can tell this is going to take a while. "What happened, Timothy?"

The story Timothy tells doesn't win Adrienne over quickly.

"I met her last night. Well, early morning. I think it was four or five in the a.m." His voice is thick with tears and he keeps clearing his throat.

"Who?" she asks.

Timothy hesitates. "She said her name was Ishtar."

"You mean, like the goddess?" Steve exchanges a look with Adrienne.

Timothy brightens with relief. "Yeah. Just like the goddess."

"What can you tell us about her?" Adrienne asks.

Timothy shrugs. He gives a description of a tiny, dark-haired woman shaped like a ballerina, but with a fierce slant to her eyes and mouth. She's beautiful, he insists, shaking his head in wonder. He describes, in detail, the brief dress she was wearing and the armload of jewellery — cuffs on her upper arms, bracelets, rings on every finger, long earrings to her shoulders. He even describes the mix of silver and gold, the eight thin strands of necklace she wore. Adrienne wonders if Timothy works in the trade. Perhaps he's a jeweller. Perhaps he's a kleptomaniac. Maybe she should take a look around the apartment.

"You were in a nightclub?" she prompts.

Timothy nods. "The Pitt. On Pitt Street. But then we came back here."

"She was here?" Adrienne's ears prick up. She glances about the room, halfway expecting to see her.

"What happened?" Steve asks.

"We talked," Timothy shrugs.

"About?" Steve again.

Here Timothy pauses, confused. After the detailed visual recollection of her jewellery, his memory isn't working so good.

"She said...she was going to make an example of me," he says. "I thought she meant...sexually."

Adrienne nods, as if this is the most obvious interpretation.

"She wanted to hear about the women I'd known," says Timothy. "She kept asking me to admit what I'd done."

"And what had you done?" Adrienne asks.

"Nothing! I've never done anything."

"You must have done something, right?" Adrienne presses. "She must've been a friend of someone you did something to, someone you screwed over?"

Chapel cuts in. "Wait until you hear the rest of the story."

He's calm, a man in his element. He smiles at Adrienne, maybe figuring she's struggling. He has that whole I-was-right-you-were-wrong look going on. Pretty soon, she's going to ask him what any of this has to do with transference, and he's going to have to admit this is a whole different bucket of crazy.

Timothy returns to the story. Ishtar kept pressing him, kept trying to get him to admit what he'd done, asking about the women in his life. Adrienne notes that down, 'women'.

"She told me she'd kill me." The tears start rolling down Timothy's face again. "She said she'd break every bone in my body."

"What did you do?" Adrienne prompts blandly.

"I didn't...I was powerless. Paralysed. I couldn't move unless she told me to. She made me...take off my clothes." The sobs return, his belly rolling under the onslaught of tears. "She was going to kill me!"

Adrienne's impatience rises. "Why didn't she?"

Timothy wipes his face with his bare hands, smearing the tears all over his cheeks and chin. "Because I don't have a penis yet."

It takes Adrienne a moment to calculate the statement.

"You're transsexual?" she asks.

Timothy nods. "Well, in three weeks—"

"She thought you were a man?"

"I am a man," says Timothy, his voice soft. "I'm just a man waiting for an operation."

"But she didn't kill you because you...I mean, she said because you...?"

She looks to Steve for help, but he's wearing his own bewildered expression.

"She said she wouldn't kill a woman who hadn't wronged her," Timothy says. "She said I could be the witness, the one to remember her. She said after what she had planned, no one would forget her. But I would be the first."

Adrienne's blood goes cold. She takes a breath and asks the question she has to; "I guess she didn't tell you what she had planned?"

Timothy shakes his head. "Something about an army."

"An army?" Steve finds his voice at last.

"She said," Timothy's sobs have stopped, "she's going to raise Hell."

They leave Timothy to his renewed crying and head outside. Darkness has fallen and the sea breeze has become icy.

"What do you make of that?" Steve asks.

Adrienne doesn't answer. The whole thing is too weird and too stupid, and she's tired. The sting has gone out of her hand where the burn has faded to skin tones, but only just. It feels raw and so does she.

Chapel comes up behind them while they're getting into the car. "Can you give me a lift?"

"Where to?" Steve asks.

"Away from here," Chapel says. "Can't stand the southern suburbs."

Adrienne's about to refuse, but Steve gestures him into the car.

They head back. The beaches are still busy, sand almost blue in the rising moonlight. Most of the crowd is simply cruising the promenades, making their way to local cafes and restaurants. Adrienne thinks Steve might turn west and go inland, but he continues up the coastal roads. A reverse of the trip they made south.

"Who the hell is Ishtar, anyhow?" Steve asks. "Greek?"

"Mesopotamian," Chapel corrects him. "Goddess of love and war."

"Did you put him up to this?" Adrienne asks.

"No." Chapel's tone is surprised. "If anything, what he's saying proves me wrong, too."

"Yeah, I was going to point out your body-hopping

transference theory just got all shot to hell."

Chapel grunts. "Some bitch goddess out for revenge instead. Who knew?"

"Sure. It's a tiny woman with supernatural powers running about killing men and raising an army," Adrienne summarises.

Steve mutters, "What's she need an army for? She's doing fine on her own."

"Maybe it's too slow for her," Adrienne speculates. "You know, killing people one by one."

Steve casts her a look. "You buying this?"

Adrienne doesn't answer. She cranes around to look at Chapel. He's playing with his phone, tapping the screen and chewing on his lip. "So what about this army?"

"I'll have to look it up," Chapel murmurs.

"Great. Okay, so get back to me when you do."

"No, I mean now. I'm just searching for a free network. But of course in a moving vehicle...never mind. Aha, here's something."

He reads out a biography of Ishtar that he's found online. Goddess of love. When she descended to Hell, all sex on earth stopped. She passed through seven gates, each time obeying the ancient law that required her to remove a piece of clothing. When she reached Hell she was naked, and she was hung on hooks for centuries. Goddess of war. She avenged herself on her lovers. One, Tammuz, she sent to the underworld for half a year every year when she found him screwing his sister.

"That's sweet," says Adrienne.

"Maybe that's why she started with prostitutes," Steve says. "They're not going to ask about those big old meat hook marks in her skin, the ones from Hell's kitchen."

"Nothing about an army?" Adrienne asks.

"Not so far," Chapel confirms.

"Killed her lovers," says Steve. "It'd fit."

"You believe this stuff yet?" Adrienne asks.

Steve shrugs. "What's it matter what *I* believe? If *she* believes it, if she thinks she's a vengeful goddess—"

"Doesn't explain how she's killing them," Adrienne interjects.

"You guys are reaching," says Chapel. "You keep making up more and more complicated explanations when the real one's simple. She's really Ishtar. She's really killing people with her goddess powers. And she's probably really raising an army."

Adrienne is about to give him an earful, but he interrupts. "Oh, you're not going to like this." He leans forward with his phone held out, screen angled towards Adrienne. "Some manuscript they found a couple years back, from a washerwoman, would you believe. Wouldn't think those bitches could write."

"What's it say?"

"Ishtar has an army all right. An army of stillborns."

"I knew it," Steve mutters.

"Gula made them. They're hibernating in caves all over Mesopotamia, waiting for Ishtar to call them into service," Chapel says.

"I'm not even sure where Mesopotamia is," says Steve, "but it's not here, and I'm glad. Plus—" he jerks a thumb at the dark ocean to his right, "we got an entire ocean between us and there. Being the world's biggest island never looked so good."

"I wouldn't get too complacent." There's a new vigour in Chapel's voice. "Ishtar made it here."

"Unless she's buying her stillborns plane tickets, I don't see it happening," Steve says.

Adrienne cuts them off. "Will you two just shut the hell up!"

Chapter Five

They drop Chapel at Hyde Park in the centre of town. Before he gets out of the car, he says, "I've got another lead for you."

He gives them a postal address for something he's come across online, a cult dedicated to 'confining the powers of the goddess of destruction'. The Lord of Lords, the cult calls itself.

"This is for a post office," Adrienne says.

"So? Aren't you the police?" Chapel says.

After he leaves, Adrienne mutters, "What in hell are we meant to do with this?"

Steve shrugs. It's getting on to dinner time, Adrienne knows. His wife is probably waiting at home.

She sighs. "May as well check it out."

They're back near Chinatown, so Adrienne phones in with the address while Steve goes for food. Then they eat hot dumplings with their fingers and wait for the database to cough up a name. Steve keeps glancing at his watch and muttering about calling his wife.

"Belongs to a Mark Davis," says the voice over the radio.

They're given an address. Steve drives one-handed, blowing on a pork dumpling while he navigates the traffic.

They cross the bridge into the north of Sydney and pull up outside an art deco one-storey house in Mosman. The man who opens the door looks like he's just home from an office job. He has brown hair and a bad suit. He's at that certain age when the body begins to trade muscle for fat.

"Mark Davis?" Steve asks.

Davis eyes them carefully until Adrienne pulls out a badge, then he looks surprised. "Has something happened?"

"What would've happened?" Adrienne asks.

Davis goes from surprise to confusion to consternation in a second. "Come in, then."

Inside the house is neat, too neat, and plain. Like Davis himself.

"We're here to ask you about the Lord of Lords, Mr. Davis," says Steve.

"Please, call me Marduk."

Adrienne hesitates. Great. More nutjobs with crazy names. "Is that your name?"

"It's my chosen name," Davis replies.

"Not your legal name?"

Davis raises an eyebrow. "You still think the state has the right to legalise names? You think that's their call? Plato said—"

"I'm sure he did, Mr. Davis," Adrienne cuts him off.

Davis sits on his faux-leather couch and glares.

Steve taps away on his phone for a minute. "Marduk. Champion of the gods," he gives Davis an impressed look. "Nice."

"Modest, too." Adrienne takes up a position in the doorway. "What does your organisation do, Mr. Davis?"

"We teach the right of the individual—"

"So you identify with who? Socialist Alliance?"

"Oh, no. We don't propose to build a relationship with one of the bigger parties—"

"Don't like playing with the other kids?" Adrienne interrupts.

Davis — Marduk — gives her a soft glare.

"Partnerships between organisations with differing goals," he says, enunciating each word, "have a habit of falling apart."

"Like cops and robbers, that sort of thing?" Adrienne says. "I've seen that one fall apart. What about you,

Steve?"

Steve gives Davis a wink. Davis doesn't respond. He's not prepared to buy the good-cop-bad-cop routine, that's clear.

"Socialism," says Davis, "frequently aligns itself with atheism. We're not atheists. Our goals are not the refusal of the gods. Just the...containment of them."

"Sounds complicated," Steve says. "How do you do that?"

Davis rolls his eyes.

"We're looking for a goddess right now, as it happens," Adrienne says.

"Oh, really? Which one?" Davis has an expression like he's entertaining the ideas of a small child.

"The goddess of goddesses," says Adrienne. She pretends to check her notes. "What do you know about someone calling herself...Ishtar?"

Davis gives his first smile of the encounter. "Ah, the two faces of the human race. Love and war. Everyone knows Ishtar. At one time, the name Ishtar came to mean simply 'goddess'. As if there was no other. She is the every-goddess. In a way, she's the mother of all of us."

"So you call home once a week?" Adrienne asks.

Steve sniggers.

Davis looks through her like he's smelled something bad and doesn't want to admit it's his. "If it's her you're after, you've got a big problem on your hands."

"We like problems," Steve says.

"Why's that a problem?" Adrienne asks simultaneously.

"She's evil," Davis says. "She'll destroy the world, just because she can."

"I never understand the bad guys that want to destroy the world," Steve says. "I mean, they live in the world, right?"

Davis chuckles. "Ishtar can take it or leave it. One of the few deities to walk into the Underworld and right back out again. She enjoys the dead."

"The dead?" Adrienne prompts.

"Ishtar," says Davis, "is always talking about the dead. She threatened her own father once. Said if he didn't do what she wanted, she'd raise the dead to eat the food of the living."

"Eat our food?" Steve says. "That's harsh."

"And I'm just betting," says Davis, "that the dead don't have the patience for farming. So when they run out of food..."

He lets the sentence hang.

"Zombies," says Steve with disgust.

Stillborns, thinks Adrienne.

"What did Daddy do to earn that threat?" Adrienne asks. She figures she should probably read up on this stuff. Maybe it will come in handy.

"I wouldn't say it was earned," Davis says. "He tried to talk her out of taking revenge on Gilgamesh. But Gilgamesh had humiliated her."

"That happen a lot, the humiliation?" Steve asks.

"Of Ishtar? No," Davis shakes his head. "By all accounts she was stunning. And powerful. No one else in history rejected a proposition from Ishtar. But Gilgamesh thought he knew better. He recounted to her a list of her abused lovers. Ishtar didn't like that."

"No sense of humour?" Steve asks.

"Do you know where we could find her?" Adrienne asks.

"Find her?" Davis echoes. "You mean...find the way to the goddess?"

"I mean something less esoteric than that," says Adrienne. "I mean find *her*, meet her. Shake her hand and tell her to have a nice day."

Davis looks nonplussed. "What?"

"Do you know," Adrienne says carefully, mimicking his earlier enunciation, "where we could find someone claiming to be the goddess Ishtar, come to avenge men and raise an army of dead children?"

Davis stares. "Jesus Christ."

"See?" She turns to Steve. "Scratch a Neo-pagan, you'll almost always find a Christian."

"Can't fight upbringing," Steve says.

"You're talking," says Davis, "about a goddess that walked the earth thousands of years ago. Do I know how you *find her* today? No."

"Don't play dumb," Adrienne insists. "You know something. Maybe you know where her spurned lover is? What's his name? Tammy Something?"

"Tammuz." Davis looks edgy.

"Is he here, too?"

"I can't say."

"You don't know?"

"When he returns, I'll know. I'll be summoned."

"You're that important?"

"I'm his chief bodyguard!" Davis' face is white.

Adrienne smirks. "Not much of a Champion of gods, then. A bodyguard. What, you just liked the name, Marduk?"

Davis looks at her sourly, opens his mouth, and apparently prefers not to provoke a cop. Adrienne thinks less of him for it.

She says, "Any chance he's spending July in Sydney this year?"

"July is the month of Tammuz," Davis looks past her. "Farming season in the northern hemisphere. Were he anywhere on earth, Detective, it wouldn't be *here*. And if I'd had a summons from Tammuz, I wouldn't be here to explain all this to you."

"So, even if Ishtar was sending an army after him, say, she wouldn't send it this way?"

"You were *serious* about the army?"

Adrienne's had enough. She turns towards the door.

Steve gives Davis a mock salute with his notebook. "Don't try to be a hero."

"That was a waste of time." Adrienne slams the car door behind her. "Davis knows less than we do. Remind me why I even listened to that crazy Chapel bastard."

"You didn't lose anything this time?" Steve asks.

"What?"

"You've been losing stuff all day," he says. "Just checking."

Adrienne checks she still has her wallet, badge, watch, notebook; all there. She wonders where her scarf is and then figures it's in the pocket of the jacket she left at the Cult of Ishtar's house.

"Where can I drop you?" Steve asks.

It's clear he's ready to call it a day. Adrienne's phone rings and its Nina. She holds up a hand to stall Steve, but he starts the engine anyway.

"I just met a man," says Adrienne by way of introduction, "who goes by the name of Marduk."

Nina's deep-throated chuckle travels down the line. "Modest, isn't he?"

"Just your regular ego-maniac," Adrienne replies.

"The God of Babylon," says Nina.

"I thought there were a bunch of gods in Babylon, anyhow." Adrienne exhausts her entire knowledge of ancient Babylonian gods in one sentence.

"There were gods *in* Babylon, sure," Nina says, "but Marduk is the patron god of the city of Babylon."

"Okay." Adrienne doesn't want to hear any more.

"Meet you?" Nina asks.

"Home time?" Steve says simultaneously.

She nods. "Drop me at a bar, would you?"

"Which one?" he asks.

"Any one." To Nina she says, "I'll text you when I'm there."

She hunkers down in her seat, resting her head. She's lived in this city, maybe not all her life, but all the most interesting and best bits of it, and she's learning now it isn't her city at all. Something else owns it, something old and powerful in ways she doesn't understand.

Chapter Six

Steve finds her an old brown pub somewhere near the centre of town and she texts Nina her location. It's happy hour, so the drinks are cheap. It's always happy hour someplace. She orders two at once to save herself another walk to the bar, and sits with her phone on the table in front of her, spinning it idly while she downs the beers.

Nina arrives while she's on her fourth drink.

"How's the supernatural world treating you?" Nina asks. When Adrienne doesn't answer, Nina nods. "Always like that the first time."

"You've seen this stuff before?"

Nina helps herself to a bar stool. "Nope, not like this. I found Candice Angers, by the way. The woman who found the body—"

"Behind the church, right," says Adrienne. "She up for questioning?"

"She's dead."

"Powdered?"

"No, not like that," Nina says. "They haven't released a cause. Officially."

"Unofficially?"

"Her heart stopped."

Adrienne wonders if the bitch-goddess has anything to do with that. "I'll see what I can find out."

She downs her drink and thinks about ordering another, but she's distracted by someone entering the dim pub. A woman. There's something familiar about her walk.

The newcomer squints into the dark interior and heads towards the bar with the rapid step of someone used to too much attention. She's wearing a long skirt and heavy boots, a gothic look probably perfected in her teens. Now she's older, the clothes are faded and less earnest.

"Want a drink?" Adrienne asks Nina, eyes on the woman.

Adrienne doesn't wait for an answer, just picks up an empty glass and goes to the bar. She comes up around the woman's right side as she's paying for her drink. Adrienne tries to lean into the other woman's line of vision. The woman ignores her for as long as it takes to get her change, then she turns with a defensive frown on her face.

"Can I help — *Jesus*. Adrienne?"

"When were you going to call?" Some barely remembered sense of familial duty tells Adrienne she should embrace her sister, but her gut is clenched and she can't seem to uncoil her hand from the empty glass.

Grace opens her mouth to respond, but collapses instead into an apologetic grin. "Wow, I barely recognise you."

"I could say the same."

It's true Grace has changed, but that's not what she means.

Standing beside her sister like a stranger, she thinks she should feel something. Fierce protectiveness mixed with equally fierce impatience; resentment from being the 'other' sister, the one who wasn't the favourite. There's a lifetime of emotional back-and-forth Adrienne should be able to draw on, but she's numb. If blood is thicker than water, she's not feeling it.

Neither woman moves to touch each other, to hug or even shake hands, to make sure of the other's reality. They stand like bridge pylons, unable to shake the history that binds them, but afraid to acknowledge it. At least, that's how Adrienne feels.

"Shall we sit down?" Grace shifts her weight from one foot to another.

The spell is broken. Adrienne buys a drink and a glass of water for Nina, then leads Grace back to the table.

"This is Grace," she says simply. "Grace, this is Nina."

Nina is the first to speak. She offers her hand. "Adrienne's little sister? Thought you were dead."

"Adrienne just likes to pretend I am." Grace sits with a grimace that she masks with a quick smile.

Adrienne sits opposite, relieved; there it is, that familiar gnawing hostility that comes from being around Grace.

"So, where've you been?" Adrienne spins her glass. She's lost the taste for beer, but such losses are usually temporary.

"Well," Grace clasps a glass of lemonade, pushes a straw around, unsettling the ice, "I was in Somalia for a while, covering the pirate attacks."

Grace looks tired. Her fringe hangs long over her eyes. The colour has seeped out of it over time, and grey is beginning to show in her little sister's hair. Her face is still young, though.

"Sounds dangerous," Adrienne says.

Grace grins. "You think it's too dangerous a job for me? It better be because I'm your baby sister, and not because I'm female."

"They take it out on women worse," Adrienne says.

"They take it out on women worse everywhere. I could be sitting in my apartment, I could be walking through a park—"

"But if you were here," says Adrienne, "we could find the sons of bitches. We could pursue them with every means available to us."

"Every legal means," Grace says.

"Whatever."

There's silence. Nina sips her water and pretends to be deaf.

"I didn't come here to talk about that," Grace says. "I'm here because of what's going on in the Persian Gulf. What the news isn't covering."

"The Persian Gulf? As in, the Gulf War gulf?" Adrienne's about to launch into another stinging attack about safety when Nina catches her eye. She eases back in her seat.

Grace says, "I snuck my camera out of the country — well, I won't tell you how. There's an embargo on this." Grace pushes her drink aside. "Brace yourself for something weird."

"Oh, great. I love weird."

One thing Grace has never been is a drama queen. Always quietly went her own way, against the grain — or with the grain as she saw fit. She reaches for her bag, some tawdry thing made of silk and ribbons. No doubt it was rainbow colours when it started, but now it's become muted and ragged. To Adrienne, it looks like a pile of sick with hairballs. She fights the urge to tell her sister to take better care of her stuff. This is Grace. She doesn't take care of stuff.

Grace pulls out a digital camera. It's battered and dusty and she gives it a cursory wipe, then flips it around and switches it on. Adrienne sees an image of green water, the canal walls behind it bleached white in the sun. A lone palm tree stands tall beside low buildings. But this isn't the detail Adrienne is meant to be looking at. On the sand is row upon row of fleshy, lifeless soldiers, feet raised like they're marching into the water.

"What in hell...?" Nina asks.

"They say it's an army," says Grace, "belonging to—"

In unison they say, "Ishtar."

"How'd you know?" Grace asks, her eyebrows high on her forehead, hitting her faded fringe.

"Long story."

"Okay." Grace looks at Adrienne expectantly, but when nothing else is forthcoming, she continues. "Well, they were seen going into the ocean at Iran, Kuwait, even as far south as Saudi Arabia and Oman."

They look like grey, human balloons, skin bloated and slippery-wet in the sunlight. Their eyes are closed, their bodies completely hairless. Some of them have fingers and toes, but not all of them. Many don't even have arms. Their necks are thick, as if the head is joined to body by a long, fat tube.

Nina leans back, looking queasy. "They look like sausage meat."

"Or pale slugs," says Grace, unperturbed.

"They're stillborns," Adrienne says.

"What?" Nina blurts.

"They're stillborn children, an army of them."

"They're too big," argues Nina.

"Wait, I've heard of this. Word among the locals is that Ishtar had a stillborn army once before," Grace says. "But if these guys are part of the same army, they're the miscarriages."

"So this is the B-team?" Adrienne angles the camera for another look.

"They were small when they came out of the caves. People on the Tigris and Euphrates were joking that they were bait," Grace says. "Thing is, they're growing. And they're growing pragmatically. You shoot one, cut it in half, then there's two of them. They develop whatever they need to keep pace with the army. They grow feet, but they don't grow a new head, or a face. See?"

She flips through more photos. Adrienne leans over to look. The tallest members of the army are shown passing a man in fatigues. He's holding a camera and pointing it down. The stillborns don't pass his knee. And they're weird. Oddly-shaped, bulbous and strange. Definitely not any kind of creature Adrienne recognises.

"Any theories on why that is?"

Grace says, "Locals believe they're monsters. That if they were ever human, they've forgotten how to be. And every day, they get a bigger. This one's being carried by one of its brethren, but you can see tiny feet — at both ends of its body." She gives her sister a queasy smile. "How sick is that?"

"Pretty sick," agrees Adrienne. "How many of them are there?"

"Thousands."

"So they've marched into the ocean—" Adrienne says, ignoring Nina's muttered blasphemes.

"Yeah, they're following a leader, I think." Grace flips to a photo of a grey skin sack with its hands towards its face. The figure stares straight ahead with bulbous eyes in its wet skin, its head like a balloon. "Look. It's sucking its fingers."

"Sweet." Adrienne tries to sound casual. "So where are they now?"

Grace is wrapped up in the story her photos tell.

"They were being tracked, but it became impossible. They went east and then..."

"Then what?"

Grace spreads her hands. "How do you track something with no heartbeat? No body temperature? No need to come up for air. They're down there somewhere, in the ocean, looking for their queen."

"And," Adrienne hesitates, "when they find her?"

Grace shrugs. "Who knows? Unholy Hell, I imagine. I mean, you only need an army if you're going to war, right?"

"And what if Ishtar is...here?" Adrienne asks. "What if they're coming this way?"

"To Australia?" Grace laughs. "Why would she be here? Heck, that's why I came home. I figured this had to be the safest place in the world, right? We're hardly a superpower. What kind of threat are we?"

Adrienne thinks it through. No near neighbours and no allies that care much about us. Australia, a desert on a rock. Perfect place to train your army away from the glare of the world's attention.

"Maybe that's the point," she says. "We're not a threat. We're easy pickings. Practice."

A training ground.

Grace finishes her drink. "Bathroom," she announces.

It's only as she gets up, her coat falling away at the sides, that Adrienne realises her little sister is pregnant. She feels sober and sick at the same time. She stares, speechless, and Grace catches her expression and grins.

"A souvenir," Grace says.

"How...long?"

"Seven months, about," Grace says. "Haven't actually gotten to a doctor yet. Life is...busy."

Grace leaves Nina and Adrienne at the table, nursing empty glasses. Adrienne realises the kind of tiredness she's feeling now is more like the beginning of defeat.

Her phone rings and she answers it without thinking.

"Where are you on Google Maps?" Steve asks without preamble.

"What are you talking about?"

"Checked your data downloads lately?"

Adrienne sighs. "I'm having a tough night. Get to the point."

"The Internet, she's a goner," Steve supplies.

Adrienne thumbs her phone to data mode and types 'Ishtar' into the Google search bar. The screen stalls for several long seconds before she flips back to her call.

"I'm getting nothing," she says.

"I know. You're getting the same thing as almost every-damn-body in the country. Something's knocked out the Internet links between Australia and the rest of the world. Whatever mirror sites we've got locally are being overwhelmed by demand."

"How in hell do you knock out the entire Internet?"

Steve lets out a groan like he's doing complicated mathematics in his head. "You don't knock out the entire Internet, just our part of it. Smash the cables on the ocean floor. That takes out most of it. Then you let the rest of us go all Fight Club for what's left. You following? Happened to Egypt a few years back."

Information warfare, Steve calls it. He says it's not a big deal to pull off, either. The data cables are only reinforced near the shore, close enough in case boats accidentally snag the line. Further out in the ocean, they're often less than two centimetres across. "You need to get right to the floor of the ocean, though. We can't reach Japan at all. Singapore, Hawaii — even New Zealand's out."

"You're a font of information," says Adrienne.

"Yeah, but I had to find all this out the old-fashioned

way. By phone."

"So right now it's just us? Australia, I mean. With busted cables?"

"Far as I can tell." His tone is dry. "But, I mean we have to call these places one at a time. You know how hard it is to get a phone line when the whole country's trying?"

"Who *can* we reach?" Adrienne asks.

She can hear Steve flipping through his notes. "New Caledonia."

"Fuck," says Adrienne.

Nina frowns, trying to get Adrienne's attention, but Adrienne holds up a hand. Steve continues, "Could be a spy submarine, if those things still exist. Or terrorism, of course. ACMA is looking into it." In case she doesn't understand, he adds, "Australian Communications—"

"I know," says Adrienne. She takes a breath. "They're isolating us."

"ACMA?"

"No. The army." Adrienne presses her fingers to her temple. "But how'd they know where to find the cables?"

"Are you kidding? They're listed on Wikipedia. So ships can avoid—"

She cuts him off, tells him to meet her and hangs up. She stares past Nina for a full two minutes before Nina says, "Bad news?"

"The worst kind of bad. This goddess of yours," she says. "She's smart."

Nina grunts. "Honey, she's not *my* goddess."

Looking at the tattoo on her hand, Adrienne wonders when she stopped pretending Ishtar wasn't real.

Steve proves he doesn't need Google Maps to find his way back to her. Adrienne feels his slap on her shoulder less than ten minutes later, and hears him claim he has a photographic memory for pubs. He nods hello to Nina and Grace. Grace nods politely in return, but it's clear she doesn't remember him.

"We were at school together," Steve says. "I guess I've put on some weight since then." He rests a hand self-consciously on his stomach, but Grace only continues to give him a polite and distant smile.

The pub has filled up, locals piling in, jostling each other for room. It's mid-evening, but the communication outages have drawn people out of their homes. They're congregating in public places, waiting for an answer, holding onto each other.

"Grace has some interesting photos," Adrienne says.

As her sister does a show-and-tell, Adrienne fills in the gaps with the Ishtar story and the army marching across the bottom of the ocean.

"So," says Steve, "you think an army of dead babies has kicked out the Internet cables so they can play war games uninterrupted at our place?"

Adrienne shrugs. "Makes about as much sense as anything else."

"Great. So she's controlling them, this Ishtar bird?"

"Who can say? She was a very powerful goddess, apparently," says Nina. "Had a habit of killing her lovers and taking her holidays in Hell. So, you know, controlling dead foetuses shouldn't be such a big deal."

"I guess we find her and ask her," Adrienne's glass is empty but she feels too queasy for a re-fill.

Grace looks from one to another. "You know where Ishtar is?"

"We've come across her," Adrienne confirms.

"What's she look like?"

Adrienne shrugs. "Human."

Grace waits, but when Adrienne falls silent she says,

"Well, I guess that makes sense. She had a human form once. All the gods and goddesses did, but they were more powerful. And they liked to be worshipped, of course."

"There's that," Steve acknowledges.

"Thing is, how'd she get here?" Adrienne asks.

"Well, the most popular way," Grace says, "is to fly."

"So you're telling me," Adrienne says, "that an ancient goddess got herself a passport, checked out a text book on modern geography—"

"Google Maps," Steve reminds her.

"—and hopped a plane to Australia?"

"Probably saw it on TV," says Steve.

"If you think about it," Grace says, "it makes sense. We have so many tools nowadays that we take for granted, right? TV, the Internet. Enter some revenge-mad goddess looking for — what did you call it? — a training ground, and hey, presto!"

"So, where is she?" Nina asks.

No one has an answer.

"One of us should tell the chief," says Steve. "He's gonna have to talk to the military. Explain what's coming if that army's really walking towards Sydney."

Adrienne doesn't respond.

After a minute Steve adds, "Flip you for it."

Chapter Seven

Adrienne argues that whatever the chief's contribution will be to their adventure, it can wait until morning. They have no evidence for their crazy theory, and no real leads on where Ishtar or her army is, apart from 'maybe somewhere in the ocean, kicking out cables'. They sit and barely talk until it's about ten o'clock at the end of a very long day.

Nina retires to her flat in the city, Grace heads to her hostel, despite Adrienne's protestations. Only Steve and Adrienne remain, making the long trek to Steve's car. Parking was hard to find with everyone heading into town — apart from the doomsday-sayers, who've fled to the mountains and ultimately, probably, the desert beyond.

Steve's parked behind the State Library on a narrow street near the strip of parkland called The Domain. It's a space largely used for outdoor concerts or visits by the Dalai Lama. In between there's often amateur football games, but at this time of night, it's empty and dark.

Adrienne feels eyes on her. She turns in a slow circle, making it look casual, making it look like maybe she's searching for a late-night coffee shop while simultaneously checking the sky for falling stars.

She sees it, a black limo. Or, not *a* black limo, *the* black limo. The one that freaky bitch fled in while Adrienne was left behind heaving her guts into the gutter.

"Ishtar," she murmurs.

"What?" Steve asks.

"Stay here."

Adrienne walks towards the old sandstone Sydney Hospital, across its courtyard and through the iron gates out onto Macquarie Street. She flaps her badge at a startled security guard with cheeks like thick pockets. Then she sprints past the rest of the historic buildings on Macquarie Street and rounds a corner, coming out onto the edge of the Domain parallel to where she estimates the parked limo to be. She's spot on.

"Police!" She slams her fist against the opaque window.

Steve is still a hundred metres up the road. He turns at

the sound of her voice and gives her a look of pure surprise. When he sees she's pulled her gun, he does the same.

The window rolls down but no face appears from the gloom of the interior.

"Come in," says a voice. It's earthy, husky, old. It has some kind of accent, but she's hard-pressed to say which one.

"You come out!"

There's silence. Then the sound of satin sliding on car upholstery. Someone emerges, a tiny woman with thick wrists and gold jewellery on every limb. She wears a long black gown with spaghetti straps and a flat silver brooch with a familiar-looking eight-pointed star in the middle of her chest.

"Name!" Adrienne's voice is louder than it needs to be, but there's something sinewy and unnatural about the way the woman moves and it's freaking her the fuck out. "Tell me your name!"

"I am Ishtar, your goddess!" The woman seethes. "And you should bow to me!"

Adrienne's knees weaken but she fights it, wobbling on her feet. Steve is at the limo by now, but Adrienne gestures him back. Ishtar mistakes the gesture for something more disrespectful. She reaches out a hand and Adrienne's stomach rolls, her vision blurs. She gasps.

"You're surrounded!" Steve must've learned that from a cop show.

It works, briefly. Ishtar turns around, chin first, the rest of her body following. She casts Steve a quick look and then raises a hand. His eyes roll back in his head and he flops to the ground.

"No!" Adrienne shouts.

She leaps onto Ishtar, wrapping arms around her shoulders, holding the gun to the woman's neck. She hopes she doesn't have to use the thing because if it goes off now, she'll probably blow her own head off, too.

Ishtar smells of snake skin, of oil and blood and the tang of something worse. She lets Adrienne hang there, and Adrienne finds she's unable to move the woman even a fraction of an inch.

"You think you can stop me?" Ishtar's voice reverberates throughout her frame like she's hollow. "You, with so little power."

Ishtar spins, knocking Adrienne off. Adrienne staggers back, but stays upright. Ishtar reaches out, too far, the skin pulling tight as her arm lengthens. She grabs Adrienne by the shirt and rips it in half, leaving it hanging from her trousers like strips of sunburned skin. Despite herself, Adrienne cowers. She raises a hand over her face as if that would help, angling her forearm in a classic martial arts defence pose. Useless, she knows that; even so, the animal brain can't help but want to live.

But Ishtar's hands only clench and unclench, a snake testing the air with its tongue.

"What's the matter?" Adrienne asks. "You don't hit girls?"

Ishtar doesn't smile. Adrienne can't imagine her smiling. But she sneers and bares her teeth and Adrienne thinks 'animal brain' all over again.

"Not yet," Ishtar says.

"What are you waiting for?" Adrienne asks.

But Ishtar turns and gets back in the car, her long gown dragging behind her.

"What are you waiting for!" She keeps shouting until the car is out of sight. Her skin is exposed, cold, her hands are still caught in the cuffs of her ruined shirt. She feels momentarily manacled, until she rips her arms free and tosses the shirt to the ground.

Steve is lying on the ground, muttering "Ow, ow, ow"

over and again.

"Lover's tiff, darlin'?" comes a stranger's voice, gruff and masculine.

"Fuck you!" Adrienne suggests.

"Aw, that can be arranged, sweetheart." The stranger moves in, eyes her sports bra, hands moving restlessly in the pockets of his trousers. He's homeless, Adrienne realises, and that's all that stops her from falling into a kung fu crouch. It's just a threat; she doesn't know kung fu. But she does know how to bring a man down with a well-placed kick or a fist to his windpipe.

"You're under arrest," she says, "for vagrancy, intent to harm—"

"Hey! You're the one with your boobs out, bitch. That's entrapment!"

"Yeah, but in court I'll be in a suit, and you'll still stink of scum and booze. Now, fuck right off."

The homeless guy propels himself away, mumbling and cursing.

There's a groan from Steve as he rolls to his side and tries to get his knees under him. Tears pour from his eyes, but he doesn't seem to realise. He stands unsteadily and looks towards Adrienne.

"What in fuck happened to you?" he asks.

Chapter Eight

It's the middle of the night, but Adrienne is high on adrenaline. Everywhere the streets are full of people equally alert, alarmed and awake. She gives Steve forty bucks to find her a new shirt, and he returns with a baby doll style black t-shirt with the pink outline of a cat on the front. The cat is smoking a pipe. For no apparent reason.

"Where's my change?" Adrienne asks.

She's sitting in the front of the car with Steve's jacket on backwards to cover her bare torso.

"You don't go shopping much, do you?" Steve asks. "You owe me ten bucks."

They head first to The Pitt, the place where Timothy, between sobs, had claimed he'd met Ishtar. There's no sign of her, so they check up and down Pitt and Bridge Streets in the CBD before heading to the famous club scene of Oxford Street. Most of the bouncers they meet don't have an interest in helping the constabulary locate a short woman in a long black dress. Most of the patrons they stop and talk to feel the same.

"Find someone else's party to ruin!" one drunk girl shouts.

Her friends drag her off Steve and they trip, laughing and screaming down the street. The pubs are loud with humanity apparently enjoying the excuse not to email home. People pull out their phones and shake their heads, unable to get through to friends and family. The atmosphere is more festival than funeral, but there's an element of both in the night air.

Steve refuses to leave her side, though he keeps one arm wrapped around his ribs. Adrienne has tried calling the office to find out about the numberplates she'd reported earlier, but there's no accessing the database except manually. Data lines even within the country are clogged with people looking for answer, and the list of requests in front of her is long.

When dawn weeps its spilt-milk colour across the sky, they're still questioning stragglers, bedraggled club-goers who stare blankly.

Finally they meet a bouncer in front of The Parlour nightclub who claims he's seen the woman they're after.

"Yeah," he says, "gorgeous. Showed up in a limo with two security guards. I thought she might be a movie star—"

"Who'd she leave with?" Adrienne asks.

The bouncer frowns. He's short and solid across the shoulders, and his arms are thick all the way down to his wrists. "Some guy, skinny little runt. Surprised the hell out of me."

"Why's that?"

"Could've sworn he was gay. Then he went home with the hottest chick in the place."

"Other guys tried, I guess?" Adrienne prompts.

"Tried, failed. Honestly? She didn't seem that interested in the guys. Don't know how this guy did it. Indonesian guy. Very..." the bouncer searches for the right word.

Adrienne's scalp prickles. She has no reason to suspect, but there's no escaping it. Plenty of Indonesians in Sydney. Doesn't have to be Chapel.

"Distinguished?" she says. "But with a goofy grin?"

"That's him," the bouncer confirms.

She describes Chapel in as much detail as she remembers, just to be sure. The bouncer nods emphatically the whole way through.

"Damn," Steve mutters.

"She had a great look going on, this bird," says the bouncer. "Dedicated Egyptian, you know? But not overkill."

"Think anyone else would know where they went?"

The bouncer frowns, spreads his hands. "Like who?"

The rest of the night is fruitless.

They head into the office just after dawn. Adrienne figures that now's the time to tell the chief everything. Someone needs to be looking after this shit, and it shouldn't be her. They need the military. They need some way to cut off the army of dead foetuses that's marching across the ocean floor and probably up into Sydney Harbour, looking for their goddess.

But the chief's office is empty, and it's still empty three coffees later.

"Nice shirt," says Campbell, a young man with a brutish personality and a clean, sharp-chinned face.

"Sell it to you," says Adrienne.

Campbell isn't interested.

She ignores whatever he says next and hits speed-dial, waiting for the chief, Douglas, to pick up.

"Where are you, boss?" she asks.

"Day off," says Douglas.

"I need to talk to you," says Adrienne. "Face to face."

The chief hesitates, asks if she's resigning.

Adrienne sits upright in surprise. "No!"

When she presses the point he explains he's heading to his son's graduation. "Bottom of the year, but at least it's a degree in engineering." Paternal pride in action.

"Which university? Can I meet you there?" she asks.

Douglas pauses. "What's this about?"

"It's difficult to explain," Adrienne stalls.

"I don't like difficult to explain. You know the KISS principle, right? Occam's razor?"

"I'm familiar."

She cranes around to see if Steve's at his desk. He is, asleep in his chair. Campbell is trying to balance a teabag from Steve's left ear. Adrienne turns back to her phone call.

"This is really big," she says.

When she won't back down, Douglas relents.

Half an hour later, they cruise into the grounds of Sydney University amidst a cavalcade of families and friends.

Adrienne drives because she's familiar with the campus from her own uni days. Plus, Steve looks like Hell. He's still refusing to get his ribs seen to. Maybe he's scared of what they'll find.

They double-park, leaving a business card under the windshield wiper. The chief is hard to spot in the crowd — he looks like every other middle-aged parent whose first child has graduated. He's overweight and out of his depth, with an uneasy smile pasted to his face.

"Chief." Adrienne nods.

The chief sighs and turns away from his family, ignoring the shooting sneer of his wife and the goggle-eyed surprise of his offspring.

"Thank God," he says. "I hear they serve sandwiches with no crusts. I hate that shit."

"One day you'll look back on this," says Steve, "and wish you'd stuck with the sandwiches."

Douglas indicates he's listening, and Adrienne takes a deep, deep breath. She starts from the beginning, from the inexplicable deaths to the damaged communication cables to the photos on Grace's camera, which she's brought along to show him.

"We think she's summoning her army," Adrienne concludes.

"Rob, they're going in!" Douglas' wife says.

The chief waves her back. "So let me get this straight. You've got a dead goddess-evil-mastermind on your hands, and you've no idea where she is, or where her army of dead mutants is going to land? Is that what you're telling me?"

Adrienne ignores his sarcasm. "Stillborns, not — but yeah."

Douglas sighs, leans back. "Ah, shit."

There's silence. No one can argue with that.

"I'm hoping you're losing your mind, Garner. It'd be

easier to accept," Douglas says.

"You know I'm not."

Douglas shakes his head. His lips are pressed tight and he has a frown so deep it looks like it's never going away. "And you want what?"

"Military," Adrienne says.

"And how do you propose we engage the might of the Australian military against an imaginary enemy?"

Adrienne thinks on her feet. "We tell them it's a biological terrorist threat. Moving across the bottom of the ocean."

Douglas rubs a hand across his forehead. "All right. I don't like it, but I don't want to be the one responsible if you're right. I'm sending this up the chain to someone else."

"Thanks, Boss."

"Lord knows I've seen the bodies, they were weird enough. But this," Douglas rattles the camera. "God help me, if you're wrong."

"I'm not wrong."

"Then God help us all," Douglas grimaces.

Steve winces, holding onto his ribs. "Tell Him to bring reinforcements."

Campbell calls from the office as they're leaving the chief to his graduation sandwiches.

"You guys meet someone called Mark Davis?" he asks, sounding confused. "Found your names in a log book at his house."

Adrienne bites back on the obvious question, 'why is he keeping a log book of visitors?'. She doesn't have time.

"Yeah, we've met him," she says. "Calls himself Marduk."

"Not anymore. He's dead."

147

Adrienne takes a breath. Steve gives her a querying look.

"How?" she asks.

She's expecting to hear that Marduk died like the others, bones turned to jelly, body an oozing skin bag.

"Starved to death."

"That's not possible. We saw him yesterday." Adrienne realises logic itself is a crazy pursuit given all she's seen, but she can't help it. It's always been her tool, her weapon.

"Yeah, doc said it didn't make any sense either. Something about," there's a pause while Campbell seems to be checking his notes, "lanugo."

"What in hell is that?" Adrienne asks.

"Body hair that usually grows on starvation victims. Bunch of other things, too, but I didn't write all that shit down."

Her temple thuds.

Ishtar.

Is she following them? Have they been looking in the wrong direction the whole time? They've been searching for her when they should've been looking over their shoulders?

She goes to hang up, but Campbell says, "I got your plates, too."

"And?"

"They're stolen," Campbell answers.

Adrienne swears.

"Limo's probably stolen, too. Got a report on that. Oh, and this one, fresh off the fax, about unusual activity at a mansion in Rushcutter's Bay. Right on the water. Big place with a big gate. And a limo parked in front. Neighbours say the owners are away. They're worried about teenage tramps, or something. Matches your stolen plates, though." Campbell chuckles. She can hear the satisfaction in his voice. He's just handed her what could be the key to her own case, and he knows it. He won't likely let her forget it, either.

"You want me to send back-up?" Campbell asks.

"Let me check it out first." To Steve she says, "I'll drive. We're going to Rushcutter's Bay."

"Posh," Steve mutters. "Think they'll even let you into that suburb?"

"Me? What about you?"

"Hey, I'm not the one with a nicotine-chugging cat painted on my shirt."

Adrienne admits the shirt might be a give-away. They swap jokes about mansions and money and confirm their bitter desires to rise above their class. They laugh and Adrienne feels a re-stirring of hope. Something she'd forgotten she was missing. Hope and relief, like this whole crazy, messed-up thing might be over soon.

Then she calls Grace, who predictably ignores Adrienne's advice to get out of town.

"Take the baby into the mountains for some fresh air," Adrienne says.

"The baby isn't breathing *air* yet," Grace replies.

Adrienne hesitates. Images of malformed, breathless, lifeless stillborns storming across the bottom of the ocean appear unbidden in her brain. She feels that unfamiliar, fierce protectiveness she first experienced in the pub. She wants to reach down the line and haul Grace to somewhere safe. But she's not sure where that is.

"Just stay away from the water, then," she tells Grace.

Her sense of hope is already gone.

She gets a text from Campbell, who's holding down the fort back at the office. No words, just a picture. It's a grainy black-and-white image of the now-familiar foetal army.

After poring over the photos in Grace's camera, Adrienne can see straight away that the army has grown. Not in numbers, in size. The navy diver caught in the upper right of one frame looks to be a foot shorter than the stillborns closest to him.

Stillborns. Their bulbous heads seem to float, their stubby hands hang in front of them, their eyes are closed.

"How deep can a person dive to?" Adrienne asks.

It's the kind of question Steve can answer, being a trivia nerd. "Solid suit, six hundred metres is the record."

Around the stillborns the dark ocean waters are shot with spotlights, revealing half-imagined creatures. The kinds of things that have always lived in the depths; skeletal figures with sharp teeth and no skin. She holds out the phone with the photo to Steve.

"It's the army," she says.

"Which? Ours or theirs?" Steve asks.

"Theirs. Hers. The army of stillborns."

"They're here, aren't they?"

She nods. "Oh yeah, they're sure as shit headed this way."

Steve is quiet.

She goes to call Campbell, but her phone rings before she can.

"Nina?"

"Chapel's gone missing," Nina says.

Adrienne hesitates. She didn't even think to call Nina when she suspected Chapel was with Ishtar. She curses herself. "We think he might be with Ishtar."

Nina lets out a volley of abuse. Her voice has a shake in it Adrienne hasn't heard before.

"Where is he now?" Nina asks.

"We don't know."

Adrienne suffers through more abuse, driving one-handed through the busy Cross City Tunnel and out into bright daylight.

She hears the scratch of a lighter, and a puff of indrawn breath, then Nina asks, "Where are you?"

Adrienne doesn't want to involve Nina any more than she has to. "I'll call you later."

She veers to avoid a car taking a corner too wide.

Steve grunts. "No point rushing. My money's on Chapel being dead already."

Adrienne thinks about making a smart-arse remark in return, something about Chapel being a pain in the neck anyhow, but she doesn't. With the walls of the world giving way, with the weirdness welling up from the other side, even Chapel is an ally. They can't afford to lose one of the team.

They wind up in a beautiful spot overlooking the bay. Daylight dances along high pale walls that guard the perimeter of the estate. Just inside the gate is a tennis court and beyond that, the house, standing high like a pale yellow cement sponge cake. On top of it is an inexplicable green dome. Maybe it's an observatory. In a position like this, overlooking the yachts and playboy speedboats of the harbour, Adrienne figures she'd have an observatory, too.

She rolls to a stop in front of the security gates and reaches out for the intercom.

"It's open," Steve comments.

She nudges the gate with the nose of the car. "Think I'll park across the perimeter. Make sure the gate stays open."

"Good idea."

She lets the car roll forward a metre, then stops. They go the rest of the way on foot.

The front door is ajar when they approach. No sign of the security guards she was expecting.

Steve calls out in a booming voice, "Police!"

He has his sidearm out and he's half-crouched by the front door. Adrienne kicks it open and peers in.

Inside is all marble floors and antique parlour chairs. No Ishtar. No Chapel.

"I'm calling for backup," Steve says.

Adrienne doesn't stop him. She's got a bad feeling in her gut. It gets worse as she peers into each room, gun arm extended. The elaborate lounge seems empty. They enter and circle the ornate gold-trimmed furniture. French style, Louis XIV. They move through into a dining room that's more like a ballroom. The green dome she'd seen from the street turns out not to be an observatory. Just a high round ceiling, shocking in its ostentation.

This Ishtar, she knows whose house to steal.

The ballroom gives way to an industrial-sized kitchen, pristine and empty. Behind the kitchen is a set of glass doors eight metres across, and behind the doors is the pool. Sunlight and water meet in an Arcadian image of serenity — except for the half-dozen women surrounding the pool. They're not lounging in swimwear. They're—

"Doing laundry?" Steve mutters.

The women are silent, wet to their shoulders, kneeling by the pool washing sheets and clothes with an unusual amount of concentration.

"I hope it's saltwater. Not chlorine," Steve says, displaying a surprising amount of domestic understanding.

"Shit," Adrienne whispers, "where is the bitch?"

Steve shakes his head. "Not here."

"Car's here." They're talking in staccato phrases. Adrienne's phone starts buzzing against her hip. She pulls it from her jacket. "Yeah?"

"It's happening, it's here."

It takes her a moment to identify the voice.

"Grace? Are you okay? What's here?" she asks.

"The army. It's in the harbour and — *Jesus.*"

"What?" Adrienne's voice rises, and she straightens from the hunch she dropped into when they entered Ishtar's house.

"They're rocking a ferry to pieces!"

"How tall are they now?" Adrienne hisses.

Grace's voice goes numb. "They're killing them."

Adrienne's heart skids to a momentary stop. She turns to Steve and opens her mouth to explain. But over Steve's shoulder, she sees something that makes everything else unimportant.

A tall, solid man in dark clothes stands with a gun pointed at them.

"Police!" Adrienne shouts.

Steve spins. He's fast enough that the stranger's shot goes clean past him. And straight though Adrienne's right arm. There's a metallic ding as it hits the row of pans behind her.

It's like her arm has been electrified. She drops her phone and screams.

Steve fires. The bulky security guard lets out a shout and drops his weapon. Blood starts pumping from his shoulder at about the same time Adrienne feels blood course down her sleeve. She's hit, *goddamnit.*

"Shit!"

Steve hesitates, stuck between his injured partner and the injured suspect.

"Grab him!" Adrienne yells.

Steve runs to the guard, who's leaking blood in wide pool. Before he gets there, Ishtar steps into the doorway. Her black hair is loose and falls over her shoulders and breasts. She wears a simple dress that covers her from her toes to her neck. She's stunning. She's horrifying.

Ishtar spies her fallen guard and gives Steve with an expression of pure, animal hate. Steve stops in his tracks. Adrienne isn't sure what happens next, not at first. Her eyes take it in, but she doesn't believe it.

Steve collapses like his spine has turned to water. His head is last to hit the floor, but it makes barely a sound. His face is liquid rubber, one eye against the ground, the other staring straight up at the ceiling, like an olive in an omelette. The wash of fluid that leaks from his mouth and ears and eyes and arse isn't red like blood, it's pink.

Adrienne steps back to avoid the rolling wave as Steve's body empties out. She makes a noise like a yelp, then a deep, shuddering cry. She trips and slams against the kitchen bench, and half-climbs it before her brain kicks back in. Quelling her panic, she raises her gun at Ishtar, expecting the same sodden fate as Steve, but she doesn't fire. She figures there's no point.

And besides, her arm hurts like Hell. The gun waggles unconvincingly in her hand.

Ishtar watches with a cool gaze. "Put away your toy."

Adrienne arm drops like the gun's a dead weight. "Why in *fuck* did you kill him?"

Ishtar frowns, delicate eyebrows pulling down over wide-set dark eyes. "He displeased me. If not, I would have spared him. There's no point in killing now."

"No? You've had a bit of a scatter gun approach going on so far. I count eight bodies."

"I should think more," Ishtar says. "What was this one to you?"

"My partner," Adrienne spits.

She slides her arse along the bench until she can leap clear of the mess that remains of Steve. She tries not to think about what she's doing. Her arm is throbbing and she tries not to think about that either. She notices the women outside haven't stopped their washing. A few of them send curious glances towards the kitchen, but otherwise they don't react at all.

"Partner? As in, lover? You can get another one." Ishtar sizes Adrienne up. "Probably."

"Bring him back." Adrienne hesitates. "Please?"

She was about ten the last time she said please.

Ishtar is unimpressed.

"Come on. You're powerful enough to kill him," Adrienne says. "Show me your real power. Show me you can bring him back."

There's silence while Ishtar stares at her. Gold flecks pepper her irises, and her eyelashes are so thick they could be strips of velvet. Adrienne can't help noticing how goddamn stunning she is, even as she busies herself hating her.

Ishtar breaks the silence by laughing. She laughs and laughs, and her laugh is hard and mean. "You think because gods come back, humans can, too? No."

Adrienne says nothing, but she wills Ishtar to stop laughing, shut up and do something fucking useful. *Bring him back. Don't waste my time. Don't waste the one thing humans don't have anywhere near enough of.*

"Humans have nothing to come back *with*," Ishtar continues, "In all my years, little human girl, in all my years, I have never seen evidence for a human soul."

"Is that what makes it okay?" Adrienne says through gritted teeth. It's not just impatience; it's the pain of her arm that locks her jaw. The whole room throbs with it. "You're okay with killing us because you figure we don't come back?"

Ishtar raises one of her fine eyebrows. "The question is irrelevant. You live such tiny lives."

"So it's not okay. It's just easy."

Ishtar's eyes spin fire and the corners of her mouth

pull back. Her teeth are stone, her throat the whole world. "I'm going to let *you* live, little human girl. I'm going to let you live, because I want you to see what's coming. I want your eyes to be open. I don't want you to miss a thing."

And then she's gone. Adrienne tries to hold herself upright with her good arm against a kitchen stool, but it doesn't work. She slides to the floor and brings the stool right down on top of her.

That's where they find her.

Steve's backup arrives, but too late for Steve. Adrienne figures she'll owe him for the rest of her life, but she's not sure how to thank a dead guy.

The officers call for an ambulance and before she knows it, she's rolled out on a gurney. Her arm and side burn like she's being eaten by fire ants. She lets out a howl of pain. In the ambulance, she's given a shot of something cold and numbing.

"Call Chief Douglas, metro. We'll need a second ambulance for Steve," she says. "He's in the kitchen."

"Which one was he?" The paramedic has a kind face and long hair, like a hippy.

Adrienne hesitates, trying to work out how to describe what happened to Steve.

"One of those guys," says the other paramedic from outside the ambulance, "looks like he's been dead for a while."

She thinks of the bloated frame leaking pus and blood.

"No," she says. "They both just..."

The other paramedic can't hear her. He continues, "His skin is riddled with stretch marks. That guy got big real fast. Like a goddamn mushroom cloud went up inside his skin."

He must mean the security guard. Adrienne sits up. Her vision goes gritty around the edges for a moment.

"Patch me up," she says. "We have to get to the harbour."

He doesn't look like he's about to oblige, so Adrienne adds, "You want more weird shit like those guys on the floor in there?"

The hippy does what he's told. He dresses her wound elaborately while the two uniformed officers who found her radio back to headquarters. Adrienne watches the washerwomen, handcuffed, being loaded meekly into a police van. No sign of Ishtar.

Her phone rings and it's Nina.

"Just in time," Adrienne says. "I need a driver."

Nina asks once where Steve is and doesn't ask again. Adrienne doesn't answer.

The officers won't let her take her gun, claiming it's evidence. She replies she hasn't shot anyone, and how in hell do they expect her to do battle with an evil goddess? She sounds like a crazy woman, but she doesn't care. It's only then Nina drags her away.

"Did you find Chapel?" Nina asks.

Adrienne shakes her head. "Not yet."

Nina takes the driver's seat while Adrienne climbs in the back. Her arm is in a sling, the skin of her hand oddly grey except for the red welt of the burn-tattoo. She moves her fingers experimentally. They still work, but the leaden thud in her upper arm makes her stop.

"Use the fucking siren," Adrienne mutters.

Nina fumbles with the siren and the spinning blue cop light, which she slaps onto the roof. They make the city fringe within twenty minutes, barely a word passing between them. Nina, to her credit, can drive like a maniac.

Adrienne is leaning back with her head on the seat, watching the sky and the swarm of helicopters like a dark, buzzing cloud. She hasn't done that since she was a kid, and she's glad to get this one chance now. It's a morbid thought, but she doesn't fight it. She blames the drugs they've pumped into her, but really it's something else. It's the sudden weight of her age. It's the fact she's gotten old enough she doesn't remember her childhood so clearly anymore. Her whole history feels like a dream. Somebody else's dream.

The closer they get to the centre of Sydney, the more her dread increases. She wonders if this is a good day to die. She wonders what it's like to be dead. She wonders what Ishtar did to that security guard, that puffed-up balloon of blood and cartilage. He sure didn't look bothered when Steve shot at him. Did he think he could survive the bullet? Or does survival stop mattering sooner or later?

She wonders, of course, what Steve was thinking.

She hasn't called his wife. She hopes Douglas will.

"You okay?" Nina gives Adrienne a worried look in the rear vision mirror. Adrienne rolls her head to meet Nina's eyes. She gives a thumbs up, but doesn't have the wherewithal to lie. They hit gridlock long before they see the harbour. Nina pushes the car forward, blue light flashing. She gives bursts of the siren. They move sluggishly into the parking lane and Nina edges forward.

"This will take for-fucking-ever," Adrienne observes.

Nina grunts. She flashes Adrienne's badge at the various official vehicles and keeps the siren going the whole way. Nobody stops them. There's precious little authority evident anyhow.

"When you see the next uniform," Adrienne says, "pull over. I want to talk to them."

"What kind of uniform?"

"Any kind."

Nina spins the car illegally right, going the wrong way up a one-way street. Horns blare and Nina conscientiously gives every one of the complaining drivers the bird. She twists the car through the small streets that edge the city, but hits gridlock again in front of St. Mary's Cathedral. She puts the car in reverse.

"Find out where Grace is, exactly," Nina says. "Circular Quay? Or the Botanic Gardens?"

Adrienne's about to say she can't possibly find out where Ishtar is. No one would understand the question. But then Nina repeats 'Grace' and Adrienne fumbles for her phone. She finds Grace's number, but the phone rings and rings. She hopes that's because Grace is busy someplace, living her life safely away from the harbour and what it's about to give birth to.

"The dead," says Adrienne.

"What? The phone's dead?" Nina says.

"No, the dead. Remember what Ishtar said? The dead shall outnumber the living. When her father refused to help her, that's what she said to him. They'll eat our food and...whatever."

"Not a daddy's girl," Nina observes.

Adrienne shrugs. The drugs make her feel like all the parts of her body are floating separately from each other.

The words hadn't meant much to her before. Now she's met Ishtar, they carry a lot more weight. They feel real. The dead and the living. "That's what the army's for. They're for us."

"Nice."

More gridlock. Nina curses the traffic, thumping the steering wheel in frustration. "Where to?"

Adrienne peers out the windshield. They're smack up against the back of the Domain. She gives Nina directions to the harbour via Art Gallery Road, but either her directions are bad or Nina's understanding is. They end up in Sydney Harbour Tunnel instead. Adrienne experiences a moment of wild panic. The Tunnel will take them underwater, right into the harbour. Where the army is.

She imagines flabby monsters tearing holes in the tunnel, imagines the tunnel flooding, cars floating until they hit the concrete roof, occupants dying in their seats, under water with no way out. At every slowdown in the traffic she breaks out in a new sweat. But they're through and back into the daylight while she imagines getting out of the car and running, running until she's far away.

"Now where the hell are we?" Nina snaps.

Adrienne's teeth chatter. She's freezing and sweating at the same time. "Turn it around."

This time she tries to direct Nina across the Harbour Bridge, back into the city CBD. Nina steers them instead around in a loop to Milson's Point. This puts them north of the Quay, across the harbour with a direct view of the Opera House and city centre.

"Forget it," Nina says, "this will have to do. There's no getting back across the bridge now."

Adrienne feels a chill when she says that, but Nina merely means the traffic back into the city is bad from all directions. They'd be stuck in traffic going nowhere if they tried.

Nina abandons the car and Adrienne tips out behind her. Nina pushes forward through the crowd of people who've gathered to watch the harbour. Adrienne keeps pace, nursing her arm. The harbour wind cuts through her light pussycat shirt.

Milson's Point is mostly a tourist destination, a great place for wedding photos. The Harbour Bridge hangs blackly to their right. From this angle it lives up to its nickname of 'the coat hanger'. There's lush red bottlebrush in front of them, a thin length of parkland, and then the choppy harbour spread out in either direction. They're separated from the city by ocean water, but close enough they can almost wave to the crowds of people on the other side of the harbour. There's usually a good view of the Opera House from here, but something else is in the way, something white and almost as large.

The army of stillborns. Their bloated bodies and bulbous skulls break the surface of the water like fleshy icebergs. And they've grown. For some, the water reaches their massive chins. But others are even taller. Adrienne estimates that if their feet are touching the bottom of the harbour the tallest must be over a hundred metres.

"Fekking hell," someone mutters.

Adrienne isn't sure if it's her.

"Some weird freakish mutant shit, hey?" says a man to her left. He's sweating and wild-eyed. "Probably nuclear waste."

Misshapen white heads, eyeless, hairless. They look like egg whites that have exploded in hot water.

"What are they doing?" Adrienne murmurs.

They're swinging their arms through the water like they're testing the temperature.

"Maybe they're dancing," says the man.

Adrienne scans the crowd, looking for Ishtar. If the army of stillborns is here, then Ishtar must be here, too. Here or on the other side of the harbour. Adrienne moves forward again. Her arm thuds against strangers and she winces, drawing a sharp breath. She makes it to the cast iron fencing that edges the harbour and to her right, six metres away, she sees her.

"Grace!" Her voice is shrill, panicked. She shouts over and over, and lunges forward to cover the distance between her and her baby sister.

Finally Grace turns. There's something dazed in her movements, like she's just waking up. She looks at Adrienne without recognition, and Adrienne's stomach lurches. She reaches Grace's side, Nina behind her.

"Grace, I've been trying to call you," Adrienne grabs her sister by both arms, ignoring her sling. "What on earth are you doing here?"

Grace continues to stare blankly. It's fear, Adrienne thinks. She considers slapping Grace across the face. It would satisfy a lifetime of resentment — might snap Grace out of it, too. Instead she gives Grace a shake. "Where's your phone?"

Understanding returns to her face and Grace reaches for something. "My bag. Damnit!"

Her bag is gone. Lost in the crowd someplace, that vomit-coloured bit of tattered cloth. Adrienne hopes Grace won't cry, because she'd be forced to promise to go find the bag. And it's not possible now, not here, not at the end of the world. Waiting for Ishtar to suck the bones out of all of them.

"Look at that!" someone shouts right beside them.

Adrienne turns, still holding onto Grace. She expects to see Ishtar, but what she sees is something else. In Sydney Harbour, the ocean is rocking. The army has learned to work in unison. They stir the harbour water with their hands, one direction and then another.

"Oh, shit."

The crowd is stunned, watching as the ocean is manipulated as easily as bath water.

"Everyone!" she calls. "Please move away from the edge of the water. Please return to your vehicles. This is an emergency. Please!"

At first she's ignored, another crazy person on a crazy day.

Nina grips her elbow. "What's going on?"

"Ishtar's found something faster than eating our food," says Adrienne. "They're making some kind of preternatural pump."

"Oh," says Nina, "shit."

The water recedes from the edge of Milson's Point, washing in the other direction towards Circular Quay. Crowds of people in the Quay begin to move backwards from the edge, climbing to higher ground. She realises many of them are in military uniform, herding people from the edge. Douglas came through. She sends someone a silent prayer of gratitude.

Where Adrienne is standing, she's twenty metres or so above sea level. But she doesn't feel safe, not if they're going to keep rocking the ocean this way and that. She's not the only one to see the implications. A ripple of nervous energy goes through the crowd and they begin to move. Every direction at once.

"Police! Evacuate in a calm and orderly fashion!" Adrienne commands. "Police. Please evacuate. Flood warning!"

She's ignored. She holds her badge high over her head and keeps yelling.

"Tsunami!" Adrienne shouts.

The emergency broadcast system starts up, the one the city installed for some visit by a US president years back. It's a siren that reminds Adrienne of old air raid movies. It's a lousy noise but it works, part of a shared memory of 'the war'. As the water rocks more and more deeply, the crowd around her moves faster. Adrienne can taste the panic. People scream and fall and run. By the time the docked Sydney ferries scrape the bottom of the harbour thirty or so metres down, there's chaos. Adrienne tries to stand firm, but she's pushed and rocked like a paper boat. Her arm thuds from every blow. Nina stands on her right, shielding her. Grace takes her other arm, the uninjured one.

Then they see her. Ishtar. Standing under the thick construction of the Harbour Bridge beside one of the huge concrete and granite pylons. Still and solid while the crowd flows around her. Ishtar, small and sensuous, with eyes that carry fire and fingers that promise it. Ishtar, with her black hair piled high on her head and a broad, tall forehead. She is Ishtar in war garb, silver-plated armour across her chest. She wears bracelets up and down her arms. Some of them are cutting her skin and blood trickles down to her wrists. She seems impervious. More than that, she seems oblivious. She turns dark eyes towards Adrienne, and Adrienne can't breathe.

Ishtar, the only calm figure on the harbour.

Above Ishtar's head, a military squadron jogs in formation over the Harbour Bridge. Adrienne wishes they were closer. She wishes they knew what they were looking for, but she's got an inkling they won't be looking for a tiny, dark-haired woman. Even though, looking at Ishtar, it can't be anyone but her, anything but her. She reeks of power and age.

Beside Adrienne, Nina says, "There's Chapel."

Adrienne notices Chapel then, standing beside Ishtar, his gaunt face pallid in the sunlight. He wears the same dead-eyed gaze that Grace had. Adrienne reaches out for her sister and her hand closes around Grace's. Neither woman moves. Then she gives Grace's hand a squeeze and tries to let her go. Grace won't release her, and in truth, Adrienne is glad. She doesn't want to face the end alone. Best to be with someone who's known her most of her life.

Then she spots Ishtar staring at Grace's pregnant belly, a sneer of domination on her face. Adrienne drives forward, rage propelling her. She drags Nina and Grace with her, though she doesn't, in the end, mean to.

Ishtar watches them come.

"Chapel?" Nina asks again.

Chapel doesn't respond. He's an empty ragdoll, all expression, all personality wiped away.

"What have you done to him?" Adrienne asks Ishtar.

"Whatever he wanted," says Ishtar. "At first."

Ishtar gestures with a finger and Chapel falls backwards, neck snapping, body breaking like spun sugar under a spoon. Ishtar doesn't even look at him.

Beside Adrienne, Nina lets out a strangled gasp. Adrienne holds onto her.

The goddess inclines her head and seems to consider them. "Give me your hands, women. To help wash this mortal mess off."

Ishtar indicates her own body, her hair, her thin dress which is whipped by the winds of the Harbour.

"Find another patsy," Adrienne says. "I'm keeping these hands."

"Then I'll take your skin."

"Go to Hell!"

Chapter Nine

There's nothing but bluster in Adrienne's words. She's seen what Ishtar can do. She knows she has nothing but her all-too-human spirit to keep the goddess at bay. She knows it won't be enough, but she decided long ago — so long ago she doesn't remember the decision — that she would die on her feet. She watched her mother's servitude and her aunts' and her grandmothers'. She watched it and vowed she would bow to no one. She would fight the whole world on her own if she had to.

"Do you know," Ishtar says, filling the space between

them with each word, "what happens to people who defy me?"

"Do you know," Adrienne returns, "that if your freakish army floods Sydney, you'll drown, too?"

Ishtar steps close so she can speak in a normal tone amongst the screaming of the crowd. "I've been to the Underworld, had my skin stripped from my body. And risen. What other god can claim that?"

"Not Tammuz," Nina observes.

"That's right," Adrienne takes up the theme. "If Tammuz is here, you'll kill him, too. Again."

Ishtar turns those black eyes on Nina. Adrienne holds out one hand protectively. Nina looks suddenly old and tiny, like life has started to seep out of her body.

"He's not here," says Ishtar. But she's not sure, that's clear. There's a brief tic of fear in her face as she stares them down.

"He might be," Adrienne says.

"Maybe he's dead already," Nina says.

Ishtar gives an almost imperceptible shake of her head. "I would feel it."

"You sure?"

Ishtar doesn't hesitate, but that gives her away more than anything. They've hit a nerve. "He's nowhere near here! I am first. I am the first and only goddess, and all others are too late. When I find Tammuz, when he comes back to me, it will be just us. I will destroy all others."

Adrienne wants to laugh. There are tears pouring from her eyes, though, and her laugh comes out as an embarrassing snuffle. She wipes the back of her hand across her face again and again.

How can anyone argue with Ishtar, a goddess, an immortal bitch? How can anyone confront that strange logic?

"So, this is all just about your jealousy?" Adrienne

says.

Ishtar looks reproachful. "What do you mean, *just*? I raised the army, an army that wouldn't be raised by its mothers," says Ishtar. "I raised and summoned them."

"Why can't you go find him right now? Skip this step."

"Who are you that you think to question me?"

Adrienne turns to look at Grace. She grips her sister's hand more tightly and Grace smiles, gives an almost-nod. A kind of blessing for whatever Adrienne has to do next. At that moment Grace reminds Adrienne of their mother. She looks to Nina, whose face gives away nothing. She's lost inside there someplace.

"Nina?"

"I don't reckon the bitch can control them," Nina says.

Ishtar hisses, hands clenched by her chest. "I do what I want. I control the oceans if I wish to. I control humans. I beat the other gods back to this earthly realm. I am the first."

Her face is contorted in a mask of joy as the wind whips her hair like a banner. Her hands are balled into fists at her sternum. She is a hideous, beautiful thing, this goddess made flesh.

Nina takes her time lighting a cigarette, taking a long drag and puffing out smoke, which is whipped away instantly. She looks sick, but she keeps sucking on that cigarette, eyes on Chapel's body.

"Bullshit," she says.

Ishtar gives her a sneer of contempt.

"I'm telling you," Nina says, "she can't do it. Go on, show us what a powerful goddess you are."

"I summoned them!"

"But then what? You're controlling this?" Nina chuckles, a dry, terrible sound.

"Nina, stop," Adrienne says.

"Ain't that the curse of motherhood?" Nina asks. "You raise them, bring them up right, and the little fuckers end up doing whatever the hell they want anyhow."

Ishtar turns, her face blank. "You'll never know motherhood. None of you!"

There's a gasp from Grace. She curls her arms protectively around her swollen belly, pulling Adrienne's hand across in front of her. She gives Adrienne a pleading look, but Adrienne has nothing left. She can't think of anything to say or do to stop this monster. She would give up the fight right now if she knew how.

"Will the water reach this high?" Grace whispers.

Adrienne feels a pang of unreasonable anger. If Grace had left town when she'd asked — but it's irrelevant. Irrelevant, too, whether the water will reach them or not. Ishtar is just getting started.

"Nah, it can't reach us," Adrienne tells Grace.

Nina catches her eye. There's reproach there and Adrienne hopes it's just for lying to her sister and not for something else, something Adrienne should've done.

By now the wave created by the stillborn army is washing up the twenty metre wall towards where they stand. On the other side of the harbour the waves rock into the high density buildings of the CBD. Ferries sway like toy boats, smashing glass windows on the far side of the harbour, and scraping against the stone wall of the embankment on this side.

And there are bodies. Dozens of bodies like broken dolls, batted by the massive hands of the horrendous army. None of them recognisable, but all of them familiar. Adrienne wants to make some comment about humanity and loss and hope, but she can think of nothing. She looks about for their own army, but they're nowhere in sight. They probably just kept jogging in formation right past Milson's Point, heading north.

Heading for the hills.

Nina takes the cigarette from her mouth and tosses it aside. She gives Adrienne a look she doesn't understand.

"Fuck this shit," Nina says.

And she leaps at Ishtar, leaps into the void because it's impossible, impossible. Impossible to stop Ishtar, the first goddess, the only god to make it back here, to the soulless earth.

The moment is frozen for Adrienne, Nina mid-air, arms flung forward, both feet off the ground, face caught in a rictus of fear and rage.

And Ishtar cuts her down.

What's left of Nina falls, losing the graceful arc it commenced. Falling like a sack, a bloody, empty thing. She falls and what hits the earth isn't recognisable as Nina.

Sometime later, Adrienne realises the screams she's been listening to are her own. She tries to clamp down on them, but there's a series of whimpers instead. She pulls herself up and moves to the edge of the void. Her knees ache and one hip clicks painfully. She can't breathe for the pain in her ribs. She is shaking all over, really hard, really shaking. But her sight is clear and she can see Nina's crumpled body dissolving into grey, face down in the muck, one exquisite cheekbone hidden. Her eyes are blank and staring.

It's not good enough, she thinks. It's not good enough for their lives life to end this way. Mere body count. She thinks of that line about how we're all playthings for gods, but that's not good enough either.

This Ishtar bitch, she would kill her if she could.

Adrienne offers up a string of barely coherent expletives to the goddess. She's only dimly aware of Grace holding one of her arms and shushing her like she might shush a child, her child, perhaps, the unborn hope

Grace carries in her belly. She wants Grace to run, but the words coming out of her mouth aren't for Grace. She wants to say, *I can't bear to see my baby sister dead*, but still all she hears is the rage.

Ishtar reaches out and wraps her long, cold hands around Adrienne's skull.

"I'm going to drown the world," she says. "You can watch with me, little human girl."

And she feeds Adrienne with such horrific images that she's left screaming long after the ocean fills her up.

Biography

Deborah Biancotti's first short story collection, *A Book of Endings*, was shortlisted for the William L. Crawford Award for Best First Fantasy Book. An Aurealis and Ditmar award-winning writer, Deborah's work can be found in *Clockwork Phoenix*, *Eidolon 1*, *Ideomancer*, *infinity plus*, *Australian Dark Fantasy and Horror* and Prime's *Year's Best Dark Fantasy and Horror,* as well as a critical essay in Scarecrow Press' *Twenty-First Century Gothic*. Her second short story collection, *Bad Power*, has just come out from Twelfth Planet Press. She is working on her first and second novels.

The Sleeping and the Dead

Cat SPARKS

It is, in most respects, an unremarkable morning, when a malfunctioning mechanical bull jerks its way into Truckstop's goat compound. *Gengis must be stoned again*, thinks Doctor Anna. *Old war machines don't usually get this close.* The thing is bucking and kicking in all directions, metal rivets glinting in the sun. Her spirits lift considerably at the diversion.

Abandoning her Stoli and cactus juice martini, she climbs down from her balcony, brandishing the cricket bat she sleeps with just for luck. Best to smash its tiny mechanical brain before the nuns catch wind of it and freak.

Those nuns freak at everything. Everything is a sign, from shooting stars to cloud formations — on days the desert's cursed enough for clouds.

The bull is nothing but a humble all-terrain load-bearing unit, wandering blind until its battery depletes. Might somebody be using it for decoy? If they are, they're being mighty slow about it.

Time was when she'd have used the thing for target practice. Not today. She's not up for wasting bullets, so she smacks the bat down hard upon its hub casing. It shudders to a standstill, quivers, indecisive in the heat. The air chokes with radioactive dust.

A dozen scrawny Nubian goats watch her sullenly from the sidelines. Beyond them, a cluster of hopeful mothers camp beside the wire. She swears at the goats. The mangy buggers will eat anything; even chipped ceramic shards of clapped-out war machines.

Swinging the bat so the goats don't get ideas, she peers up at the lookout tower. Gengis waves. No doubt he's been watching the whole performance, but when she responds, he signals back in their private code, the sign that means *there's something interesting out there.* She gestures to the goats and the smashed-up bull, but he signals back again. More urgent. Same message.

Fuck the goats then, this must be important. Takes a lot for Gengis to give a damn.

She runs to the tower, discards the bat and climbs the spindly rungs hand over fist. Tries not to get too excited. It's probably nothing, but all the same, she feels her heartbeat quicken.

Gengis is standing when she reaches the top, hash pipe abandoned on his sagging canvas chair. His eyes are wide and blue — the only lively feature in his craggy, toothless face. "Reckon some of them stories must be true."

"What stories?" Anna snatches the telescope from his arthritic fingers. No need to ask him where to point the thing. A metallic gleam in the middle distance. There it is again.

She raises the scope and adjusts the lens, the battered bronze casing warm between her palms.

"Fuck me," she says, and she means it.

In the lens, three men stagger across the baking flats, scrawny and sunburned, but men they are, with ragged vestiges of youth clinging to their tortured frames. Still men enough to potentially be of use, not like old Gengis here, withered and wasted twist of wire that he is.

"Sister Daisy's not getting her mitts on these ones," she mutters underneath her breath.

"Reckon they dug 'emselfs up from their graves?" says Gengis.

When Anna finally lowers the scope, he's sucking on the hash pipe, cheeks hollowed.

"Now why'd you go and say a thing like that?"

"Legions of the Underworld," he croaks through plumes of blue.

"I told you not to smoke that shit near me."

Gengis shrugs, settles back into his canvas chair, legs creaking beneath his feather weight. Angles an inch more into the shade of the battered beach umbrella poised above.

Anna's already climbing down the tower, revolver tucked into the back of her pants. In her excitement, she's forgotten all about her cricket bat.

Venus peers weakly through the glare, wasting her grace on the endless, dusty plain. In the distance, storm clouds sully the horizon. Vast, voluminous boiling things, cauldrons of corrosive isotopes and acid flashback. If it rains today, they'll be in trouble. Rainy season isn't due for weeks. Anna keeps an eye on them anyway, seasons being what they are. High on the list of events no longer to be trusted.

It's Doctor Anna's lucky day. The nuns are in the ossuary chanting at their skulls. They'll sniff the men out soon enough, but not before she's had a chance to claim them. She takes up a position near the goats, doing her best to feign protracted nonchalance. *Thomas won't be one of them. Darling Thomas is long dead.*

It takes another hour for the men to cross the sand. Once they see the goats, nothing will stop them. She stands, revolver at the ready, but she doesn't want to shoot. Not yet. Not before she's heard their stories. Finds out where they've been hiding all these years.

They were soldiers once, judging by the khaki rags still clinging to the ropey sinew of their limbs. *Not just the green*, thinks Anna, when she's close enough to be sure the three aren't apparitions after all. They carry themselves like enlisted men. Broken, beaten, battered, yet still possessed of a military mindset. She'd known it once. Even married it for a time.

The nearest one stares her down with sunken eyes. His torso features a hideous scar. For a moment, it looks like he might drop to his knees and cry. She can't assess their ages through the grime and deprivation — anywhere from twenty-five to fifty.

Anna glances back up at the tower, makes the sign for water, clear, so Gengis sees. He takes his sweet, stoned time descending, ambling across the hard-packed sand, water skin slapping hard against his thigh.

He tosses the 'skin across the stretch of sand between them. The men fall upon it like starving dogs, which they are, Anna reminds herself, regardless of apparent human forms. They shove, claw and elbow, but somehow each one gets to drink. That done, they fall back on the sand, exhausted.

Mere moments earlier she'd been sure they'd kill the goats. Has their strength given out, or do they see her as a benefactor? Someone who'll offer food and shelter?

"Delirious," says Gengis, his face deadpan as always. "The sunstroke's on 'em. Surprised they ain't sunblind."

"But where are they *from*?"

"Hell," says Gengis. "Like I already told ya."

She cajoles the three of them into the clinic's waiting room with the promise of cold corn mush. They eat with their fingers, shovelling food in great greasy gulps like there's no tomorrow. So far as these men know, there isn't. Best to eat up while the eating's good. Doctor Anna watches them at it, enjoying the greedy glistening of their fingers. The sounds they make are almost sexual.

She wants to talk, but the food has made them docile. *Damn!* She should have made them sing for their supper.

Soon they're snoring loud enough to wake the dead. Anna watches them twitch for an hour or two, the unsteady rise and falling of their chests. Coughing and wheezing, farting in their slumber. Perhaps they've travelled further than the hopeful mothers? Not so much *come here* as *escaped from somewhere else*. Finally safe enough to snatch some fitful sleep. She pities them. They don't know the truth. How much safer they'd have been in the crow-pecked wilderness.

She shuts the door and goes outside to brood, leaving them dead to the world. Twelve good hours and they'll be right to talk. Her mind's already clocking possibilities. They've come from *somewhere*, which means *somewhere* exists. A place with men and law and ammunition. There's a half-life to their current harmlessness; they'll be crazy when they wake. Anna knows she must be on her guard.

She has plans for the three of them, plans she doesn't yet fully understand herself. They raise intriguing possibilities for the clinic. If their seed is fresh, there'll be no more need for frozen embryos. But where have they come from? Those ragged military uniforms have piqued her interest. There are no bases within miles of this place. Just the bulls, clanking and creaking, shitting spent ammunition casing across the blasted wasteland.

Scant breaths of tepid wind bear snatches of the nun's familiar banter from the ossuary. Drumming and chanting. Singing — if you could call it that. *An eighth year, a great year,* so they've been claiming for weeks now.

Cosmologically auspicious, astronomically advantageous; the planting cycle, the birthing circle, on and on and on, like a hammering headache.

She watches nuns dancing in the dust, spinning and twirling as if the stuff's not killing them. Necromaidens. Fallout wraiths. Praising absent gods for their blisters as well as their dreams. Like her, they have no formal training. Their cult has grown organically, exponentially as the years have dragged. Anna became conscious of the neatness of the skulls long before glimpsing the girls' demented Tinkerbell antics around the gritty edges of Truckstop's barbed perimeter. She might have dismissed the girls as ghosts — the barren landscape groans beneath the breathless, phantom weight of them, but no, the nuns are solid. As solid as forty-five kilos of half-starved girl can get.

The men sleep on, oblivious to the danger. Anna chews her fingernail, revolver on her knee. *You're too late. The world's already dead.* That's what she wants to scream at them all, the hopeful mothers and the mindless irritating nuns. *Go home, all of you. Crawl back into the dust.* But somehow, somehow, she never seems to say it. Not to the huddled masses, anyhow. She whispers to the corpses on the days she gets it wrong. When she botches an insemination or gets bored halfway through. When she wanders outside for a precious cigarette. But mostly, she keeps her feelings to herself, saving them for the windstorms or the open road or tomorrow and the thousand years of nothing left to come.

The fertility clinic stands proud and lonely, ringed by clumps of withered palms. International style, with its *brise soleil* screens of patterned concrete blocks. A monument to forgotten vintage modernism, harnessing the desert's stark vistas and light. The awnings are long gone, blasted to shreds by the elements.

Doctor Anna's work is in the basement. She loves the dark recesses of the earth. What coolant still exists is piped down to the lab. When the pumps fail, that'll be the end of it.

All her work will have been for nothing. It's all for nothing anyway. There's not much left to save.

The clinic's generator is on its last legs. Do frozen embryos have souls? The hopeful mothers think so, dragging their weary bones to Truckstop across a hundred miles of heat and dust.

Women worship at her feet. The walking dead whose wombs still pulse with blood. They leave stones in place of flowers, as nothing grows. Lingering just long enough to ensure the baby sticks, then they leave to make the epic journey home.

Some of them have walked so far just to die upon her doorstep. Others she will kill herself — the ones who can't be saved. Still others arrive already pregnant, hosts to multi-limbed monstrosities. They're the ones she tosses to the nuns. Doctor Anna has no time to spare for monsters. She's not sure what the nuns want with them either. Do they dance and sing and sacrifice them on altars? They can't possibly want more skulls.

Days like these, in the pauses between moments, Anna thinks of Thomas and the world the way it was. Time and indifference have colluded to corrode detail. She fears imagination might be filling in the gaps. Anna remembers shopping malls: vast, glorious, inviting. Celestial music softly piped and a thousand different types of bread. Landscapes littered with useless things.

She hates the functionality of the present. Every tool exactly in its place. Nothing ever gets lost. The past is a phantasmagoria of single-use syringes and sweet, nutrient-free foods in shiny wrappers, make-up, swimsuits, and manicures for dogs. Pets you didn't have to eat when times got tough. Or rather, tougher. Things haven't been merely tough for years.

When she pictures Thomas, he's always smiling. Handsome, forever twenty-one. Always with his shirt off. That's not wishful thinking on her part — he was like that. Half-naked, a glossy sheen to his taut, tanned hide. The kind of guy who could fix motorbikes and cars. Animal musk mixed with engine-oil cologne. Signed up because he wanted to jump out of planes, not because he had it in for Arabs.

Army boys were her type back then. These days anything with a hard cock will do. Not so easy to come by. She prefers them with hair, but the atmosphere decides. She likes tattoos inked before the fall. Everything from hot rods to baby feet. Jesus, naked ladies, dragons.

When Anna takes the three men breakfast, they trade their names through the window bars. The leader gives his as Rocco. The scarred one is Jimenez, the other, Skunk. Food has knocked the crazy from their eyes. A scrub and clean clothes might render them halfway human.

A line of nuns snake past their holding cell, balancing baskets on their heads, white sheet robes flapping listlessly in the heat. Wide awake now, the men scrutinise the girls with military precision, eyes shining. When they glance back at Anna, everything has changed. She can smell the lust in them, feel them straining to focus on the salvation of corn-mush porridge and gritty bread.

The nuns keep a wary distance, as if an invisible barrier holds them back. In their eyes, men destroyed the world and conspire still to pollute what little there is left of it. Their death cult or life cult, depending on your perspective, is a wholly female affair. Men are only good for certain things. They're nasty about it too, with their shivs of sharpened human femur. The nuns keep well clear of Gengis, though. Gengis belongs to Anna. She's told them he's some kind of golem, hacked from living stone and sand. He looks as weatherworn as time itself, face crisscrossed with scars like Martian canals. Sunken eyes like tar pits. No, as far as they're concerned, Doctor Anna can have that one.

The nuns go back about their business, ignoring the men as if they were rocks or goats, blessed as they are with short attention spans.

"You think they're pretty?" asks Anna, her voice laced with artificial innocence. "You think those girls are sweet?"

"Girls is girls." Rocco shrugs. "Looks like plenty to go around."

"Looks can be deceiving."

Rocco smiles, squinting from the sunlight in his eyes. "That old man in the tower's no threat."

"You got that right," says Anna. "Gengis hasn't killed a man in years. But those girls have skull power on their side. You are only three. Sure you want to mess with odds like that?"

He's not listening. Men never listen.

When the nuns have gone, the three lay back, sated, clutching at their groaning stomachs. Anna asks a few distracting questions in her best clinician's voice. Obvious questions. One thing about Armageddon, it cuts through all the need for small talk.

"So where the Hell have you come from?"

Rocco looks at her slyly, weighing her up. Calculating how much he can score in exchange for information. "You run this place all by yourself?"

Anna doesn't answer.

When they realise silence isn't going to get them

anything, the men start speaking of a realm below where the light is weak and feeble. Of cold cement inset with crumbling cracks. Of a man who is part demon-lord, part major.

"What's his name?" asks Anna, suddenly interested.

"He goes by many...Master, Daddy, Jesus..."

The three men joke between themselves, private signals she can't understand. Not the funny kind of jokes — none of them are laughing.

"He was God and we were his lieutenants."

"Yeah," says Skunk, and they're silent after that.

Eventually, the men want to know when she's going to let them out. She needs to put some thought into that one, so she climbs back up the watchtower to see what Sirius has to say about it. Her Dog Star confidante, invisible now, in the sunlight, but shining every night to give her comfort.

Anna watches storm clouds boil along the far horizon. If there's any sign of movement, bells will peal. She's not worried. You don't survive this long out here by chance. Lately though, she's been seeing ghosts. Nothing strange in that — the desert claims them all in its good time. But these are not *her* phantoms. She didn't summon them; deprivation didn't drag them screaming from her psyche. These windborne apparitions linger like imprints, remnants of better places, better days. She's sure they're real in their own way, and that it's the prescience of storms that brings them on.

How long has it been since she bathed or changed her clothes? She probably stinks, and it shames her to acknowledge she only cares because three men have come. There's a splinter in her palm from when she bashed the bull to death. Radioactive dust, she reminds herself.

She kicks her ragged threads into a corner, empties a pitcher into a large tin basin, stands in it and soaps. The liquid is soon rust-coloured. Old blood, she thinks. Old ways.

Anna dresses before her mirror, puts on jewellery. Every piece she owns. A sapphire pendant to match *his* eyes. Earrings. Forty bangles of the finest Mexican silver.

The clinic endures, which is more than can be said for the city of her birth. She's hazy about those details, too. Where she's lived, the places she spent her youth. She must have had a childhood, yet she can't remember one. Not a single warm and fuzzy moment.

Truckstop's provenance, too, is dim and distant. It once sported a pretentious name, some kind of exclusive resort. Deluxe cosmetic tourism. She smiles at the resonance of elegant ladies reclining on crisp, white linen sheets awaiting surgeons to tailor vaginas to match their lips. In the future, nothing is white and bony shoulders are nothing to be proud of.

The nuns like anything smooth and shiny. Crap that glitters. Cellophane or gold, they see no difference. Lately, they've taken to drawing Anna's sign, the eight-point star, which is set above the clinic archway. The dumb fucks think it's holy. Anna knows it's just some corporation logo from before, but she claimed it as her own the day she saw how much it mattered.

The nuns consider her some kind of angel. She's not even a qualified doctor, but hasn't the heart to admit it. She managed to get her head around insemination tech, that's all. Knows how to hold core temperatures steady, knock them out and bring them back alive. Doctor Kamali chose her for her steady hand. Everyone was drunk back then, still living out of cans. The cans ran out long before the booze and hope.

Kamali checked out with the last of the morphine. Couldn't bear the shame of bringing babies into being. What's the fucking point? she screamed, even when sleeping — especially when sleeping. But there had been a point back then, and Anna took it.

The nuns collate their scriptures from a myriad of ancient sources: celebrity cookbooks, women's magazines. That glossy paper made it right through Armageddon, barely blackened by the pyres of burning Bibles. Doctor Kamali rolled cigarettes from the pages of *Revelation*, her faith commensurate with her dwindling tobacco stash. When she died, they made a nest of her old library, plugging cracks in the brickwork with paper pulp.

The only thing that shits Anna more than women is men. Men brought about the end, but they didn't stick around to see it through. Their busted war machinery still litters the landscape, churning dust till the batteries expire. But the men themselves? Where did they go? Anna never did work that one out. To war, she guessed, but which war? How many were there? Was anyone victorious?

Anna had been powerful once — that much she could be sure of. Real power, not this pitiful masquerade. And she'd loved him — Thomas — whoever he might have been. The man with the lion tattoo.

She's lingering at her own reflection when commotion snaps her back into the moment. Ugly laughter. Sound carried swiftly through dead air. "Daisy!"

The nuns have deceived her with feigned disinterest. What had she been thinking? As if they wouldn't want three men for themselves.

Anna hurries down the stairs, sandals slapping hard

on weathered slate. "Idiots," she spits. "Never should have...too hard to protect."

By the time she makes it to the front, the waiting room's surrounded. Nuns occupy every spare inch of balcony, packing in tightly, craning their glass-shaved heads for a better view through the office window's bars. She pushes through the dirty linen mass of them, glad of her own broad shoulders and impatience.

Inside, Rocco has Daisy backed against a wall. Her sheet is torn. The girl bunches ripped fabric against her breast, eyelids lowered demurely in submission.

Rocco's laughter resonates. A deep thing, assured and utterly revolting.

"Step away quickly and you won't get hurt," says Anna calmly.

"I'm thinking that one's fine just where she is."

"I'm not talking to Daisy," says Anna. "Step away, Rocco, while you still have a chance."

He's not listening and neither are his friends. The other two hang back. Silence bloats to fill the space, stifling and oppressive. Beyond the window, placid faces gawp.

"What you've got here is paradise," says Rocco, picking at flecks of grit between his teeth. "A whole town made of nought but little girls."

"Different from the girls you've known," warns Anna.

"Thing is," says Rocco, "we ain't known so many."

"Are there no women in your bunker?"

Skunk's face cracks into a smile. "There's women. Old and skank and butt ugly as all fuck. Which is what he keeps 'em for, natch."

"Incentives," cuts in Jimenez. "Rewards sometimes. If you're really lucky."

"Ain't been so lucky in a long time," says Skunk.

Jimenez's features cloud. That scar on his chest looks

anything but lucky.

Seems like it should be Rocco's turn to speak, but his eyes are fixed on Daisy.

"Been dreaming all about her," he whispers.

There's no point warning him to be careful what he dreams of. Rocco is long gone, his mind his weakest aspect. He's fixed on little Daisy with such beady calculation. One move and he'll be on top of her. The other two will do whatever Rocco does. Dogs will always follow bigger dogs.

All three shift their gaze around to Anna. Seeing her as if for the very first time. Most likely true. Yesterday the men had been half-crazed with thirst, half-blind with sun and terror and exhaustion. Anna feels the pressure of their eyes, senses the spell of her authority evaporate.

It's Daisy who makes the next move, as Anna knew she would. She smiles, performs a little pirouette, takes Rocco by the hand, her prayer wheel of human ivory abandoned on the floor.

"Don't be an idiot," says Anna.

Rocco tips an imaginary hat, allows the girl to lead him to the door. The mass of nuns part to let them through.

Still Jimenez and Skunk pause, weighing up their options. Long enough for Anna to make a move of her own. She steps up to block their way with her body. Holds her palm up like an old time traffic cop.

"What the fuck?"

"Why are you here?" she asks them bluntly. "What have you come looking for?"

"Home," says Jimenez.

"Yeah," says Skunk.

"Home," Jimenez says again, like he feels the need to reinforce it.

"Nothing grows here," Anna says, stepping closer.

"Even ghosts can't permanently imprint."

Jimenez shrugs. "Those girls don't look like ghosts." It's then that he sees it. He gestures at Anna's eight-point star tattoo, visible since she changed from shirt to singlet.

Skunk has seen it too and is clearly shaken. Both of them stare, wide-eyed. They've forgotten all about Rocco and lovely Daisy.

"Where did you get *that*?"

"Why — what does it mean to you?" She angles her arm so they can get a better look.

Jimenez swallows dryly. All she sees is terror in its purest form.

"Venus," mumbles Skunk in a low whisper.

"The star?"

"The lady."

A look from Jimenez confirms he's said too much. The men have lost their derring-do, dumbstruck by a symbol.

"There's a lady in the bunker?" Anna thinks she'll have to starve the data from them, or beat it, maybe. Whichever way is quicker. "It's just a star," she says and they both cringe.

A piercing shriek from outside sets her teeth on edge. The anguished cry is barely human, gender indeterminate. The nuns take it as their cue to leave, padding softly across the faded linoleum floor.

"I warned him," says Anna. "I warned you all."

Taking advantage of their confusion, she steps back, slamming the door in both their faces.

The trapped men hammer on the sturdy wood with balled fists, yelling out obscenities. Anna's prepared to be a little patient. It's not the first time her clinic has served as a jail. Eventually their arms will tire and they'll try their luck with the barred window.

Somewhere across the sun-baked sand, cruel laughter resonates. The men are hammering so hard that at first they don't make sense of what they're hearing. Rocco screaming, a symphony of pain.

"Tell me more of Venus and the star," Anna shouts through the door, but the men are far too filled with rage to hear her. Their hammering continues, as does Rocco's agony. The latter eventually overpowers the former.

"There's nothing that can be done to save him," Anna cautions. "I can't stop the things those sisters do."

Eventually the pounding stops.

"What are they doing to him?" calls Jimenez, his voice unsteady.

"Practising their religion. *Performing* it. Those girls aren't much in need of practice."

"Which religion?"

"The one that suits their mood. Forget about it. Your friend is dead. There's nothing you can do."

Another scream and the hammering starts up again.

"Whatever," she says, wandering back around to the kitchen to get a drink.

When she returns in half an hour, the men have fallen silent.

"Tell me about the Major," she says, lowering herself to sit cross-legged on the porch.

Occasional screams of torment still echo across the landscape.

"I'm sorry," says Anna. "Really I am." Then she asks again about the Major. "Does he wear a mark like mine?"

Jimenez and Skunk aren't talking. Both are far too horrified for words.

"But he's an ordinary man?" she asks them. "Like you?"

No answer. Not so ordinary then. They don't trust her. They're never going to trust her. They think Rocco's misfortune is her fault. She keeps on at them with questions, but the screaming doesn't stop. The men clam up, concentration shot to Hell.

She leaves them be. She'll come back and let them out tomorrow. There's a trail of red leading to the ossuary façade, but she ignores it. Such details have long ceased to be her business.

She walks the camp perimeter, binoculars dangling, useless, half-hoping to spot another bull. This time she's up for target practice. Blowing the damn thing's head off would improve her mood. But there's nothing past the line of passive, waiting mothers. Nothing but endless sand and sunlight.

Let the storms come and boil away tomorrow. At least that way she won't have to care.

Just past sunrise, the two men still stand defiant. The resonance of Rocco's screams hangs about them like an all-enveloping fog. She's brought a jug of water and two enamel mugs. Holds them high so they can see them through the bars.

"Where the fuck is Rocco?" asks Jimenez through the window.

"Describe the Major and maybe I'll let you out. Take you to him too, if you behave yourselves."

She takes their silence as a yes, pours, then passes each man a mug. They snatch them and quaff gratefully, gulping without spilling anything.

She holds the jug ready in anticipation. "The Major," she reminds them with a waning smile.

"White guy. Maybe forty. Maybe fifty."

"Blond hair, bright blue eyes. Tattoo."

They stare at her eight-point star while they're talking, still mesmerised by its apparent significance.

"Like this?" she asks, baring her bicep for closer inspection.

Jimenez shakes his head. "Nothing holy, Ma'am. He's got a lion."

A lion.

She almost drops the jug. "What kind of lion?"

"Big."

"Where?"

"On his back."

"Holding a flag in its paw?"

They don't answer quickly enough, so she screams: "Is the fucking thing holding a pennant?"

Skunk nods almost imperceptibly.

It's holding a fucking pennant. She stands there, jug gripped tightly, her mind elsewhere. *The lion changes everything.*

Questions chitter through her brain like locusts. Why did she never search for Thomas below the earth? Bewitched by a glamour, the sleight-of-hand of solid rock. Rock can be blasted. Caves can be created. She pictures swarms of men tunnelling through honeycomb like ants, each new chamber comforting and womb-like.

When she's ready, she goes to speak with Sirius. It's not his time yet, but she always knows he's there.

The would-be mothers watch from beneath their ratty awnings. Some days it's their silence that bothers her the most. They think she should be planting babies in her clinic. Making half an effort to save the future from the past. But she can't think straight since the men walked into camp. She hates the way they've turned things upside down.

"There's something I'm forgetting," she tells her Dog Star friend. "Some big secret I'm supposed to know."

The threat of storms has abated. One less problem she has to care about. A lick of breeze against her neck, teasing of coolness yet to come. Perhaps she should kill the men? Put them out of their misery. Forget the shiny illusions they have to offer. The women, too, the queue of hopeful mothers. She could end their suffering so cleanly.

She hears the splintering of wood, comprehends its great significance, yet cannot bring herself to care. The lion lives. He lives. *He lives*, over and over and over in her mind. That lion tattoo is the sign she's been waiting for, a thousand tiny candles flickering in her head. The message from Thomas, a purpose after all these wasted years. Truckstop wasn't the end but the beginning! The kick-off point for a glorious new season.

The skin beneath her own tattoo tingles — the dove on her back, not the eight-point star on her arm. She recalls a Hong Kong backstreet. Crowded, the stink of fish. The lion and the dove. They'd been inked together, side by side as the smoke-choked night filled with stars. Rockets, too. Brilliant fireworks as they kissed beneath the needle's burning repetition.

That was the night they felt no pain. No, the pain would come later, tiresome decades of it, or had it been longer? Who could say? Who bothers counting years when time itself is at a standstill? Only those crazy nuns with their great skull abacus and the ivory hourglass and the blanched bronze sundial, its symbols as worn and faded as history itself.

The nuns. She snaps herself back into the moment, hurries to the makeshift prison to find a splintered door. The stupid men have kicked the damn thing down. Back out on the sand, the nuns are circling poor Skunk and Jimenez like jackals, sniffing their stink, ever vigilant, ever hopeful.

"Where's Rocco?" spits Jimenez, defiant, despite the terror in his eyes.

"I warned him," offers Anna by way of an apology.

"Why don't we go and visit him together?"

Reluctantly the nuns fall back. Daisy is with them. They'll do whatever Daisy says. Anna suspects her own safe days are numbered.

What's left of Rocco's corpse has been hammered haphazardly to a cross. The shape is incidental; Anna doubts these girls have heard of Jesus. Jimenez and Skunk stop dead, speechless, even with the nuns too close for comfort.

The girls have spread his innards on a rattan mat, lungs and liver separate. The liver may be the seat of the soul, but poor Rocco's speaks of little but misfortune. Perhaps they ripped it too eagerly from its housing? Between life's fading and the immanence of death sit those precious moments where truths are told. Rocco screamed for hours, but in the end, his passing came as swift as starfall.

A wall of turbulence obscures the horizon, broiling acid clouds spitting caustic phlegm upon the silicon sea.

Jimenez steps forward, fists clenching and unclenching. Anna gestures to the lookout tower where Gengis trains a high-powered rifle on him.

"Tomorrow," says Daisy, interrupting. "Dawn of the eighth year begins tomorrow."

Then, abandoning Rocco's shredded frame to the vultures, Daisy and her entourage hurry to consult the ossuary's great skull mothers, arms overflowing with sticky male entrails.

"You sure about this?" Anna asks the men, eyes squinting in the ochre afternoon glare. "A lion with a pennant. No chance you could be mistaken?"

"What the fuck is the matter with you? Those bitches tore our buddy limb from limb!"

"No mistake," says Skunk, staring straight at her. Anna notes the milky cast of his eyes. Both of them have it. Whatever bullshit they might or might not be sprouting, they've definitely done time away from light. She's amazed they can see at all, what with the glare and the sun-bleached forever. That they saw enough to get as far as Truckstop.

"More water." Skunk holds out his cup.

Anna isn't listening. She's thinking about Daisy's dawning eighth great year, a date of auspice and serendipity. A year when time itself will be tested, debts collected, promises made now answered for.

Not that Anna gives a damn if an occasional throat gets slit in a show of penance. A splash of red looks pretty on the washed-out rocks. But whatever the fuck year they'd thought it'd been, it's *her* year now, goddamn it. Year of the lion and the dove. Reunited like they'd never been apart.

"Take me to your Major and his lion tattoo."

The men pale visibly as the words escape her lips.

"Not in a month of Sundays," says Jimenez. "Not if it was the end of the world."

"The world died thirty years ago, taking all your Sundays with it," she says. "Nothing left here but ghosts and undead friends."

Jimenez shakes his head. "You don't know what you're asking. You don't know."

"I'm asking you to take me as far as the Underworld gates," says Anna. "After that, I don't care where you go."

"Wouldn't even if I knew they way," says Skunk, defiant to the last.

But she knows she'll knock it out of him. A day or longer, maybe three. It doesn't matter. Only the lion matters. "Take me to the Underworld, or I'll throw you to the nuns."

No answer. She isn't expecting one. Perhaps the men

no longer care, for what's left for them to care about? Walk another hundred miles or get crucified outside the ossuary? If the nuns are what remain of civilisation, barbarism doesn't bear thinking about. Better to die in the shade by their own hands.

But their hands are trembling far too hard to hold a blade, even if they had a blade to speak of. So they stand in the sun, feeling their bones bleach and fade beneath their meat.

An hour later when Anna calls their names, they haven't moved.

"Come inside," she whispers gently. "Eat and rest. Forget about your friend."

This time they do as she commands, walking like the condemned men they are, eating a final meal, then sleeping the sleep of the dead.

There's a giant ghost serpent only Anna can see. She feels it shift beneath the sands, tunnelling through the hard-packed silica fines. Other times it coasts above the surface, moody and bucolic, its rainbow sheath refracting shards of sky and sunset. Colours faded before the rise of man. The thing is blind. It flicks its tail in shiftless grace. Soaks up sun. Heat is the one thing it can never get enough of.

Despite its flimsy corporality, she stays indoors on the days the serpent moves. The would-be mothers have no sense of it. They cross its shadow, pass oblivious through its discontented flesh.

The nuns can't see it either, but they know it's there. They merely wait, charting plans for its massive, elongated skull. A figurehead for their beloved ossuary. It has to die eventually. Everything does.

But today the great ghost serpent sleeps. The men and

Anna await the rise of Sirius, the only sigil Anna ever trusts, before setting off on their journey. The others don't yet know of her intimacy with the Dog Star, the dialogue continually running in the substrata of her mind.

The men freeze when they see the bed sheet retinue waiting patiently beyond barbed wire barricades. Seven scrawny nuns, Daisy chief amongst them, flanked by two hardy red-eyed Nubian goats.

Jimenez throws a backward glance at the clinic's cold white walls. "You never said nothing about them nuns coming too."

Anna shrugged. "You reckon I'd know how to stop them?"

Daisy has the raptures upon her, eyes fluttering upwards in her tiny shaven head. Her sisters pay no more attention to the men than to the goats. Each clasps a skull and, apparently, the skulls are speaking.

"They've forgotten Rocco," Anna whispers. "Short attention spans. You don't have anything more to fear. For now."

A gleam of metal catches their attention. Gengis stands guard atop the watchtower's skeletal frame. Utterly motionless against the skyline, as if carved from the very dirt itself.

"What's his story?" mumbles Skunk.

Anna stares beyond the tower, far out across the insipid, pallid blue. She sees old Gengis as the envoy of Sirius, star stuff moulded human, but she'd never tell him that. Soldier of fortune, Armageddon escapee. Last man standing when the dust finally settled. All those things and several more besides. Or is he something else entirely? So deeply tanned, his race long rendered indeterminable.

But he doesn't quit and he doesn't whine and he can hold that rifle steady in a howling tempest. His needs are simple, his problems very few.

"He keeps us safe," is her eventual answer.

Skunk doesn't bother asking safe from what. Perhaps coming to comprehend the pointlessness of questions, he turns his back on Gengis and starts walking.

The slender line of hopeful mothers raise shrouded faces as Anna's expedition strides past. They've learned better than to stand and make a fuss. The ones who've made it this far understand the need for waiting. They sit passively as all their future hopes march north into the desert.

Anna knows they'll be sitting there when she returns. And if she doesn't? Will they die there in their straggly encampments, sunburned faces wrapped against the wind? What will happen when storms inevitably set in?

Not her problem. Very little is, these days. Her own destiny has taken a turn for the better. Finally, there seems a point to all she's seen and done. The clinic has been a holding pattern, sanctuary from the ravages of time. Perhaps she's finally ready to rejoin the world?

Will Thomas remember her? Of course he will. True love is all the Earth has left. Their separation has been a test. An endurance, or perhaps some harsh initiation rite?

Thomas will be a man now, not the smiling youth embedded in her memory. Half-forgotten, yet never quite let go. They were meant to be together beyond fire and flame.

They walk for hours, sunlight dazzling their eyes. Three nuns up front, four bringing up the rear. Anna's doctor's bag weighs heavy, but she's brought it for good reason. She pats its scuffed black leather for reassurance.

"I don't trust 'em sneaking along behind us," grumbles Skunk.

"Their singing shits me," adds Jimenez.

Anna hasn't heard the singing, she's so wrapped up in

her private thoughts. But she hears it now, so gentle, bittersweet. Mournful, hopeful, all mixed into one.

The air before her shimmers with the faintest trace of ghosts. Battle scenes. Cars and tanks. People running, screaming through the flames. Rubble raining as buildings crumble. The usual sort of thing. She's long stopped wondering where the pictures come from. Resonance or residue, aftershock...afterbirth. All roads led to death, no matter how you look at it.

Sister Daisy is slung with reliquary beads carved from a polished human femur, threaded on string plucked from ancient carpets. Scrimshandering has become the holiest vocation. Many fine clinic scalpels have been liberated for the cause, high art being far worthier than surgery. Anna never argues. She leaves Daisy to her business. Daisy might be crazy, but she's smarter than the rest. All Anna has to do is wait. Time will deliver. All will return to the dust from which it came. She throws a parting glance to the ossuary, a gleaming monument to the end of days. The end of time itself, for past the end of days, who's counting? Does time still flow when all the clocks are broken?

Once some swanky kind of bar, all sandstone, chrome and glass bricks, that ossuary became as good a place as any to store the dead. A sturdy tower of gleaming skulls and bones, if somewhat scoured by relentless desert dust. That dust clings to everything: skin, stone and soul. On a bad day the air swirls thick with it. On a good day...*but ah*, thinks Anna, *there are no good days anymore.*

Venus sits sullen in the powdery dawn sky, offering little commentary, as is her way. All today's ghosts are from the cities. Sleepwalking, listless in the tide. They chatter to the void, hooked up to the electronic whisper, muttering mantras under faded breath.

Anna recalls metropoli, those vast and shining jewels.

Sheer towers, wind blasted corridors, massive fingers of chromium and glass. Once she walked amongst them, invisible in the slipstream, relishing her anonymity. Banked-up cars from here to doomsday. Gridlocked regularity, spores on crusted macadam. She can smell the gasoline stench, the acrid belching choke of it. The image fades, soaked up by the sand. Patina on retina, industrial residue.

It had been the end of days, although they hadn't known it then. Always autumn, whenever she thinks back on it. Cool breezes, gusts of wind stirring up the leaves. She suspects the seasons past of trickery. There are no changes anymore, only baking heat by daylight. Freezing chill at night when the sun fades.

But some things she is certain of, the startling turquoise of Thomas's eyes, the gleaming smile, the cocksure tilting of his head. Young love so strong you know you're both immortal. Powerful enough to transcend death itself. Only it doesn't. Transcend anything. Thomas shipped out the night the fire rained, all their pointless promises forgotten. *I'll find you,* he told her, although he never did. But he looked for her. She knows for sure he tried.

She's brooding on this issue as she puts one foot before the next, lulled by repetitive patterns of her fellow travellers' footfall. She stares at the dust-baked earth, trusting the nuns to watch the skies and the horizon and all the nothing lying in between. They like to watch with their sharp little eyes, minds alive for signs and portents. Now and then they pause to evaluate the significance of details all but invisible to Anna and the men: the twist of a skeletal sparrow's spinal column, burnished shards cracked off a rogue bull's metal casing.

The men stick close to Anna, as if understanding they'll never feel safe in this life again. Understanding the world as they knew it is long gone.

All portents aside, Anna continues to see ghosts, knows that they're imprints more than signs. Moments imprisoned by the heat and glare, doomed to eternal repetition and playback. Right now, she sees an army march across argent sands, foreign colours streaming from spear tips. Their breastplates, once golden, are hammered and stained. Lost in time as well as destination. Above their helmets, a plane plummets, earthbound. When it crashes, the sand trembles from impact, yet there is no plane, just as there are no marching soldiers.

Other times, through tears, she sees naked children frolicking with dogs. Their dusky skin repels the glare, teeth as white as reliquary ivory. They're not real. They've never been real. These are island babies, scrabbling for coconuts and shells. They smile at her through a thousand summers. No one told them the world has ceased to be.

The visions become more corporeal, more intense. She feigns indifference, but the mantle's getting thinner.

"Tell me about the Major," she asks the men who trudge beside her. Did they see the plane? She's too afraid to ask.

"Fucking crazy," Jimenez offers after a time.

"Who isn't after what we've all lived through?" She hates the way her voice sounds, the way she speaks like one of them.

"There's crazy and there's crazy," Jimenez says.

Anna can see he won't elaborate unless she forces him. He doesn't want to be the one who calls it. There's no way to dress up words like *psychopath*, but he surely will, if it will keep him alive.

The singing stops, sudden silence jarring. The men freeze in their tracks like startled rabbits.

Anna brings a finger to her lips, mouthing a soundless *shhhh*. Unnecessary. All know something's wrong.

They drop to a crouch, no need for instruction, all but the nuns. They sniff the air like dogs.

If it's a storm come early, they're done for. Nowhere to run and hide. The sand a few feet ahead erupts. The scent of burning ozone, the air alive with sparks.

"Rogue bull," says Anna, climbing to her feet.

The nuns are already onto it, swinging rifles from their shoulders, fanning out in three precise directions.

"It's just a bull," says Anna to the soldiers. "Good target practice — those things can't aim for shit."

But the men don't get up immediately. Jimenez's got the shakes. Skunk crouches, eyes flitting side to side.

"Suit yourselves." Anna moves forward for a better view. She's seen this show a hundred times, but it's not like there's much else to look at.

It's just an old SUGV, 30mm Mk 44 chain gun quadruped. Waterproof and shockproof, but miles away from nunproof. The bull calibrates its sights on Daisy but it isn't quick enough. By the time it's done, the girl has ducked away. The thing is on its last legs, all pretence at stealth corroded. That it can still shoot is miraculous.

The nuns duck and weave their way around it, freezing whenever it gains one in its sights. Then all of a sudden they let fly with rocks. They squeal with glee when they score a strike. It doesn't take long for the bull to fall. The tired old thing collapses on its side, twitches in the sand, battered and undignified.

Though it has never truly lived, it dies a creature's death.

"Fucked up little witches," Skunk mumbles.

Anna's mind drifts as each rock strikes home. The shimmering heat reflects off the sand. Through the gloaming wash, she flashes back to younger days and

Thomas, who's vaulting over spike-capped palace walls.

She'd been bathing with her slaves in a marble pool strewn with rose and lilac petals. First the gasps, then the stifled giggles of the waterbearers. Olive branches trembled as Thomas thudded heels first into soft grass.

The three slaves stared aghast at this forbidden male intrusion. But it soon became clear that Anna did not mind. She stepped from her bath, rivulets trailing down her soft brown skin. When she ran to him, the slave girls closed their eyes, turned their faces from the couple's wild abandonment. What they couldn't see they couldn't be forced to tell.

Stray dust particles in her eye make Anna blink. What the Hell memory was that supposed to be? Women's quarters? Slaves balancing amphorae? But it had been Thomas, clear as day. Not her usual flavour of fantasy — she'd never been the slave girl type — but new environments brought new feelings, she supposes. Something in the northern dust or the way the sky has changed.

She can see so much further than she used to.

Seven days pass before they see more clouds, a boiling bank of thunder smothering the horizon, end to end. The goats bleat, nervous. They can smell the air's deceitful chemistry. That night the moon is at its thinnest, bled out by the tainted pallor of dusk.

The nuns drive their skull sticks deep into the ground.

"Which way?" asks Anna.

The men remain tight-lipped. They know, of course. She knows they know. Their steps have been slowing, more hesitant, more wary.

"Why do you want to go below?" asks Jimenez in an uncharacteristic surge of bravado. Perhaps he knows his time is near, his days are marked and numbered.

"You wouldn't understand," says Anna.

"The fuck I wouldn't. I've been there. Twenty stinking years beneath the earth. Darkness like you couldn't even dream."

They've been through this routine so many times by now.

"But that's where *he* lives, so that's where I must go."

So simple, when she says what's on her mind.

"Major Thomas?"

"My Lionheart."

Jimenez scratches at the sand lice in his hair. "That Major never had a heart to speak of."

"Oh, but that's where you're wrong," she coos. "You don't know him. Nobody knows him like I do."

"Like you did," chimes in Skunk. "Like you did. Maybe. And maybe he was sane before the fall. Maybe I could picture that if I had a gun to my head. But twenty years in darkness sucks the kindness from a man. The man you loved is barely human now."

"You don't know anything about the man I love!"

She's angry now, and the men shift their weights uneasily from foot to foot, eyes on those twitchy, deadly little nuns with their sharpened skull sticks and human femur shivs. The goats keep whimpering and whining in the heat. They can smell the wrongness. They know something bad is about to happen.

Then Daisy starts to make a racket, jibbering and jabbering in tongues, pointing to something tall and glinting. So slim and distant, they all might have missed it.

"Ruins!" exclaims Anna. The men's downcast eyes confirm she's right. They know which way, and now she knows it, too.

Recognition unfolds as they approach. Not much left

of the busted-up brick wall: a crumbling tower with a sand-scored plastic sign. The symbol, once familiar. A logo of some kind. She knows she used to know what it was for, but it's gone now, as with the accompanying words and whatever significance they once held. She doesn't care; the words aren't important.

They make the ruined place their camp, skull sticks staking out a perimeter. A fire is struck, bitter lizards roasted upon twigs. A pockmarked canteen passes from hand to hand, metallic-tasting water shared in meagre gulps.

The men sense the futility of their futures; stare at their battered, dusty shoes. The moon is nothing but a sliver now, a frown against the angry carbon sky. When the nuns start singing, Anna wanders off alone.

The stars are bright, but there's not much light to see by. Doesn't matter, she's not going far. She just wants to be alone to talk to her faithful Dog Star friend.

The air's still warm and heady from the day. Something cloying about it, too. Something familiar. It takes her a while to recognise the scent: wildflowers, deep and sweet and true. It's her memory, of course, playing tricks. Nothing has grown out here for years. A handful of scrabbly cactus plants perhaps, desiccated thorns and tumbleweeds.

But wildflowers? Surely she must be dreaming. "What of it?" she says to Sirius. He's bright tonight, watching over her as always. When the moon is insubstantial, she needs him most.

Another scent beneath the heady sweetness. She frowns as she does her best to recall its name. Something...living. Something earthy. A flock of black-faced sheep, of all things!

Then suddenly she's on the shaded mountainside. Young with skinny legs and ropy braids. And he's there, too, staring at her sun-bronzed skin. She can smell the musk of him at fifty paces.

They fuck under a shady cedar. He smells of sheep but she doesn't give a damn. Afterwards, she combs stray leaves from her hair with fingers splayed. He lays still, abdomen glistening with sweat.

"You're mine," she tells him. "You must never love another."

He laughs. "Twenty girls from town say you're too late."

She cradles his head in her lap and strokes his hair, aware of the power beneath her fingertips. With the slightest pressure she could end his life. But she doesn't. She loves him as silly village girls are wont to do.

"I can make you mine forever. I can make you do whatever I want."

"If you say so," he says, drifting into a sated slumber.

And he did sleep, too, for a thousand years. Or so it seems to Anna, out here beneath the stars tonight. The memory is confusing. It isn't hers. It can't be. But it feels so real, as real as anything else.

Truth is, she's been waiting here so long she'd almost forgotten him completely. Thomas, her lover, her friend. Her soulmate, if survivors still wore their souls. His absence left a cavern in her heart, but soon it shall be refilled.

The nuns have stopped their singing and the night is cool and still. The gate she seeks cannot be far away.

"I want to remember more of him," she tells Sirius. "I want to see him just the way he was."

And then suddenly she's angry, although she's not sure why. The years she's wasted out here in the dust. The broken-down clinic, seeding all those salted wombs. What the Hell did she think she was trying to prove? She was never about healing. The women who walked to her were doomed. So why did she keep planting all those years?

Sirius winks through the stratosphere. Beneath, a meteoroid burns hollow, trails to nothing.

"I was waiting. Waiting for him."

She turns and hurries back to camp, almost tripping over stones in her haste. She wakes the soldiers and they do not thank her for it.

"He gave you something to bring to me," she says. "I want it."

Asleep not long, their minds are fogged with exhaustion.

"Who?" says Jimenez, blinking grit from his eyes.

"Thomas, you idiot. He must have given you something."

"Lady, we escaped," said Skunk. "Lucky to get this far at all."

"Dug our way up. Bribed our way out to the surface." Jimenez cuts himself off sharply — perhaps he thinks the now-silent nuns are listening.

"But you found me so easily!" Anna says. "He must have told you where I was. Offered guidance."

Her tone suggests she's past the halfway point of reason.

"Maybe it's not him?" Skunk offers. "Maybe he's not your guy?"

She can't even hear him, that's how far she's flipped.

"Can't be a coincidence," she mumbles over and over. "Hardly a chance thing — what would be the odds?"

She finds herself a private space, lies back to study constellations. They changed their names the day the Earth caught fire. Banished are the old guard: the bull of Heaven, the goat-fish, the great one. Tonight she sees shapes close to her heart: the lion, the lovers, the dove. The Dog Star, winking conspiratorially, approves of all her visions. In the background, the periodic bleating of goats and soldiers bickering in low whispers is punctuated by the howling of distant wild dogs. She tracks lonely satellites through the early hours, deaf and dumb, doomed to circle silently forever. She drifts to sleep, a smile upon her face. Imagines Thomas's arms around her own.

The morning light is weak and chill. Tracks bleeding off to the east reveal a tale. Skunk has run off in the early hours. Took a canteen, blanket and a knife.

A nun crouches near his scuffed sand tracks, leans on her skull pole for support. Her name is Wattle and yes, she saw the soldier leave.

"Why didn't you try and stop him?" Anna screams.

Wattle shrugs. "The boy is marked for death."

"Says who?"

"Says Madame de Bethune!" She shakes her stick and the skull swings round to face them.

Anna stares into the skull's cavernous depths.

"Madame says he shall be feeding crows by noontide."

"Not a lot of tide 'round here in case you haven't noticed." But Anna leaves it there. Wattle will not be moved. She lives for that skull on its whittled branch. She'd die for it if she thought it was what the skull wanted.

Meanwhile, Jimenez stews in disbelief. "You ain't even gonna hunt him?" he whines.

"What for when I have you?" She points north. "Is this the way?"

The soldier's sullen shrug indicates she's guessed it right. She's seen a subtle twist of macadam through her spyglass. Up closer, they notice how cracked and warped it has become, boiled and blistered from excessive heat.

Further beyond, a stiff shale ridge, gnarled like a crocodile's back.

"Over there," whines Jimenez. "Sure as fuck, you don't need me."

"We need each other," Anna insists.

The walk takes longer than expected. Hours longer under ruthless sun. Too hot for singing. Even the nuns drag their feet, skull sticks trailing swishes in the sand.

Anna's excitement increases incrementally. She half expects a five-point flange of sleek jet fighters to burst out over the ridge in salutation. Fact is, she can see them if she really wants to. Clear as she can see the sand and sky.

As they get closer, Jimenez begins to crack. "I'm not going back down there. You said to the gate. That's the gate ahead. He'll kill me for running out on him. Plenty of men get hooked up for less."

"But you're the messenger!" Anna offers brightly. "I barely remembered anything before you came. Thomas will reward you. Promote you. Shower you with gifts. He'll love you, soldier boy, for bringing home his girl."

But Jimenez is crying as the rock ridge looms ahead. Anna frowns, expecting something grander. An archway, perhaps? Something akin to the ossuary's antique splendour. At the very least, an orifice leading down into the earth's cool recesses.

She's been hoping he'll be there to greet her. Waiting with his handsome, rugged smile. Older, of course. A little gray around the temples. Wiser, too. More worldly than before.

Jimenez keeps blubbering.

"Shut up," Anna snaps.

"Not going back," he whimpers.

"You're going where I say you're going."

She's not really listening. All she's thinking about is that missing doorway as he mewls and blubbers like a baby.

It happens swiftly, no time for contemplation. In a second, Jimenez is leaping. Wattle collapses in a heap upon the ground, her precious Madame de Bethune rolling free of its shaft.

Jimenez manages to liberate her knife. He slits his own throat before anyone can stop him. Does a decent job of it too. Wattle sprawls beneath his bulk, open-mouthed, recipient of warm baptismal blood. His eyes have whited over. He's dead, but he's still kneeling.

Anna's furious she didn't see this coming.

Wattle crawls away on bleeding knees, leaving the soldier's frame to slump all the way to the ground.

The others merely stare in silence. A pause before the prayers. Such deep commitment guarantees no going back. How dull their gaze is. How estranged from living women they have become. Standing there as silent as their skulls, as useless as the mountain ridge before them.

Jimenez's corpse twitches as the last of his fluid drains.

"Thomas would have blessed you." Anna whispers into his ear. She sits with him to catch her breath while the nuns set up a campsite, milking goats and baking damper as they brew a billy full of bitter thornbrush tea.

Anna sees the soldier's suicide for what it is — a sign. Thomas isn't waiting by the gate to let her in. Things might be tougher than they seem, but that's okay. Decades in the sun have taught her patience.

The soldiers regarded him as some kind of warrior king, a pharaoh of the lands beneath the dirt. Even the kindest pharaohs could have cold-stone hearts. To go down there love-blind might be foolish.

She walks off on her own to think. The skyline streaks burnt umber, and for a while it seems there'll be no moon at all. But the moon is there eventually, not far from faithful Sirius.

"What must I take with me?" she asks.

But she knows the answer already. Knew it days before they set out on foot. She brought it with her in her doctor's bag.

Insurance.

It's not that she doesn't trust beloved Thomas, but his minions — who can say? Best be on the safe side. Best make sure she's covered.

The nuns are boiling porridge. Smells like seeds and grass and clay. Tastes like it, too, but it quells the bellyache. After eating will come time for prayer. A few solid hours of pantomime, interpretive dance and religious mumbo jumbo. That's when she needs to act. They think she's holy; she takes great pains not to disappoint them.

The skulls look wise and ancient in the flickering firelight, watching sagely from atop their sharpened sticks. Daisy and her nuns insist the skulls aren't silent. They whisper secrets from the future and the past. Give names to keep track of potential prophecy. Some are helpful, others downright liars. It matters little in any case — the stupid bitches do whatever their hollow-headed bony masters tell them. Drink the stormwater, it's perfectly safe. Dance naked in it while you're at it, don't worry that the acid strips your flesh.

Anna ducks behind a rock, applies the *Essential Oils Sheep Placenta Collagen Mask, with grape juice and green tea extract.* Something scrounged from the back of the clinic's storeroom. She hums a little tune, rocking back and forth as she waits for the stuff to harden.

Apparently such things were commonplace in the world before. Who today would waste a rich sheep's placenta on anything so frivolous as skin? The clammy cling of it reminds her of better days.

Taking care to ensure her tattoo is exposed — both of

them, the eight-point star and the dove — she joins the nuns at their fire. They all gasp and make the sign. Beneath the mask, every word Anna speaks is prophecy.

She's known for some time that words themselves don't matter. It's all about the ceremony. The ritual. Gestures and incantations. Flourishes and exaggerations. Nuns gape, open-mouthed as she pulls the pneumatic hypodermic from her coat folds.

"What's your name, little sister?" she asks each one in turn. Firelight has rendered them identical. Mindless creatures of the swarm, like fish or bees — not that she's seen either of those in years. Daisy and Wattle. Hibiscus, Dandelion, Flax, Eithne and Anemone.

"Sting of scorpion, fang of snake." She hisses and spits, making claws of her hands.

Then she's on her feet, dancing between them, kissing cheeks and tugging arms. She jabs each one and they barely notice, hollering witchy nonsense as she reloads.

When the deed is done, Anna slinks into the shadows, peels the sheep's placenta from her face. She'll cast the mask into the fire when the others sleep. She won't sleep — tomorrow is too near. She'll spend the night with Sirius in darkness.

With the tepid dawn comes something new. The pressure of unseen eyes. One pair or a hundred — Anna can't be sure. She can smell it, too, the scent of unwashed flesh. The nuns are busy ministering to their skulls. Their needs come first even when there might be danger — and when is there ever no danger in this world?

The ridge juts defiantly in the sharpening morning light. Less of a crocodile's back this morning, more an impassable wall.

Out in the open they're vulnerable. Exposed. But it's

too late — the eyes have already seen them. Is the doorway hidden, embedded in the living rock? Is it somewhere else entirely? Was Jimenez lying all along?

No, his blood is the truest certification. Not that there's much left of it; the sand is scuffed, the red stain but a memory. Something must have crept up in the night. Sucked the iron from the silicon granules. Took the body, too.

Her reverie is broken by the sounding of a gong. Dull reverberations of wood upon metal shattering the air's sullen quiet. She's been expecting this — an invitation, or something like it. A grand pronouncement signalling connection between two worlds.

She takes her time in getting up, brushes sand and grit from her garment's folds. Allows each beat to guide her to its source.

Her shoulders slump when she sees it's only Daisy, hammering on steel with a gnarled tree stump. Throwing her whole weight behind each blow, the resultant sound much deeper and louder than it ought to have been.

Could this steel slab be a door? It has no handle, window slit, nor hinge. When Daisy glimpses Anna, she stops to catch her breath. Starts again as Anna checks its welds. Knobs and rivets infest its farthest edges like hardy boils.

Not a door. A seal. To keep us out or something else inside?

Daisy eventually tires of her exertions. Anna stands lost in private reverie as the last reverberation melts away to silence.

No army of demons burst forth from the ground. The sky does not darken, the wind does not howl. The desert behind her is as still as it has ever been. The ridge remains an oppressive, threatening weight.

She turns to see nuns scurrying like ants, each bearing items essential to their acceptance of the new situation. In moments they have transformed the giant metal plate into a shrine. Somehow they've found flowers in this dead and dreary wasteland. Tiny mean-looking things reminiscent of the nuns themselves. A shrine is always their first response, followed closely by requisite prayers, chants, dances and incantations. They'll strut their stuff until exhaustion claims them, but the door will stay firmly shut. It has been fused to the living rock for a reason. They don't care. Reason has long been the least of their concerns.

Anna's heart sits like a stone. Has she come so far to let mere steel obstruct her? It seems there'd been a time when anything was possible. When the mere sound of her voice could bring a mountain crashing down.

Was she ever a goddess or a princess or a high priestess? It hardly seems to matter now the world is drowned in dust. The water poisoned, clouds so thin and still. The men all limp, the women crazy. Anna doesn't know why she's come here. If she ever had a plan, it's lost to time.

"Let me in or so help me, I'll raise the dead!" She pummels the steel with balled fists, shrieks insults into the tepid wind. Her words evaporate unheeded. Languid whispers tossed from breath to breath.

She leaves the sisters to their silly games, returns to the embers to sketch circles in the sand. The skulls stare down at her in a non-committal fashion. Past death, small details become so irrelevant.

Sudden movement catches her attention. Dandelion scampering along the rock face like a nimble goat. Perhaps the girl has heard a noise. Not far beyond where Anna sits, the hobbled Nubians bleat in nervous bursts. Whatever it is, they've heard it too; or perhaps they can sense or smell a foreign presence.

Moments later, Dandelion's stealthy investigation is

backed up by both Wattle and Hibiscus brandishing bone shivs. Anna settles back comfortably to watch. She likes it when the nuns turns into huntresses; the gleam in their eyes at the promise of fresh meat. How much better they are this way; an army swarming like crabs across the rocks to take a city.

Anna's picked her favourite. Wattle would be hitting puberty right about now if she could bleed. Why these children were burdened with such hopeful post-apocalypse monikers, she can't imagine. Anna vaguely recalls a Dawn, a Melody and a Sunshine going back a couple of years. There was even a Rainbow, a buck-toothed horror who'd had the good grace to die of dysentery.

Wattle somehow manages svelte rather than bone-grating skank. She's got a spring in her step and a swivel in her hips. Yes, there are hips, somehow, occasionally visible beneath those dust-encrusted hotel sheets the nuns appropriate as robes.

She's a catwalk model, an MTV rapper. Doctor Anna remembers those things and is occasionally grateful for small mercies. All that tempest of clamour and noise. Apocalypse couldn't have rained down soon enough.

She doesn't stay watching by the embers for long. The cries tell her they've found something of interest. Anna goes to join them, picking over the sharp rocks, wishing she had a little more light to see by.

The girls have found a secret cave. A tunnel sloping downwards. Footprints not their own. A few discarded items. Evidence of occupation. Recent or not — that's the tricky question. Daisy and Wattle light torches bound with pitch. Flax is frightened, wants to go back for her skulls. She and Daisy argue. Not in English. They're jabbering prayer talk but Anna's heard it all before.

"It's a hidden tunnel," she explains. "Passage to the

Underworld!"

Flax doesn't care. She breaks from the rest of them, hurries across the rocky waste to the safety of hearth, skull and goat. But she doesn't get far. Something whistles through the air, fells her swiftly, her pale skin and robe splattered red. The sky is spitting rocks. The others sprint for the tunnel mouth and its meagre shelter. Rocks rain down on them, sharp-edged, well aimed. By the time they reach the tunnel, all are bleeding. All but Anna. Miraculously, she has escaped without a single scratch. She would wonder about it but there's no time. The injured nuns are cut and terrified, separated from their skulls, left with nothing but strings of reliquary bones to protect them.

Their babbling continues, punctuated by unbridled shrieks of terror. Soon, a competing noise strikes each one silent. Outside on the sand, something is being slaughtered. Might be the goats, but the terrible gurgling sounds could equally belong to poor little Flax.

Terror keeps them pinned within the comparative safety of the overhanging rock. In time, their attackers begin to show themselves. Black shadows enveloped in the stench of blood. Silhouettes stark against the brightening skyline. Matted hair, bodies wrapped in skins. *Wildmen*, thinks Anna. Her next few words must be chosen carefully.

"We're here for Major Thomas," she tells the one who stands a little ahead of the others. Taller. More sure of himself. The silhouettes step up into the torchlight, blood-soaked bundles slung across their broad shoulders. They carry meat, hopefully the flesh of goats. Their lips and mouths are stained with red, their eyes unfathomably white.

"Do you speak?" she asks, her voice too soft. Too gentle.

The big man looks like he's emerged from the dawn of time. A place where words such as *reason* or *truce* do not exist.

"The road is closed," the wildman says. "Best be off before he gets wind of it."

To her great astonishment, he speaks with a cultured English accent. The sort that used to grace late night talk shows; dimly lit faux lounge rooms with guests in comfy chairs.

"Major Thomas is my husband," says Anna, most determined. "He sent three messengers across the sands to find me."

A throaty muttering escapes from the rest of them, silenced swiftly with a twitch of the headman's hand.

Somehow Anna understands it is the number three that speaks truth for her rather than the unsubtle lie of *husband*.

"I see no messengers," he says, angling his head from left to right.

"They died protecting me."

Not entirely a lie, not exactly the truth. Either way, the headman's next response is silence. She tries to assess how many stand behind him without appearing to be counting. Feels the silence corroding her resolve.

"You want to be remembered as the man who kept the Major from his wife?"

The headman smirks. Memory is not high on his agenda. But it's the only thing that matters to her — that and the chance to put the pieces back together.

"You'll take me to the Major or you'll get out of my way."

He's not buying it. She pictures his foul-smelling soldiers raising spears against the skyline. Feels the soft scattering of sand grains blown against her skin.

Where is Thomas? How can this be happening?

The nuns stand, pale-faced, shoulders slumping, eyes trained on the gritty dirt. They make no sound, afraid the slightest noise will draw attention. Hell, it seems, has caught up with them at last.

Then suddenly rough hands appear from nowhere, stripping their burdens: shoulder bags, weapons, tools. The nuns shriek in agony when the men lay hands upon their reliquary bones. Anemone faints, weakened from blood loss.

The headman gestures. Anna looks. Behind her, the tunnel beckons, a dark gash in the ridge's granite spine.

Anna turns her back on the fallen girl. There's nothing she can do for her. For once, the remaining sisters take her lead.

One of the wildmen tugs on Anna's shirt. As he points a grubby finger at her earrings, Anna realises that *he* is actually female. Small breasts apparent beneath the tunic fashioned from scraps of stinking hide.

"Here you go, honey," Anna says, unhooking a silver hoop from each ear. "You need all the pretty you can get."

She expects a blow in trade for the insult, but the wildwoman smiles, revealing jagged teeth. She's still smiling as she stabs the blunt post of each hoop through her earlobes without flinching.

The road to Hell is paved with flaming torches. Not enough of the damn things, though, so they trip and slide through that first hour. The passage smells of damp and dank. Slippery lichen covers everything; it's even in the air. Anna feels like she's breathing in great globs of it. The nuns whisper softly as they stumble over loose rocks. The earth is open, swallowing them whole.

The passage twists and turns around bends and

corners. Anna misses all the little things she's come to trust. Stinging sand and the biting cold of twilight. Her beloved Sirius and the context of the sun. Is it days they've been walking, or merely hours? No day nor night nor gradients in between.

Will she ever see the light again? She daydreams of it — funeral pyres, orange ochre flames licking Armageddon sunsets. Evenings nestled on the clinic porch with its glorious clear view across the way. High magnification binoculars trained on the ossuary façade. Tasteless art, obscene art, a hundred thousand lovingly polished skulls, display racks packed tight with the damn things, solid as a dry-stone wall. Each one cherished, special, loved.

Not much love going on down here. The wildmen reek like rotting carcasses but, mercifully, don't speak, nor push and shove. All they have to do is keep on moving, which is fine by Anna. Down below to Thomas is where she wants to go.

The passage eventually widens into a cavern filled with others. She thought the wildmen stunk until they met this lot. The reek of shit and unwashed flesh is overpowering. It fills the space entirely, every crevice, every crack.

The new ones are much thinner than the wildmen. Dirtier, too, if such a thing is possible. She thinks they might be children, or runts, or outcasts. Whoever they are, they're blocking the passage downwards.

"We belong to Major Thomas," Anna says. She doesn't trust their wildmen escorts to speak for them or cut a deal on their behalf. Everyone must hear his name just so they understand. *Fuck with me, you're fucking with the boss.*

A toll, it seems, is required of them. Anna removes her silver bangles, casts a glance at her pathetic, disappointing nuns. The journey underground has stripped them of their substance. Not to mention other things: Flax and Anemone and poor old Madame de Bethune. Without their skulls, the girls have nothing. Reduced to little more than frightened children, hungry, hurt and helpless. All their prayers have turned to babble. They stink of urine and abject, blinding terror.

The tunnel people wrench the bones from round the nuns' necks. Their clothing, too, what little there remains. When they pull off Anna's shirt, a gasp is heard, echoing off the hollow cavern walls. The wildmen escort backs away.

Anna's so angry at being stripped after volunteering her own silver, it takes a moment to work out what's going on. The star tattoo! Eight dull points stained deep into her flesh. Why does everything come back to that damn thing?

They've obviously seen it before, and it scares them half to death.

"I'm the queen of Heaven," she growls like a rabid dog. "Don't you people know who you're dealing with?"

The runts are standing well back now, so she figures they know something. They let her keep her bra and underpants. They're keen to give her a wide berth from this point forward.

The naked nuns whimper. Anna holds her head up high as they're ushered forward into claustrophobic darkness.

When she glances back, the nuns have disappeared without a trace, as if they've never been. She experiences a sudden, unexpected surge of affection for them, stupid and pointless and useless as they were. Anger begins to boil beneath her skin. *How dare they take my nuns away and treat me like a dog! Do they not know who I am?*

Who *is* she, exactly? For a second she almost remembers something important, but as another moment passes, the thought evaporates.

She is made to walk until she's sure she can walk no more. Then, in a blinding stumble, all of a sudden she is there, the Underworld spread out before her like unravelled cloth, a gaping cavern blasted from solid rock. New stench overpowers the cloy of shit and lichen. She knows the stink of stale human defeat. A cocktail of diesel, grease and abject misery. Stretching high above her head, the walls are slick with slimy phosphorescence.

Anna knows this is the Hell of Bosch and Dante and St Theresa of Avila and Fatima and St Faustina. Whitfield's Eternity of Hell's Torments, that world of agony and pains. A place scoured by the baying of the hounds of death, where time destroys all life and wakes the sleeping.

Inferno spreads below her feet, microcosms of suffering and oppression. The groan and squeal of great machines, scalds of steam, bitter sweat, stale air, all tainted with despair and hopelessness. Stink, reek, fug, stain. Nightmare distilled to its bare-boned essence.

Below her, workers toil in gangs, chipping away at the walls with picks and mallets. Gnawing their way through solid rock, widening the Hell pit slowly, inch by inch. The cavern seems to stretch for miles. Anna can't even see the end of it. But this place holds the man she knew and loved. He has need of her and so she has come to him, all but naked into the vile and stinking earth. This fearsome vista is testament to his need. She knows now she is late by several decades. She should have sought him out when the world caught fire instead of brooding in her desert of bleaching bones.

She is not alone. A blue-clad welcoming committee of three tosses her crumpled clothing into a heap at her feet.

"What have you done with my girls?" she asks, snatching up her garments. The heat is stifling, but she puts her things back on.

These three — all men — look like Rocco, Jimenez and Skunk. Practically indistinguishable, if she didn't know for sure those men were dead. They don't answer her question and she smiles to herself, smug and sure. *Idiots, like men everywhere. They'll all get what's coming to them.*

They lead her down a bank of rough-hewn stairs. Hell looks even worse up close than from above. These are not men toiling before her in chains; these are living skeletons wrapped in perished hide. Scraps of khaki speak of who they used to be. The three who'd come to her across the sand had been princes by comparison. The elite. Officer class, not worker drones. Men who had once been trusted.

And as for the women — oh, the women! Ancient sour drudges every one. She felt their hatred and ill-use, scar tissue fused with sinew to the bone. Anna hopes her little nuns are safely dead; their tiny minds are too ill-equipped for the horrors of this place.

How long has it been since Anna danced? Rhythmic movement fell by the wayside, lost like all those other things she once swore she could never live without. Decades endured without the beat of a drum, the strum of a chord or the haunting seduction of a flute. The nuns danced, performances without accompaniment, but their movements were never the stuff of life.

Yet she hears life now in the hammering of stone. Repetition like the heartbeat of a slumbering machine beast. Singing too, if you could call such mournful lamentation song.

A soldier leads her forward. She stops, presses a finger to her lips. "Shhh."

The soldier pauses, glances upwards, taps his foot. He

moves forward but she does not. The one behind her shoves.

"Shhh," she says again, louder this time. "I'm listening."

The heartbeat's regularity intrigues her, as does the sombre annotation of the singing. The men are willing themselves to death as they chisel further through the mantle of the earth. All the while the beast sleeps on, regardless. Oblivious to their endless suffering.

"It's beautiful," she says.

When the soldier behind her gives her one more shove, she turns on him, spinning quickly to reach and pull the shiny dagger from his belt. She ends his life with one quick thrust. Eyes fluttering, he crumples to the rock. The other two step back to give her room. She grips the knife, warm blood oozing over white-clenched fingers.

A low wall separates the path from the pit below where the ragged men toil. She vaults over the side, landing squarely on both feet, still clutching the knife as she regains her balance. The toilers shuffle to give her room. They stare intently. *An unfamiliar woman is amongst them. A woman wielding a bloodied knife.*

She moves between them, falling into rhythm, hips swaying gently to the beat. They don't touch her, not yet, but she can feel lust boiling like a tide beneath their skins. One touch means death. Not from Anna — at most she could take out two or three before the mass crushes down on top of her. No, death is commanded from above. The rocky platform high above their heads.

The heartbeat continues, syncopating with her own. She slips between them, lets the knife fall to the ground. Each man stiffens, becomes a soldier in her presence, willing to thrust his life into her hands. She splays her fingers, holds them out on either side, fingertips brushing ragged khaki like anemone fronds. Carnality soaks through her skin like radiation. Hush falls across them, dark as shadow. A final shudder as the sleeping beast falls silent. No chipping, no hammering, no excavating.

She sees this army as the men they might have been. Long stone shadows playing tricks upon her eyes. Broad shoulders, straight backs, imaginary rifles at the ready. As she lays her hands upon pallid flesh, eyes roll back in silent climax. She infuses each orgasm through her pores, each tiny death a strengthening of her core.

A new sound. Drumming. The music of war. Feet on concrete, palms slapped hard against taut thighs. She dances for them, a montage of lust, sweat and seed, hips gyrating, belly rounded, breasts that heave and swell. Her own skin glistening slick with perspiration. Building to her own epiphanic climax, when at last they are graced with *his* presence; the lone figure high above on the rocky platform looking down.

She has played out the reunion scene in her head a thousand times. All the clichés patience has made accessible: running along a moonlit beach, fields of gently swaying grasses. Atop a mountain sheltered from wind and rain. The light is always perfect, the temperature mild. Sometimes there's music, sometimes her own joyful laughter, like the playful peal of little silver bells.

Stinking underground caverns packed tight with the living dead was never on the cards. But the setting doesn't matter. Nothing else matters when love is true and strong. Not the ravages of time, nor the cruelties of truth — small things so insubstantial in the face of passion and divinity. When you love so deeply and completely, flames cannot be diminished. Nothing can hold you back from destiny.

When Anna's dance is finished she sets her sights on

the rocky platform. Stairs hewn into the living stone, flimsy without rails. She's guessing few invites are issued to Thomas' lair.

Nobody stops her. Nobody dares. The figure stands on the platform, watches for awhile. She doesn't return the favour, all attention focused on the climb.

Though she wills it not to, Anna's pulse begins to race. Flushed with the power of her dance, she's blushing at private memories, love and lust intertwined. A lot can change in twenty years — or is it more like thirty? Time-wise, the fires of damnation haven't left her much to work with. She knows she should be bracing herself for impact and potential disappointment. He's still a man, no matter what this place has made of him. No matter what he thinks he's made of himself.

She's almost at the top before she notices the hooks. Fearsome twists of rusted steel, spaced evenly, suspended from the cavern's roof. For meat, she imagines. A few more paces and she's figured out the truth. The *meat* stuck on the farthest hook is living. Agony has forced all sound from the man's grossly pierced torso. He flips and twitches like a worm tormented by ants.

Jimenez's scar. No wonder the poor devil chose to bleed himself into the sand.

When she reaches the top, a guard of honour pauses to salute. She nods her acceptance of the situation, that she's graduated from *prisoner* to some kind of *guest*. She pauses in the entranceway, takes a deep breath, blinks.

What if it isn't him?

What if it's someone else?

What if?

She turns, takes one final look down into the cold hard cavern filled with desperate men, cowering from the light like it might burn them. What do they think they're waiting for down there? Forests and fields and streams to reclaim the land? The future holds promise of no such luxury. It takes love to recreate the world. Love and light and peace.

And with that thought, she steps across the threshold.

It's dim. Even dimmer than outside. Takes a moment for her eyesight to adjust. When it does, by the light of half a dozen lamps, Anna beholds what is probably the last fat man left upon the Earth. He's wearing jeans, a shoulder holster and one of those blue wife-beater singlets once so popular amongst the tradesman castes. Behind a heavy wooden desk, a wall of crates is stacked high to the ceiling. Mostly liquor and canned pineapple labelled *Guangdong Eat Strong Food Industrial Co., Ltd*, wherever the fuck that used to be. To the left, a low red velvet divan. Upon it lounge two skanky whores, both well over forty, dressed in lingerie that, just like them, has most definitely seen better days.

She'd have known him anywhere, even though his piercing sapphire eyes had dulled. Even though his face had aged and she couldn't see his back. The lion tattoo would be in place, she didn't need to see it to know it.

"Hey Tom," she says, half smiling. Teasing. "How the fucking Hell have you been?"

The man cocks his head, squinting in the dim green luminescence.

"Anna," she prompts him. "Anna Ishtar."

The name feels strange coming off her tongue. Back at Truckstop, nobody bothered much with surnames. She'd been plain Doctor Anna for so long.

The skanks on the couch hurl daggers with their eyes. He's still staring with his mouth half-hanging open.

"We met at Glastonbury," she says, not bothering to mask her irritation. "Dancing before the Pyramid stage. Remember?"

She can literally see him strain to conjure images. The stone circle. A hundred and fifty thousand screaming fans.

"You moved to Edinburgh," she extrapolates. "I followed. And then we had that stupid, crazy fight."

He nods. One thing he can comprehend, clearly. A woman following him somewhere. The rest he seems unsure of and, quite frankly, so is she. Did she come to this country to escape him? What about all those years of tiny, insignificant moments, each one threaded together with the dedication of her longing. The hope that there's somehow been a point to all of it.

"Thomas, it's Anna — your Anna. Don't you remember? The Earth was green and you told me you loved me!"

There's a pregnant pause as he almost sees her. Tries to blink the bleakness from his eyes. Reaches out as if to remember...something, then it's gone. He doesn't know her. She's going to have to show him the dove tattoo. She undoes her top button — a slow burlesque performance. Knowing that his women are watching, she pops another one, pretending to fumble. Playing out the tease. She shucks the shirt and turns so he can see her back. She already knows what's going to happen and how much she hates him for it.

"Venus!" he whispers. "Almighty goddess of my heart."

For a long, sweet moment she indulges the illusion that he might actually mean her. But as she turns to glimpse the light of madness in his eyes, she understands it's not about her at all. Nor had it been the dove tattoo. He doesn't even remember the dove. It's the other one, that damned eight-point star. He's been forewarned about it. His eyes are glazed and he's babbling like the nuns. All this rubbish about his regal lady love which, quite clearly, isn't her or the two old broads on the divan.

No, he's talking about her rival. The one that steals the space she's supposed to own.

"Who the fuck is Venus?" she asks. "The one who's sucked up all the fondness in your heart?" He doesn't mean the star. The star is in the Heavens, not cowering in a pain-filled bunker underground.

He barks at the skanks and they scamper from his sight. So does the rest of the soldier guard that snapped at Anna's heels all the way up the stone staircase.

"I been waiting my whole life for you," he says.

Oh Thomas. My Lionheart.

He doesn't take his eyes off her as he walks to a wooden chest beside the divan. He bends, rummages inside, pulls out something shimmery and white, throws it for her to catch. A nightdress or an underslip — whatever the difference might once have been. The cleanest garment she's touched in years. She slips it on, kicks her filthy trousers off. He's still staring like he's never seen a woman dress before.

He's holding a thick ribbon of blood-red satin. Coils it firmly around his palm, eyes locked with hers. She knows something's wrong, but she can't bear to move. Not now, she tells her psyche. *Not when all my dreams are coming true.*

He moves. She thinks he's going to kiss her, but in one swift movement he binds her wrists. Tight and strong. He's done this before. Then he's pushing her ahead of him out onto the rocky platform. A cheer goes up from the crowd below, thousands of starving salivating men all chanting *Major! Major! Major!* like they mean it.

He raises his arms in a victory salute. The crowd shouts louder, more hysterical, more severe.

"Venus walks amongst us!"

She stands there in the underslip, dishevelled hair,

wrists bound. Numb on the inside, because this man hasn't got the first fucking clue who she is.

"My name is Anna," she says.

He doesn't hear her.

"Venus!" he hollers and everybody screams.

"Major! Major! Major!"

Anna can hear chanting, too, but not the words they're speaking. The sounds she hears are from an ancient time. One name uttered over and over and over.

Ishtar...Ishtar...Ishtar...

Her name.

And then Major Thomas makes calming motions with his hands. Everybody's shushing, waiting for what comes next. Will he let her speak? Or will he make some kind of statement in her supposed honour?

Thomas speaks. "As one great man once said to another, success is going from failure to failure *without* any loss of enthusiasm. I know that I must fight for the mytho-political paradox. Inside the wire, we're faced with a choice: either accept the presemioticist paradigm of reality or conclude that the task of the modern soldier is deconstruction, given that a regime change is the equivalent of a surgical strike."

Anna blinks. The cavern has fallen as silent as the grave. The men below are sucking this crap up like a sponge.

"Ask not that the journey be easy, ask instead that the Mother of All Bombs be worth it. Reality forms part of the fatal flaw of narrativity. If I do not believe I can do a thing, I definitely can't. So, I choose to believe, then act in accordance, regardless of potential collateral damage."

As the crowd goes wild with whooping and hollering, she stares at him sideways. "What the fuck are you talking about?"

He can't hear her. He can't hear anything but the

stamping and shrieking and repeating of his own "Major! Major! Major!" bouncing off the slimy cavern walls. What's left of his soul is a vacant space. Just a shell. She could rattle of magic memories to him for hours and he'd remember some of them, yes, he probably would. But for him, they'd been mere chance encounters. Places they went. Stuff they used to do. Like he'd done stuff and been places with a hundred other girls. Back when the world was lousy with supple, sweet young flesh.

"What have you done with my friends?" she asks him coyly. The nuns had become her very dearest the minute they'd been taken away.

He doesn't answer, but she notes the unmistakable outline of his cock hardening in his pants. How many minutes will be wasted like this in pointless reverie? The audience has fallen to stamping and clapping. No rhythm to it this time. No heartbeat.

He makes his victory sign again. "I answered the call," he tells the air.

Dear gods, is that a swagger in his stance?

"What call might that have been?" she asks so innocently.

Which imaginary government does he think he's serving? Which hallucinatory flag hangs limply in the cavern's flaccid air?

For a moment he almost smiles, almost remembers, almost seems like a reasonable human being, after all. But then, like everything else she ever cared for, that spark of light is gone and she's on her own, stumbling through the ruins of his incomprehension.

"Reality may be used to reinforce class divisions unless it has gone to Blackwater. If dialectic materialism holds, we have to choose between constructivism and decapitation strike discourse!"

She smiles at him sweetly.

He nods and returns the favour. "Knew you'd see things my way, darlin'."

"Yes, Thomas, of course you did."

Anna lunges suddenly and shoves him off the platform. The crowd goes wild once more as he flails and tumbles. When he splats on the stone they leap upon him, tearing him limb from limb with hands and teeth. As chaos erupts, she makes a break for the narrow staircase, hands still bound before her like a slave.

Ragged wide-eyed soldiers leap out of her path. Spread below, the vista of Hell is just as it ought to be: a belching, bleeding catastrophe of pain.

Halfway down, she glances up to check her options.

Memories return in silvery shadowplay, gradually overwriting the last few decades' harm and lies. Anna Ishtar has been stuck fast like a luckless bug in amber. Sleepwalking, locked in soulless repetition.

The staircase flattens to a passage, winds its way along the crumbling rock face. Below, a sea of blood-red angry eyes. One by one their owners grasp their tools, gawp up at her, a chorus of gnashing teeth and salivation. Such a familiar feeling to it, this passing-by parade. She knows she's been this way before, strutted her stuff before endless adoring admirers. Worshippers bowed on bended knees. Songs of praise back then, not heavy breathing. Her ankles had been ringed with bells, her hair braided thick with garlands.

It's the star tattoo protecting her — they choke when they catch sight of it. Trace a pointed symbol in the air. A ward against whatever. One simple talisman protecting her from a thousand harms. *A mighty powerful queen you've got, this Venus, whoever she might be.*

Anna Ishtar can't quite picture her, but she knows

enough to hate. The bitch that stole her place in Thomas's heart. Drove him crazy with unfathomable desires.

The pathway leads her ever downwards, further, deep as death into the earth, then along a wide ledge built for heavy traffic. Rail tracks embedded in the living rock. Overhead, power cables dangle in silvery impotence. Then, all of a sudden, the space above her widens. Anna freezes at first sight of the queen.

She's beautiful, just as Thomas promised. Slim and chic and glowing like the dawn. Five hundred feet of gleaming chrome rocket; of course his Venus would turn out to be a big steel phallus. The world might have died, but not that much has changed. And there, etched on the rocket casing, an unmistakable eight-point star. Exactly the same as hers, down to the shading.

Oh Venus, lovely Venus, so beautiful, yet flawed. Cock teaser, wallflower, debutante, *Decameron*, everything they've ever wanted all rolled into one. Whoever brought her here must have had a real good sense of humour, for, with no opening above her head, the beast remains stillborn. Can't be launched, no matter what they do. She stands, abandoned like a naked store window mannequin in an age when stores and windows have long past.

Major Thomas's Venus is a dud. No machinery to arm her. The fool thought blood and poetry would be enough. There's no way out, but it doesn't matter. She won't be going anywhere. But they will.

She clambers up the gantry base, amazed that no one tries to stop her. Hooking her arms through tarnished wire, she has a better view. She can see things Thomas died never knowing about. Something's wrong. Around her, men foam at the mouth; his workers drop like flies, they have a plague upon them. *That stuff's a lot more potent than I realized.*

The air stinks more than it did when she first got there. A sour reek, far worse than unbathed flesh. Now it's Ishtar's turn to say a prayer, small words of thanks to her lovely, lovely nuns who carried tiny passengers within their blood. *Just a little pre-war special, something we girls cooked up through the night. En route* to death, they'd served her well. Done what she required of them.

But the nuns aren't all dead. Three survive, shackled to the rocket's portal. Daisy, Wattle and Anemone, pale ghosts of who they used to be. The fight's gone out of them and the singing and the light. Ill-gotten, ill-used, robes stained with blood and vomit, yet somehow they still stand.

Men push and shove each other as panic takes a hold below. Anger, too. Each man turns upon his brother, no holds barred. They fight with tools, with knives, with claws. Their cries infuse, meld to form the howling of a single beast.

She's wondering why no one's shooting at her. Shots are being fired, but nothing seems to hit. Ancient weapons, lousy aims. Reluctance to fire a bullet at their Venus? Whatever. Not her problem. Good riddance to the masses. Not one amongst them is worth the trouble of saving.

Not a one.

And then, in a blinding flash it all comes flooding back. All she was. All she had ever been. The first one. The holy one. Monarch of a billion mothers, holy lover faded beneath artificial suns. Discarded by the animals who'd once named her sacred. Lulled into a false sense of humanity, tricked into delusions of humility and servitude.

The monsters had fired upon her stillborn army, murdered her babies as they emerged still-dripping from the sea. Ever growing, yet they set the flames upon them, an expression of human unity unparalleled.

You came together to kill my children and, in the process, killed yourselves. You burnt the Earth, scorched air, boiled water. Sent your soldiers scurrying for shelter. And here they are, decades later, burrowing like mutant cockroaches chewing their filthy way to freedom, bellies lined with gravel, minds completely shot. And all for what? Can you even recall reasons? Hatred of all I had to offer, despair at that which I could not?

She's given them everything they'd ever asked for. Sex and death and death and sex. Life and lust. Liberty and loss. Still not enough. Nothing was ever enough.

Suddenly, she's sick of the sight of them all. Poor dead Thomas. His men. All men. All history. Mankind itself and all the violence it has wrought. She can see no further point to any of it.

Daisy chews the blood red bindings from Ishtar's wrists. Once freed, the goddess hugs the three remaining nuns against her breast, quietens their whimpering with her steady beating heart. *Poor little girls, so ragged and so broken. Look what this filthy world has done to you.*

Goddess Ishtar turns her back upon the crowd. She holds her palms up high, feels them glow with white-cold fire. Flames of creation and destruction. Places each hand against the rocket's metal skin.

"I told you I was the queen of Heaven. You dumb fucks really should have listened."

The end of the Age of Pisces. The dawn of a new age. Yeah, another one, though there hardly seems a point to it. She's clocked time on various calendars, worn costumes as various gods: Egyptian, Babylonian, Mayan, Hijri. A couple of other favourites. Time ended with the last of the cities, so who cares about the date? Who's counting?

Ishtar stands until the dust has settled, waits for the sky to dare to show its face. Where is Sirius? Her Dog Star, her best friend?

"It's not polite to keep a lady waiting!"

But she waits.

The Dog Star emerges when he's good and ready. Bright as ever, winking through the storm.

"My, didn't you make a mess of things," he tuts.

"Shut the fuck up. It's my world."

"That it is. That it is. So what you going to do with it now it's broken?"

Ishtar shrugs. She's still rattling with righteous indignation and outrage. *All her love, yet Thomas spat it right back in her face...*

It takes awhile to notice all the other stars are missing. Even Orion, the true shepherd, the Dog Star's loyal friend. There's only her and Sirius, just like in olden times.

"To death and rebirth!" he toasts, raising an imaginary glass.

"Indeed," she answers, staring sadly out across scorched dirt.

Just the two of them now and for all the years to come. She's not quite sure what happened down in Thomas's Underworld. An explosion, sure, but it's not like the world hasn't seen plenty of those. She and Sirius argue about it incessantly, back and forth, back and forth. Soon she's lost track of continents as well as time. Without stars, it's difficult to navigate. Difficult to hold a thought. More difficult to care.

"So you reckon that fat guy was your boyfriend way back when?"

"Kind of. Yeah, I think so. Maybe. Perhaps he was my husband. Or my brother. Or my son."

She's brooding, so Sirius lets her think on it for a moment before he goes on. "But you waited thirty years to find the truth?"

"Happens to the best of us." She nods.

The weathered sentinel of Gengis still stands guard in his tower, keeping watch on the weary horizon. Turns out he was made of stone, after all.

They walk a decade or two in contemplative silence. Miasma settles down on them like fog. Storms have swept the landscape barren, torn up anything that looked like grass. Even ghosts are fading from the world. She misses them much more than she misses people. Baby Nubian goats, she misses most.

"I liked their ears and their funny little bleats," she tells him, just to break the ever-awkward quiet.

"Can't quite see the attraction myself," he replies.

Storms rage fierce as dragon's breath, tearing great chunks of crust from pole to pole. Fissures belch and fart sulphurous magma. Stepping between hot glaze, she barely feels it.

"Sirius, do you think I might be dead?"

He would have shrugged if he'd had shoulders. "Hard to say. Not much to compare life with now, is there?"

"No," she agrees. "There isn't."

"You could always give them another chance."

"What for? The fuckers don't deserve it."

Over time, their talk turns to other things, not just endless looping feedback of the past. As Thomas and her pride consign themselves to the substrata of mnemonic sediment, small black flowers start to push up through the cracks. Such hardy things, these little petals, sucking moisture from the bone-dry air. Shooting tendrils across the parched terrain, probing ever-gently for foothold.

"Would you look at that!" says Sirius.

"Shhhh," she says. "I'm listening."

"Listening to what—" he starts, but stops midstream. He can hear it, too, the gentle trickling of water. Dribbles glistening over granite, piss-weak spittle gathering in pools. "I told you life would find a way," he says after a time.

"Liar. No you didn't."

"It always does."

She's going to argue further, but instead she holds her breath as one by one the stars fire up again.

Biography

Cat Sparks is fiction editor of *Cosmos Magazine*. She managed Agog! Press, an Australian independent press that produced ten anthologies of new speculative fiction from 2002-2008. She's known for her award-winning editing, writing, graphic design and photography.

Cat was born in Sydney and has traveled through Europe, the Middle East, Indonesia, the South Pacific, Mexico and North America. Her adventures so far have included winning a trip to Paris in a *Bulletin Magazine* photography competition; being appointed official photographer for two NSW Premiers and working as dig photographer on three archaeological expeditions to Jordan.

A graduate of the inaugural Clarion South Writers' Workshop, she was a Writers of the Future prizewinner in 2004. She has edited five anthologies of speculative fiction and 60 of her short stories have been published since the turn of the millennium.

Cat has received 15 combined Aurealis and Ditmar awards for writing, editing and art, including the Peter McNamara Conveners Award 2004 for services to Australia's speculative fiction industry and the Best New Talent Ditmar in 2002. In 2011 the Literature Board of the Australia Council for the Arts awarded her a grant for Young Adult Literature.

She is currently working on a YA biopunk trilogy and a suite of post-apocalypse tales set on the New South Wales south coast.

Her story 'All the Love in the World' was reprinted in Hartwell and Kramer's *Year's Best Science Fiction,* Volume 16.

http://en.wikipedia.org/wiki/Catriona_Sparks
www.catsparks.net

About the Editors

AMANDA PILLAR is a speculative fiction author and editor who lives in Victoria, Australia, with her partner and two children, Saxon and Lilith (Burmese cats).

Amanda is an award-winning editor and has had numerous short stories published. She co-edited the anthologies *Voices* (2008), *Grants Pass* (2009), *The Phantom Queen Awakes* (2010), *Scenes from the Second Storey* (2010) and *Ishtar* (2011). She is currently working on the collections *Damnation and Dames* (due early 2012) and *Bloodstones* (due 2012).

Visit Amanda's website at www.amandapillar.com or read about her adventures at:

http://amandapillar.livejournal.com

KV TAYLOR is an avid reader and writer of urban fantasy and dark speculative fiction, even though the only degree she holds is in the history of art. (Or, possibly, because the only degree she holds is in the history of art.) Originally from the Appalachian foothills of West Virginia, she currently lives in the D.C. Metro Area with her husband and mutant cat. In her spare time she enjoys comic books, Himalayan Buddhist art, loud music, her Epiphone and Black Bush. She lives at kvtaylor.com, edits for Morrigan Books, and collects *The Red Penny Papers* (http://redpennypapers.com/) in her dining room.

Available Now:

The Even by T.A. Moore

In the Even — a city built in the intersection between the real and the not —ruled by the iron whim of the demon Yekum where treachery brewed amidst the ever-changing streets. Ancients dwell in the city who have out-lived their purpose and grown jaded with their immortality. They want only to die and they will take the whole world with them if they have to: suicide by Apocalypse.

Only Faceless Lenith, goddess, cynic and gambler, stands in their way. The fate of the world rests on her shoulders and mankind did not conceive her to be wise.

www.morriganbooks.com

Available Now:

How to Make Monsters
by Gary McMahon

Since the dawn of mankind, we have always made our own monsters: the terrors of capitalism and corruption, the things between the cracks, the ghosts of self...terrible beasts of desire, debt, regret, racism...of family ties, and the things that get in the way of our aspirations...the familiar monsters of our own faces, of tradition, rejection, and the darkness that lives deep inside our own hearts...

Can you identify the component parts of your own monster?

Can you afford to pay the dreadful price of its construction?

www.morriganbooks.com

Available Now:

"A brilliant premise of horror confined in twelve hotel rooms."

- Australian Horror Writers' Association

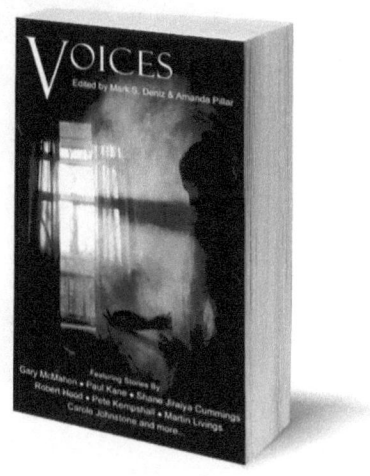

Voices
edited by Mark S. Deniz & Amanda Pillar

In every room, there is a story.

In this hotel, the stories run to the wicked and macabre.

Well crafted psychological and supernatural horror offerings await you, each written by a master storyteller. Whether you are looking to be shocked, disturbed or out-right frightened, *Voices* will have something to titillate your nerves and make your hair stand up on end. Leave the lights on and brew a strong cup of tea, the voices in the room plan on keeping you up all night.

www.morriganbooks.com

Available Now:

Dead Souls
edited by Mark S. Deniz

Before God created light, there was darkness. Even after He illuminated the world, there were shadows — shadows that allowed the darkness to fester and infect the unwary.

The tales found within *Dead Souls* explore the recesses of the soul; those people and creatures that could not escape the shadows. From the inherent cruelness of humanity to malevolent forces, *Dead Souls* explores the depths of humanity as a lesson to the ignorant, the naive and the unsuspecting.

God created light, but it is a temporary grace that will ultimately fail us, for the darkness is stronger and our souls...are truly dead.

Available Now:

The Phantom Queen Awakes
edited by Mark S. Deniz & Amanda Pillar

The Phantom Queen, goddess of death, love and war, returns to strike fear into the hearts of mortals in the anthology, *The Phantom Queen Awakes*.

Meet a washerwoman on the shores of the river; cleaning the clothes of the soon-to-be-dead; try to bargain with the capricious goddess of war; hear the songs of the dead as they cry for justice; walk with heroes of the past

Revisit the world of the Celts; a land of mystical beauty, avarice, lust and war through stories told by Katharine Kerr, C.E. Murphy, Elaine Cunningham and Anya Bast, among many other talented authors.

Available Now:

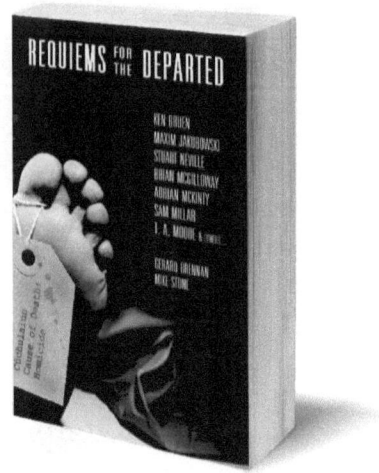

Requiems for the Departed
edited by Gerard Brennan & Mike Stone

Requiems for the Departed contains seventeen short stories, inspired by Irish mythology, from some of the finest contemporary writers in the business.

Watch the children of Conchobar return to their mischievous ways, meet ancient Celtic royalty, and follow druids and banshees as they are set loose in the new Irish underbelly, murder and mayhem on their minds.

Featuring top shelf tales by Ken Bruen, Maxim Jakubowski, Stuart Neville, Brian McGilloway, Adrian McKinty, Sam Millar, John Grant, Garry Kilworth, T.A. Moore and many more.

Available Now:

Scenes from the Second Storey
edited by Amanda Pillar & Pete Kempshall

Each story in this collection has been inspired by a track from the God Machine's album of the same name. Quirky, dark, insightful and sometimes downright disturbing, these tales reflect the emotions and images our authors experienced when they heard 'their' song from *Scenes from the Second Storey*.

In *Scenes*, you will meet a girl struggling to find cleanliness in a world full of corruption with Kaaron Warren; follow the twisted mental pathways of the egocentric with Robert Hood; watch two men search for enlightenment down a dark path with Paul Haines; and dance with a girl struggling to find her role within society with Cat Sparks.

www.morriganbooks.com

Available Now:

The Whisper Jar
by Carole Lanham

Some secrets are kept in jars — others, in books. Some are left forgotten in musty rooms — others, created in old barns. Some are brought about by destiny — others, born in blood.

Secrets — they are the hidden heart of this collection. In these pages, you will encounter a Blood Digger who bonds two children irrevocably together; a young woman who learns of her destiny through the random selection of a Bible verse; and a boy whose life begins to reflect the stories he reads...

Most importantly, though, if someone should ever happen to offer you a Jilly Jally Butter Mint, just say "No!"

Bibliography for
'The Five Loves of Ishtar'

If you would like to read Enheduanna's poem, please go here:
http://www.womeninworldhistory.com/lesson2.html

Allard Brooks, B., 1923, 'Some Observations concerning Ancient Mesopotamian Women', in *The American Journal of Semitic Languages and Literatures*, 39: 3, pp 187-194.

Anonymous, 2006, *An Old Babylonian Version of the Gilgamesh Epic*, Translated by: Clay, A.T., Edited by: Jastrow, M., The Project Gutenberg eBook: http://www.gutenberg.org/files/11000/11000-h/11000-h.htm.

Black, J.A., 2000, *A Concise Dictionary of Akkadian*, Eisenbrauns: Winona Lake.

Burke Hammons, M., 2008, *Before Joan of Arc: Gender Identity and Heroism in Ancient Mesoptoamian Birth Rituals*, Nashville: Graduate School of Vanderbilt University.

Collon, D., 2003, 'Dance in Ancient Mesopotamia', in *Near Eastern Archaeology*, 66: 3, pp 96-102.

Cuto-Ferreira, E., 2010, *Aetiology of Illness in Ancient Mesopotamia: on Supernatural Causes*, Barcelona: Unversitat Pompeu Fabra.

Galt, C.M., 1931, 'Veiled Ladies', in *American Journal of Archaeology*, 35: 4, pp 373-393.

Goodnick Westenholz, J., 1989, 'Tamar, Qĕdēšā, Qadištu, and Sacred Prostitution in Mesopotamia', in *The Harvard Theological Review*, 82: 3, pp 245-265.

Kramer, S.N., 1981, *History Begins at Sumer*, Philadelphia:

University of Pennsylvania Press or online at http://www.gatewaystobabylon.com/myths/texts/kings/shulgi. htm.

Lang, A., 1913, *Myth, Ritual and Religion Volume 2*, London: Longmans, Green and Co.

Læssøe, J., 1963, *People of Ancient Assyria*, London: Routledge & Kegan Paul.

Lerner, G., 1986, 'The Origin of Prostitution in Ancient Mesopotamia', in *Signs*, 11: 2, pp 236-254.

Marcus, M.I., 1994, 'Dressed to Kill: Women and Pins in Early Iran', in *Oxford Art Journal*, 17: 2, pp 3-15.

Mendelsohn, I., 1948, 'The Family in the Ancient Near East', in *The Biblical Archaeologist*, 11: 2, pp 24-40.

Oppenheim, A.L., 1956, 'The Interpretation of Dreams in the Ancient Near East. With a Translation of an Assyrian Dream-Book', in *Transactions of the American Philosophical Society*, 46: 3, pp 179-373.

Pangas, J.C., 2000, 'Birth malformations in Babylon and Assyria', in *American Journal of Medical Genetics*, 91: 4, pp 318-321.

Stol, M., 1995, 'Women in Mesopotamia', in *Journal of the Economic and Social History of the Orient*, 38: 2, pp 123-144.

Troy, B., 2004, *Legally Bound: A Study Of Women's Legal Status In The Ancient Near East*, Master of Arts, Miami University.

---

[i] Kramer 1981: http://www.gatewaystobabylon.com/myths/texts/kings /shulgi.htm.